Praise for Alexander McCall Smith's

NO. 1 LADIES' DETECTIVE AGENCY SERIES

"There is no end to the pleasure that may be extracted from these books." —*The New York Times Book Review*

"[McCall Smith is] a master. . . . There's beauty and revelation of one kind or another woven expertly into every line." —*The Christian Science Monitor*

"Entrancing. . . . A tapestry of extraordinary nuance and richness." —*The Wall Street Journal*

"Besides being amusing, these adventures offer up universal truths about human nature and remind us of life's simplest pleasures." —*The Chronicle Herald*

"In Mma Ramotswe, [McCall Smith] minted one of the most memorable heroines in any modern fiction." —*Newsweek*

"The best, most charming, honest, hilarious, and life-affirming books to appear in years." —*The Plain Dealer*

Alexander McCall Smith

PRECIOUS AND GRACE

Alexander McCall Smith is the author of the No. 1 Ladies'
Detective Agency books and a number of other series of nov-
els. His works have been translated into more than forty languages and have been bestsellers throughout the world. He
lives in Scotland.

www.alexandermccallsmith.com

BOOKS BY

ALEXANDER McCALL SMITH

PRECIOUS AND GRACE

PRECIOUS AND

GRACE

A NO. 1 LADIES' DETECTIVE AGENCY NOVEL

Alexander McCall Smith

Vintage Canada

VINTAGE CANADA EDITION, 2017

Copyright © 2016 Alexander McCall Smith

Published by Vintage Canada, a division of Penguin Random House Canada Limited, in 2017.
Originally published in hardcover by Knopf Canada, a division of Penguin Random House
Canada Limited, in 2016, and simultaneously in the United States by Pantheon Books,
a division of Penguin Random House LLC, New York. Originally published in Great Britain
by Little Brown, an imprint of Little, Brown Book Group, a Hachette UK company, London.
Distributed in Canada by Penguin Random House Canada Limited, Toronto.

Vintage Canada with colophon is a registered trademark.

www.penguinrandomhouse.ca

Library and Archives Canada Cataloguing in Publication

McCall Smith, Alexander, 1948– , author
Precious and Grace / Alexander McCall Smith.

(No. 1 Ladies' Detective Agency series ; 17)

ISBN 978-0-345-81192-9
eBook ISBN 978-0-345-81193-6

I. Title. II. Series: McCall Smith, Alexander, 1948– . No. 1 Ladies'
Detective Agency series ; 17.

PR6063.C326P74 2017   823'.914   C2016-903159-4

Image credit: Iain McIntosh

Printed and bound in the United States of America

2 4 6 8 9 7 5 3 1

Penguin
Random
House

VINTAGE CANADA

This book is for Linda Kandel.

PRECIOUS AND GRACE

CHAPTER ONE

A GOOD FRIEND IS LIKE A HILL

DRIVING TO THE OFFICE in her battered white van, down the Tlokweng Road, past the stand of whispering gum trees, Mma Ramotswe, founder and owner of the No. 1 Ladies' Detective Agency, allowed her mind to wander. It was easy for your thoughts to drift when you were doing something you did every day—such as driving down the Tlokweng Road, or spooning tea into the teapot while you waited for the kettle to boil, or standing in your garden looking up at the wide sky of Botswana. These were all activities that did not require total and undivided concentration, although her husband, that great *garagiste,* Mr. J.L.B. Matekoni, stressed that driving demanded your whole attention. Mma Ramotswe, though, felt it was perfectly possible to drive carefully and yet at the same time let the mind wander. There was not a driver in the country, she imagined, who did not think of other things while driving—unless of course there were, somewhere or other, people who had nothing at all to think about.

That morning she thought of what she would cook for dinner. She thought of letters she might receive and of the replies she should write. She thought of how she knew this road so well that she could drive it blindfold if necessary, and still get to her destination unscathed, or largely unscathed. She thought of how month by month, year by year, the traffic had got worse, as traffic always seemed to do. Was there nowhere on this earth where traffic got better; where the lines of cars thinned; where one could park virtually anywhere, as one could in the old days? And she thought of the people in her life, the people she would see that day, and the people she would not.

The people in her life . . . These, she felt, were of two sorts. Whatever further classifications might suggest themselves, at the outset people could be divided into those who were late and those who were still with us. The ranks of the late were legion, but each of us had a small number of late people who meant something special to us and whom we would always remember. She had never known her mother, who had died when she was still an infant, but her father, Obed Ramotswe, she had known well and still missed as much as ever. Every day she thought of him, of his kindness and his wisdom, of his ability to judge cattle—and men—with such a perceptive eye; of the love he had borne for her and of how his passing had been like the putting out of the sun itself.

There were other late people, of course: there was Seretse Khama, first President of Botswana and patriot; there was Mma Makutsi's brother, Richard, who had been called to higher things— as Mma Makutsi put it—from his bed of sickness; there was her favourite aunt, whose cheerful and irreverent remarks had been a source of such joy; there was that unfortunate man in Mochudi who had stepped on a cobra; there were so many others.

That was the group of late people. Then there was the other group, made up of those who were not late; who were, in some cases, only too obviously present, who touched her life in some way or other. These were her family, her friends, her colleagues, and finally those who were neither friends nor colleagues.

She considered herself blessed with her family. Some people had family members who were always burdensome, who wanted things, who found fault, who complained about this, that, and the next thing. Or they had family members who were an embarrassment—who prompted the making of comments such as, "Well, he's not all that close a relative—very distant, in fact," or even, "We have the same name, yes, but I don't think we're related."

She had no need to say any of that. She had a fine husband, Mr. J.L.B. Matekoni. She had various aunts in villages outside Gaborone, she had several cousins whom she always enjoyed seeing; and of course she had the two children, Motholeli and Puso, who, although technically foster children, were considered by everybody, including Mma Ramotswe and Mr. J.L.B. Matekoni, to be her own. She had lost a baby—but that had been a long time ago, and in so far as one could ever get over such a thing, she had done so. She could now think of that baby without being overwhelmed by sorrow; she could think of the brief moment during which she had held her child, that tiny scrap of humanity, and of the inexpressible, overwhelming love she had felt. She could think of that now without her heart becoming a cold stone within her.

To start with friends: prominent among these was Mma Sylvia Potokwane, matron and stout defender—in every sense—of the orphans entrusted to her care. Mma Ramotswe had known Mma Potokwane for many years and their friendship had been firm throughout, although she could not recall when, and in what circumstances, they had first met.

"But you must remember where you met her first," said Mr. J.L.B. Matekoni. "She is not one of those people one could easily forget."

That was, of course, true: Mma Potokwane was certainly not easily forgotten, but still Mma Ramotswe could not remember any occasion when somebody had said, "Mma Ramotswe, this is Mma Potokwane."

"I really do not remember, Rra," she said. "I just feel that we have known one another forever. She has always been there—like Kgali

Hill or the Limpopo River. Do you remember the first time you saw Kgali Hill?"

"But that's quite different, Mma," he had said. "You can't compare Mma Potokwane to Kgali Hill."

Mma Ramotswe considered this, and the more she thought about it, the more she felt that one *could* compare the redoubtable matron to Kgali Hill. Both were solid; both were unchanging; both would not be budged from where they stood.

Of course there were other friends—Mma Ramotswe was well known in Gaborone and could rarely make a trip to the shops without bumping into somebody she knew, and most of these would be friends of one sort or another. There were old friends whom she had known all her life—people with whom she had grown up in Mochudi— and there were newer friends, those whom she had met during her years in Gaborone: neighbours, friends of friends, fellow attenders at the Anglican Cathedral, members of the Botswana Ladies' Winter Blanket Committee. This last group met in the months immediately preceding winter and planned fundraising events for their annual blanket appeal. People forgot that Botswana had a winter and that there would be people, poor people, who felt the cold. Just because a country was drenched in sunlight did not mean that the temperature could not drop when the sun went down, especially on the fringes of the Kalahari. On a winter night, with the sky clear and filled with white fields of stars, the cold might penetrate to your very bones, as a dry cold can so easily do. And that was when you needed blankets to wrap yourself in, to make a cocoon of warmth to see you through to the morning.

So there were the ladies of the Blanket Committee, and they were all her good friends, as were the ladies who attended to her at the supermarket bakery and who always kept the freshest bread for Mma Ramotswe, even though she protested that she did not want any special treatment and would take her chances like anybody else.

Then there was the man in the Vehicle Licensing Department who invariably clapped his hands with delight when Mma Ramotswe came in to attend to business on behalf of Mr. J.L.B. Matekoni, and who would shout out, "My favourite lady has just come into the office! Oh, this is a very happy day for the Vehicle Licensing Department!" That had embarrassed her at first, but she had become accustomed to it and took it in her stride, laughing along with her admirer's colleagues. She realised that if you worked in the Vehicle Licensing Department, then you might need your moments of levity, and if she could provide those just by stepping in through the door, then she was happy to do so.

Friends were different from colleagues, of course, although colleagues could also be friends. Being self-employed, Mma Ramotswe did not have a large number of colleagues; in fact, she only had one full-time, permanent colleague, so to speak, although she had a part-time colleague in the shape of Mr. Polopetsi and another, if one took a liberal view of the definition, in the shape of Charlie. Fanwell, the former apprentice and now assistant mechanic, was not really a colleague in the strict sense, as he worked in the adjacent garage owned by Mma Ramotswe's husband and was really Mr. J.L.B. Matekoni's colleague rather than hers.

The full-time colleague was, as everybody knew, Mma Makutsi—Grace Makutsi, former secretary, graduate *magna cum laude* of the Botswana Secretarial College, where she achieved the mark of ninety-seven per cent in the final examinations; born in the remote and unexceptional town of Bobonong; survivor . . . Yes, Mma Makutsi had every right to be called a survivor. She had survived poverty; she had survived the battle for an education; she had lived with a slightly difficult skin and with the necessity of large spectacles; she had struggled for everything she possessed; and at last her ship had come home, unambiguously and magnificently, when she had met and married Mr. Phuti Radiphuti, a kind man, and a wealthy one too, being the proprietor of the Double Comfort Furniture Store. And together they had had a baby, Itumelang Clovis Radiphuti, a fine young son, and the only purring baby in Botswana.

That was Mma Makutsi, and Mma Ramotswe, thinking of her now, could only smile at her ways, which were well known, and perfectly tolerable once you became used to them. Mr. Polopetsi, her part-time colleague, was in awe of Mma Makutsi. He was a very mild man, a chemist with a chequered career, who worked in the agency on a voluntary basis because he needed something to do. He had now found a job as a part-time chemistry teacher at Gaborone Secondary School, a job that brought in very little money as it rarely required more than a few hours of his time each week. But the pay did not matter: his wife, a senior civil servant, was the main breadwinner. She preferred her husband to be occupied, and so was happy for him to spend his time on his poorly paid teaching job and his unpaid detective work in the agency.

And it suited the agency too. "Mr. Polopetsi may not be a great detective," observed Mma Makutsi. "But he does understand the scientific method and the need for evidence. That is important, Mma Ramotswe."

Charlie, by contrast, understood very little—at least in Mma Makutsi's view. He had been an apprentice in the garage, but had lost his job when Mr. J.L.B. Matekoni had been obliged to cut staff. That had been done only when all other avenues had been explored; money was tight, and many cars were now being taken to the larger garages where their complicated needs could be addressed by specialist equipment.

"They are not making cars for people any longer," said Mr. J.L.B. Matekoni. "They are making them for computers. If something goes wrong, they just take out the part and throw it away. Nobody can fix anything these days."

Charlie had his faults. He was impetuous, being given to making inflammatory remarks in the presence of Mma Makutsi, and his thoughts seemed to dwell almost exclusively on girls. In spite of all this, though, Mma Ramotswe had been unwilling to see him cast adrift and had employed him in the agency as what Mma Makutsi insisted on calling a Junior Probationary Apprentice Detective. Her insistence on this humiliating title rankled with Charlie, but he was grateful for such scraps of status as the job gave him, and even Mma Makutsi had to admit that he was making an effort. There was a long way to go, though, and she was watching him.

Those, then, were the categories of friends and colleagues. That left those who were neither friends nor colleagues, a group that in turn was divided into those who were simply unknown—people who clearly existed but who had yet to be met—and those who were known. It was this last set that was most delicate and troublesome, as it embraced those whom some might assume were enemies. That was not a word that Mma Ramotswe liked. She did not think of others in this way, as from an early age she had been imbued with the message that one should love one's enemies, and if one loved one's enemies then surely they ceased to be enemies. That message of love had been taught at Sunday School in Mochudi, when, along with thirty other children, the young Precious Ramotswe had been taught to recite the precepts of the good life. You respected your father and mother, along with a large number of others including teachers, elderly people, government officials, and policemen. You were not greedy, envious, or impatient, although you might feel all of these with some regularity. You never cast the first stone nor did you notice the mote in your neighbour's eye when you so clearly had a plank in your own. And of course you forgave your enemies.

Mma Ramotswe had tried to live according to these rules, and had, for the most part, succeeded. But if asked whether there was anybody who might be unfriendly towards her, she had to admit that yes, there was somebody to whom that description might be applied, although she had not asked for her enmity and had never sought to perpetuate it. This person, Violet Sephotho, was regrettably an opponent, but only because she—not Mma Ramotswe—had decided to adopt that position, and were peace to be offered Mma Ramotswe would willingly accede. And there was another thing: although this person was hostile to Mma Ramotswe, her real target was Mma Makutsi, who had no compunction at all in declaring that between her and Violet Sephotho there existed a state of hostility that was to all intents and purposes undeclared war.

Violet Sephotho had been at the Botswana Secretarial College at the same time as Mma Makutsi. Their respective attitudes towards the college could not have been more different: for Mma Makutsi the college represented the Parnassus to which she had long aspired— the institution that would deliver her from her life of poverty and struggle and equip her for a career in an office. For that she was profoundly and unconditionally grateful. She was completely committed to her studies the day they began; she never missed a lecture, and always occupied a seat in the front row; she completed every exercise and assignment on time and absorbed every piece of advice given by her tutors. At lectures she listened in respectful silence, writing everything down in the blue-bound notebooks that cost more than she could really afford—the purchase of a new notebook meant no lunch for a week; buying a textbook meant the forgoing of transport for at least a month. And when she graduated, on that unforgettable day, amidst the ululations of the proud aunts, she swore to herself that she would never forget the debt of gratitude she owed to the college and its staff.

Violet Sephotho felt none of this loyalty. She had taken up her place at the college because nothing else had turned up. Her examination results at school were indifferent, and had she applied to the University of Botswana she would have been summarily rejected. She might have secured a place on a vocational course, perhaps being able to train as a nursing auxiliary in a clinic or as a hospitality assistant in the hotel trades school, but both of these involved commitment and willingness to work, which she simply did not have. For

Violet, the Botswana Secretarial College was distinctly beneath her dignity—it was a place more suited to dim provincial nobodies like Grace Makutsi than to the likes of her. The college lecturers were, in her view, a sad bunch—people who had obviously not found real jobs in commerce or industry and who were content to spend their time drumming useless information into the heads of young women who would never be more than the second-rate occupants of dead-end jobs.

Mma Makutsi had been scandalised by Violet's behaviour. She found it hard to believe that anybody could so blatantly paint her nails during accountancy lectures, blowing ostentatiously on her handi-work to dry it more rapidly even while the lecturer was explaining the principles of double-entry book-keeping. Nor could she believe that anybody would keep up a running conversation with like-minded companions, discussing the merits of various men, while no less a person than the vice-principal of the college tried to demonstrate how a properly devised system of filing could save a lot of trouble and anxiety in the future.

Violet eventually graduated on the same day as Mma Makutsi, but while the latter covered herself in glory and was singled out by the principal herself in her address, Violet scraped past with a bare fifty per cent, the lowest pass mark possible, and only awarded, everybody suspected, because the college authorities could not face the prospect of Violet repeating the course and being on their books for another six months.

In the years that followed, Violet Sephotho lost no opportunity to put down or decry Mma Makutsi. And when Mma Makutsi was taken on by the No. 1 Ladies' Detective Agency, she transferred her venom to Mma Ramotswe and the agency in general.

"The so-called No. 1 so-called Ladies' so-called Detective Agency," Violet publicly sneered. "No. 1 Disaster, more likely, with that Grace—I call her Graceless!—Makutsi from somewhere up in the sticks. Bobonong, I believe—what a place! And that stupid fat lady who calls herself Precious but is really just a big waste of space, thinking she can solve people's problems! Far better go to a decent witch doctor and get him to sell you some powder than take your issues to that dump! Boring! Big time!"

Mma Ramotswe was aware of all this, and bore it with patience. She had always believed that people who were nasty or unkind to others were only like that because there was something wrong in their lives, and that people who had something wrong in their lives were not to be despised or hated, but were to be pitied. So although Violet Sephotho was in one sense an enemy, this was not of Mma Ramotswe's making and she would gladly have had it otherwise. Mma Makutsi was not of this view. She thought that Violet Sephotho was the way she was because that was how she was ordained to be.

"You cannot make a jackal into a hyena," said Mma Makutsi. "We are what we are. That is just the way it is."

"But sometimes we can change," said Mma Ramotswe. "That is well known."

"I do not think so, Mma," said Mma Makutsi. "And by the way, Mma Ramotswe, when you say that something is well known, I think that you are just saying what you think. Then you say that it is well known so that people will not argue with you."

"That's not true," said Mma Ramotswe. "But let us not argue, Mma, because I believe it's time for tea and the more time you spend arguing, the less tea you can drink."

Mma Makutsi smiled. "Now *that,* Mma, I think, is certainly well known."

CHAPTER TWO

THE DOG WAS ALMOST LATE

THOUGHTS ABOUT FRIENDS and colleagues could—and did—occupy the entire journey from Zebra Drive to the offices of the No. 1 Ladies' Detective Agency. But now, as she parked her white van behind the building they shared with Tlokweng Road Speedy Motors, Mma Ramotswe stopped thinking about the people in her life and began to contemplate the tasks of the day ahead. There were several complicated invoices to draw up, and that, she thought, would take the entire morning. Some weeks ago, at Mma Makutsi's instigation, the agency had introduced a new system of calculating fees. In the past they had simply charged what they thought a reasonable sum—often, Mma Makutsi observed, on the low side. This was based on the complexity of the enquiry and a rough—indeed, very rough—idea of how much time the matter had taken. Few clients had complained about this, but Mma Makutsi had decided that such a system was no longer acceptable in an age of transparency, when people wanted to know exactly what they were being charged for.

"The days of just thinking of a figure are over," she pronounced. "These days, people charge by the hour—by the minute, in many cases. That is the way the world is going. Itemised billing is what they call it, Mma."

Mma Ramotswe had not been enthusiastic. "I do not like those detailed bills. 'For answering the telephone, 50 pula,' and so on. That is not the way things were done in the old Botswana."

"But the old Botswana is no more, Mma," retorted Mma Makutsi. "This is the new Botswana now. You cannot live in the past."

Mma Ramotswe wanted to challenge her on that. Why, she wanted to ask, could one not live in the past? If enough people were determined to live in the past, then surely that would keep the past alive. You could go to an old-fashioned hairdresser who braided hair in the way in which they used to braid hair in the past; you could go to a doctor who dressed and behaved as doctors did in your childhood, wearing a white coat and carrying a stethoscope, as doctors used to do; you could patronise a butcher who sold old-fashioned cuts of meat and then wrapped them up in brown paper parcels and tied these parcels neatly up with white string, as all butchers used to be taught to do; you could go to a bank where there was an old-fashioned bank manager who actually knew your name, as bank managers once did . . .

But she kept these thoughts to herself. Had she expressed them, she was sure that Mma Makutsi would have made much of it and gone on at great length about modern practices and the need to be competitive. On that point—the need for competitiveness—Mma Ramotswe had difficulty in working out just with whom they needed to compete.

"We actually have no competitors, when it comes down to it, Mma," she had once said. "We are the only detective agency in Botswana—certainly the only one run by ladies. So who is there to compete with? The Bank of Botswana? The national airline?"

Mma Makutsi had looked pained at the levity of these remarks. "It doesn't matter if there's no actual competition," she said. "Competitiveness is a state of mind, Mma. It shows that you are aware of the client's interest. It is all about efficiency and value for money."

"I think we are very good value for money," countered Mma Ramotswe. "Sometimes we do not even charge anything at all. I have sent out many bills like that: 'Grand Total, 0 pula.' What better value for money can there be?"

"To somebody who has not had commercial training, perhaps. No disrespect, Mma, but when I was at the Botswana Secretarial College we learned about some of these very complicated matters. Some people have not had that opportunity—not that I'm saying it's their fault, Mma. No, I'm not saying anything like that."

In the end, Mma Ramotswe had agreed to the new billing system and had been instructed by Mma Makutsi as to how to keep a note of every moment spent on a client's affairs.

"So if you are thinking about a case, Mma—just thinking—you should still bill the client for that."

Mma Ramotswe expressed astonishment. "Should I write: 'For thinking about your case for 18 minutes'? Should I write that sort of thing?"

Mma Makutsi nodded. "Yes. But perhaps it's best not to use the word *thinking*. Some people would imagine that thinking is free. So you should put something like: 'For consideration of your affairs.' That is a very useful expression. Or you might write, 'For reviewing your affairs.' That is even better."

Mma Ramotswe looked thoughtful. "But what about drinking tea? Let's say that I want to think about a case and I decide to do so over a cup of tea. Can I charge for that? Can I write: 'For drinking tea, 50 pula'?"

Mma Makutsi laughed. "Oh really, Mma Ramotswe! No, that would not do. The client would say, 'Why should I pay them for drinking tea?'"

"So what should I write?"

"If you are talking to me about it while we're drinking tea, then you should write 'Case conference.' That is a good way of describing it." She looked defiantly at Mma Ramotswe. "I am not making all this up, Mma. This is the way it's done these days. I'm simply bringing you into the present—that's all."

"What was wrong with the past?" asked Mma Ramotswe. She intended the question seriously. There were too many people who took the view that the past was bad, that we should rid ourselves of all traces of it as soon as possible. But the past was *not* bad; some of it may have been less than perfect—there had been cruelties then that we had done well to get rid of—but there had also been plenty of good things. There had been the old Botswana ways, the courtesy and the kindness; there had been the attitude that you should find time for other people and not always be in a desperate rush; there had been the belief that you should listen to other people, should talk to them, rather than spend all your time fiddling with your electronic gadgets; there had been the view that it was a good thing to sit under a tree sometimes and look up at the sky and think about cattle or pumpkins or non-electric things like that.

But an argument of that sort would never prevail against the march of modernisation, and so Mma Ramotswe just thought these things, rather than expressed them. Nor did she put up much of a fight against the new billing system, which had all the authority of the modern behind it—and the endorsement too, it would seem, of the Botswana Secretarial College. And so her day started that morning with the making up of a bill of the new sort. *For taking instructions . . . for writing a letter of enquiry (2.5 pages) . . . for attending for consultation with client (25 minutes) . . .* It was tedious work, and by the time they were ready for mid-morning tea, Mma Ramotswe was looking forward to a break. And it was then that Fanwell came in from the garage and made his unexpected announcement.

"I have found a dog, Mma Ramotswe."

Fanwell said this as he came through the door, wiping the grease off his hands with a piece of the absorbent blue paper that Mr. J.L.B. Matekoni had introduced for such purposes.

Mma Makutsi had just turned on the kettle and was laying out the teacups in descending order—Mma Ramotswe's, her own, Mr. J.L.B. Matekoni's, Fanwell's, and finally Charlie's. Mma Ramotswe had two cups—her everyday one, white china and nondescript, and her more formal one, with a portrait of Queen Elizabeth II under a crown motif, now faded; Mma Makutsi herself made do with only one, a green cup with matching saucer. She looked up sharply as Fanwell spoke.

"A dog?" she asked. "A stray dog?"

Fanwell tossed the used blue paper into the bin, missed, and bent down to pick it up.

"Yes, it's a stray dog." He frowned. "Or, maybe not. How can you tell?"

"Stray dogs look very thin," said Mma Makutsi. "They often have no collar. They are very ill-looking dogs, usually."

"I don't think this dog is a stray dog, then," said Fanwell. "He is not so thin that you can see his ribs. He looks as if he has had enough to eat."

The water in the electric kettle started to boil. Mma Makutsi spooned tea into the pot.

"Where did you find this dog?" asked Mma Ramotswe.

"I saw him on the road. In fact . . ." Fanwell hesitated. "In fact, I ran over him. Charlie and I were coming back from fetching spares and he ran across the road. It wasn't my fault . . ."

"These dogs are always doing that sort of thing," said Mma Makutsi. "Phuti ran over one the other day. It came running out of a driveway and started trying to bite the wheels on his car. He couldn't help but run over it. Stupid dog."

"Some dogs can't resist chasing cars," said Fanwell. "Those dogs never last very long."

Mma Ramotswe was interested to find out what had happened.

"I felt a bit of a bump," said Fanwell. "So I put on the brakes and got out of the truck to see what had happened. I thought I might have burst a tyre, or something like that. But it was this dog. I'd hit him."

"And?"

"And he was under the car—not squashed or flattened or anything like that. He was just sitting there under the car, looking a bit dazed. So I got him out from under the truck—I had to drag him, but he didn't seem to mind. I think one of his legs hurt a bit, as he yelped when I touched him there, but otherwise he was all right."

Mma Makutsi began to pour the tea. "He must have lived somewhere round there. I suppose he just walked home. We could find out where he lives—we could ask about."

Fanwell shook his head. "No, Mma. There are too many houses over there. He could come from anywhere."

This was greeted with silence. Mma Ramotswe glanced at Mma Makutsi. Although he was considerably more responsible than Charlie, Fanwell was vulnerable; he tended to get himself into difficult situations, sometimes through kindness, or, more frequently, through naïvety.

"What did you do, Fanwell?" asked Mma Makutsi. "You didn't . . ."

Fanwell looked shifty.

"Did you bring him back here?" asked Mma Ramotswe.

Fanwell nodded. "I couldn't leave him, Mma."

Mma Ramotswe sighed. "No, you're right, Fanwell. If we run over something we can't just walk away." She paused. "Where is this dog now? Is he outside?"

Fanwell pointed towards the door. "He's out there."

"Then I suppose we'd better take a look at him," said Mma Ramotswe.

Fanwell led the dog in. He had improvised a collar for him out of a piece of old bicycle tube, cut and tied round the animal's neck, and to this he had attached a piece of string folded double upon itself. The dog was medium-sized—of an indeterminate breed, but the characteristic ruffled hair along the backbone showed Ridgeback blood somewhere in his past. He had a rather ungainly snout, with folds of flesh merging into exposed black gums around the jaws. Several teeth protruded from the mouth, imparting a somewhat savage look. But the expression in his eyes was not hostile—nor was the frantic wagging of his tail as he entered the room, looked about, and immediately crossed the floor to nuzzle at Mma Makutsi's feet.

"He likes you, Mma," said Fanwell, tugging at the string leash.

In spite of herself, Mma Makutsi smiled. "He is a very odd-looking dog, Fanwell," she said.

Charlie now appeared in the doorway. Spotting the dog, he clapped his hands enthusiastically. "So, you've all met Fanwell's dog. The latest member of the agency staff."

"What's that?" said Mma Makutsi.

"Fanwell says that you'll give the dog a job," said Charlie. "If the police use dogs, then why can't private detectives? Stands to reason, if you ask me."

Mma Makutsi crossed the room to hand Mma Ramotswe her cup of tea. "Nonsense," she said. "An office is no place for a dog. And anyway, that dog is not Fanwell's—it is a dog that was run over, that's all. It can go back to its owner now."

Charlie shrugged. "Fanwell doesn't know who that is, do you, Fanwell?"

Fanwell scowled at Charlie. "I'm not quite sure. That's why I'm looking after it."

"At your place?" asked Mma Makutsi. Fanwell lived with an uncle and his family in a small house in Old Naledi—a couple of rooms, Mma Makutsi believed. There would be barely enough room for the people in that house, let alone a dog.

"I'm not sure," said Fanwell. "I haven't thought about it."

Mma Makutsi returned to her desk. She placed her teacup in front of her, contemplated it for a few moments, and then fixed Fanwell with a firm stare.

"Fanwell," she said, "when you picked up that dog, did you think about what's involved in looking after a dog? Did you think about what you were going to do with it?"

Fanwell looked sheepish. "I was worried about him, Mma."

Mma Ramotswe came to his rescue. "He had run the dog over, Mma Makutsi. He had some responsibility."

Mma Makutsi's large round glasses caught the light. This was always a danger sign. "All he had to do was to check that it wasn't too badly injured," she said.

"Or that it was not late," offered Charlie.

"Precisely," said Mma Makutsi. "Once he had done that, then the dog was not his responsibility."

"But I couldn't leave him where he was," pleaded Fanwell. "He was looking very confused, Mma Makutsi. His head went round and round like this. And he had a sore leg. I couldn't leave him."

"Well, it's much better now," said Mma Makutsi. "You've done what you needed to do. Now you can take it somewhere and let it loose. It'll find its way back to its home, wherever that is."

Mma Ramotswe was more sympathetic, although she had always been slightly wary of dogs and could be nervous in their presence. This came from an incident she had witnessed during her childhood in Mochudi. A rabid dog had wandered into the village and created panic with its looping gait and strange, whooping howls. It was a Saturday morning and the young Precious had been making her way to the informal vegetable market set up by small farmers from the surrounding districts. The soil was dry and would yield some crops only where irrigation was available—for the rest, offerings were slight: pumpkins and melons, maize cobs, and sorghum that could be made into a staple porridge.

She had seen the dog at a distance, and had pointed it out to her father's cousin, who helped look after her. The cousin had looked anxious.

"But it's only a dog," said Precious. "It's not dangerous—it's not a hyena."

The cousin had taken her hand and began to shepherd her to safety. "There are some dogs that are many times more dangerous than a hyena—or even a lion," she said. "Look at the way it is walking—it's going sideways, Precious, and that means only one thing. That dog is a very bad dog—very bad."

Word had got out, and within a few minutes a police truck came bumping its way down the road. It slowed down when it was opposite the cousin, and a window was wound down.

"Over there," said the cousin, pointing to where the dog had lurched off into the scrub bush a few minutes earlier.

They watched as the truck drove on to the point where, its brake lights suddenly glowing red, it stopped. They saw a barrel point out of the window, swing about for a moment, and then slowly rise. They saw the puff of smoke first—a tiny cloud of white issue from the barrel, and then they heard the report. It was like the cracking of a whip above the heads of a team of oxen—a sharp, decisive sound.

A short while later the two policemen had climbed out of the truck and made their way into the bush. After a few minutes they emerged, dragging the body of the dog by its front paw.

Precious had gasped. "They have shot that poor dog!"

The cousin sighed. "It was very ill. It would have died."

She turned away and cried. "It was not biting anybody," she sobbed.

"It would have," said the cousin. "That poor dog would have bitten somebody, or even some cattle."

They heard later that it had already bitten cattle, and the cattle themselves had had to be shot.

"Rabies," said the cousin. "You see. That is what rabies does."

Mma Ramotswe put the memory out of her mind. Turning to their present dilemma, she said, "I think Mma Makutsi's got a point. We can't have that dog here and you don't really have room at your uncle's place for a dog. I think it best to see if the dog will find its way home. Somebody must be that dog's people. Most dogs have people somewhere."

Now she offered to help. "Is that place far?" she asked. "The place where you ran over this dog?"

Fanwell explained that it was only a couple of miles away.

"I'll take you in the van," said Mma Ramotswe. "After tea, you and I will take the dog and set it free."

Fanwell looked at the dog, who stared back up at him intently with wide, rheumy eyes. For a brief moment its tail began to move in a gesture of friendliness, but caution—the attribute that had enabled it to survive thus far—took over, and it rolled over in submission, as if waiting for a blow or kick.

"I think this dog likes me," Charlie said. "Even though Fanwell ran over him."

"He thinks you're going to give him something to eat," said Mma Ramotswe. "Dogs think with their stomachs."

"Like some young men," said Mma Makutsi. "Not that I'm thinking of any young men in particular."

Mma Ramotswe looked at her watch. "I will have another very quick cup of tea and then we shall go. There's somebody coming in at . . ."

Mma Makutsi looked at her diary. "At twelve o'clock," she said. "There is a lady from Canada."

"We shall go very soon," said Mma Ramotswe. "Then I shall be back in time for the client."

"What does this lady want?" asked Charlie.

Mma Makutsi had taken the call. "She is looking for something," she said. "That's all I know."

"We're all looking for something," said Charlie.

"Girls, in your case," said Mma Makutsi.

"Did you hear that, Mma Ramotswe?" complained Charlie. "Why should I have to put up with that sort of remark?"

Mma Makutsi smiled. "Because it's true, Charlie. That's why."

Mma Ramotswe brought the tea break to an end. "Let's not argue," she said. "Let's get this poor creature back to its home and its people." She stood up. The dog watched her, trying to work out what was happening; which was what all dogs seem to do, thought Mma Ramotswe. They try to make sense of a world that is full of things they cannot understand; just as we humans do—if not constantly, then for much of the time.

THE DOG WAS RELEGATED to the back of the van, where it tried valiantly to keep its footing, but from time to time fell over on its side. In the cab at the front, Fanwell directed Mma Ramotswe along a narrow road that fingered its way into Old Naledi, the crowded poorer suburb that was home to newcomers to the city and to those who, although no longer newcomers, had remained at the bottom of the heap. At a point where this road intersected with another, Fanwell told her to stop.

"It was here," he said. "I was driving along here and the dog came running out from over there."

He pointed to a scruffy hedge, behind which there were several small lean-to shacks.

"Maybe that is where he lives," said Mma Ramotswe, nodding in the direction of the shacks.

Fanwell shook his head. "I asked those people," he said. "They saw what happened and when they came out I asked them. They said they had never seen the dog before."

Mma Ramotswe found herself wondering what Clovis Andersen might recommend in a case such as this. Was there any alternative to allowing the dog to find its own way home? Would even Clovis Andersen be able to do anything more constructive than that?

"We should put the dog out," she said to Fanwell. "It will probably run straight home, you know. Dogs are like that. They don't forget where they live."

She parked the van at the side of the road and emerged from the driver's side, leaving the engine running. Fanwell got out of his side, went to the back of the van, and lifted the dog out, putting him gently down on the verge. Bending down, he stroked the dog's head, allowing the confused creature to lick his hand.

"We must say goodbye," said Mma Ramotswe.

"He will be very sad when we leave him," said Fanwell.

"It is always sad to say goodbye," said Mma Ramotswe.

She waited for Fanwell, who gave the dog another pat on the head before turning round to get back into the van. The dog followed him, and as he opened the door of the van it tried to leap up onto the seat inside.

"You must stay," said Fanwell. "You cannot come with me."

The dog looked up at him, its eyes wide, its mouth open to allow its large pink tongue to extrude.

Mma Ramotswe slammed the door behind her. Pushing the dog away with his foot, Fanwell closed the passenger door behind him. "We can go now, Mma," he muttered.

Mma Ramotswe drove the van slowly back onto the road. As she did so, she heard barking. Glancing in her rear-view mirror she saw the dog beginning to chase after her.

"He doesn't want to leave us," said Fanwell. "He's not going to go to his place, Mma."

Mma Ramotswe pressed down on the accelerator. "He'll give up, Fanwell. Once we get onto the main road, he'll be unable to keep up with us."

Fanwell turned in his seat. "He is just behind us, Mma. He is running very fast."

Mma Ramotswe sighed. "We can't stop, Fanwell. We can't let him catch up."

Fanwell's voice became strained. "He is very sad, that dog," he said. "He has nobody to love him. You can tell when somebody has nobody to love him."

"They'll love him in his own place," said Mma Ramotswe. "He will have people there."

She looked again in her mirror. The dog was still to be seen, although he was a good distance behind them now, his ears flapping in the breeze created by his headlong lurch in their direction. She lowered her head, looking again at the road ahead. The dog had entered her life little more than an hour ago, but this seemed to her to be a real abandonment, a cutting loose of a creature who had nobody else to turn to. The world was like that, of course, and sometimes it seemed particularly so in Africa, where there were so many who needed the support of others and had no others to give it. She sighed. They could not take on every ownerless dog—that was obviously impossible; Fanwell was a kind young man, and it was much to his credit that he had bothered to do something about the dog, but he was in no position to see that gesture through and had to be protected from the unsustainable consequences of kindness, as did others who allowed their hearts to prompt them. She thought it strange, though, that she, a woman, should be the one to tell a young man that he could not do what his heart wanted him to; were women not the ones who listened to their hearts, while young men thought only of . . . of the things that young men thought of? Or was that part of the unfair prejudice that men had to struggle against? Was it not the case that men could weep as readily as women? Was it not the case that men could be as gentle and as caring as any woman, if only they were given the chance to show these qualities? She thought of Fanwell, and she thought of Mr. J.L.B. Matekoni. Both of these were kind, sensitive men who were as understanding of the feelings of others as any woman she knew; and who were every bit as gentle.

But then Charlie came to mind, and that made her think again. Charlie was not aware of the feelings of others, or very rarely showed such awareness. It was possible, of course, that he felt more than he let on, but even if that were true, he could not by any stretch of the imagination be described as a new man. She had seen that term used in a magazine article she had read recently, and she had been intrigued. There were certainly new men around, but there were plenty of men who were not new men. You only had to go into any bar in town to see these men by the score, by the hundred, whereas if you went out in search of new men, it was difficult to know where to look. Were they the ones who were doing the shopping for their wives? Were they the ones who were collecting the children from school? Possibly; but when you went to the supermarket or the school, there were often rather few men to be seen—new or otherwise.

They finished their journey in silence. When they came to a halt under the acacia tree at the back of the office, Fanwell pointed to a small blue car parked near the agency door. "That car must belong to your client, Mma," he said. "She has already arrived."

Mma Ramotswe looked at her watch. They had returned well in time. "She is early," she said.

"That means she will be very worried, Mma," said Fanwell. "If somebody brings a car into the garage before the time you've agreed with them, that means they are very anxious about their car." He looked at her intently, as if to ascertain that she had understood. "Same thing with people, Mma. Same thing . . . I think."

Once out of the van, he went over to the blue car and started to examine it. Mma Ramotswe watched him; she was puzzled.

"Something wrong, Fanwell?" she asked.

He touched the side of the car gently, as if to answer some unspoken question.

"This car has been resprayed on this side, but not on the other."

Mma Ramotswe could not see any difference, but then cars never meant a great deal to her. She loved her own van, but beyond that cars were an alien tribe—important and necessary, but not to become too exercised over.

"I think this car has had an accident on this side," Fanwell continued. "I'd take a very careful look at the steering if I were driving it. Sometimes they don't balance the wheels properly, you see—after an accident, that is. There are many bad mechanics, Mma. Every day, more bad mechanics arrive." He paused, while he peered through the driver's window. "And this car has many drivers, Mma."

She frowned. "How can you tell that, Fanwell?"

"Because it is a rental car," Fanwell announced.

Mma Ramotswe whistled in admiration. "You are quite the detective, Rra! A car detective, perhaps."

Fanwell's face broke into a broad smile. "Thank you, Mma. I can tell that it's a rental car because . . . well, because the rental agreement is lying on the passenger seat."

Mma Ramotswe laughed. "All the best clues are very obvious," she said. "That's what Clovis Andersen says."

"Your book?" asked Fanwell.

"Yes. *The Principles of Private Detection.*"

Fanwell nodded in recognition. "That book says everything, doesn't it?" He paused. "It's a pity that we mechanics don't have something like that. *The Principles of Cars.* That would be a good book, that one, Mma."

She smiled. "*The Principles of Cars,* by Mr. J.L.B. Matekoni. That would be a very good book, I think. 'Chapter one: Listen to what the car is trying to tell you.'"

Fanwell clapped his hands together in delight. "Oh, that is very funny, Mma. The boss is always saying that to us. It's one of the first things he said to me when I started my apprenticeship. I don't think I understood then."

"But you do now?"

"Oh, I do understand now, Mma. It is very true. A car will tell you if it is suffering. And it will often make it very clear where the problem is."

Mma Ramotswe nodded. "And chapter two of Mr. J.L.B. Matekoni's book—what would that be?"

Fanwell thought for a moment. "Chapter two would be: 'What to do next.' I think that would be a good title for it."

"Well, maybe we should suggest it to him, but now I must go inside and meet this new client."

She straightened her dress, which had become crumpled in the van. There were dog hairs that showed against the dark red of the material, and she began to brush these off before she went into the office. She thought of the dog, and its vain attempt to pursue them after they had dropped it off. Perhaps it had no home after all and was now wandering the streets of Old Naledi, sniffing around for some scraps of food, for some sign of the human interest or affection it yearned for but that was not forthcoming.

As she brushed off the last of the hairs, from inside the office she could hear Mma Makutsi's voice and then, less distinctly, the voice of the client. She stopped; she was standing just outside the door, which was slightly ajar. The voices inside were clear now, and she could hear exactly what was being said. She put her hand on the door handle, and then took it off again. She had not intended to eavesdrop, but she could make out exactly what was going on inside, and this made her hesitate.

Those who listen in to what others are saying hear no good of themselves. Her aunt had told her that when she was a girl, and she had always remembered the advice. But this was not listening in—this was overhearing something because you were about to enter the room in which the conversation in question was being conducted. She could not help but hear what was being said in the office—and she could not help her mouth from opening in astonishment. So this was what Mma Makutsi said when she was not there to exercise restraint, when she was not in a position to protect the cause of truth . . .

CHAPTER THREE

I WANTED TO SEE THE PLACE
I LOVED SO MUCH

Y ES," Mma Ramotswe heard Mma Makutsi say, "you were right to come to us, Mma. You were so right."

Something was said by the other woman that Mma Ramotswe did not catch.

"Indeed, Mma," continued Mma Makutsi. "Indeed that is true. And you asked about how long we have been established. The answer is a long time, Mma, a very long time. You see I thought—back in those days when we set up the agency—that there was a need for a business like this to help people, Mma, to help them with the problems in their lives. Those were my exact words, Mma. You know how businesses have mottoes these days—things like 'We are here to serve,' that sort of thing. Well ours is 'We are here to help people with the problems in their lives.' And you know something, Mma? Once we started we were overwhelmed with enquiries . . ."

Mma Ramotswe caught her breath. Overwhelmed with enquiries? That was simply not true; had Mma Makutsi forgotten what it had been like? Did she not recall how they had waited and waited for people to come in the front door under the newly painted sign, and for days nobody had come? At one point some chickens had wandered in and pecked at the ground around their feet, and she remembered saying to Mma Makutsi: "At last we have some clients, Mma," and Mma Makutsi had not seen the joke because in those days her sense of humour had not been much developed. It was something to do with having been born and brought up in Bobonong, where presumably nothing amusing ever happened. Now, of course, she had a much better sense of humour, although sometimes Mma Ramotswe still had to explain the finer points of some humorous remark; but then we all had our weaknesses and one should not dwell on the failings of others.

But how could she say "when we set up the agency . . ."? *I* set up the agency, Mma Ramotswe thought, and although I don't expect credit, nor would I ever fish for compliments, the simple historical truth was that Mma Makutsi had come to ask for her job *after* the agency had been established. And she was in those days a secretary in the old-fashioned sense of the word. Secretaries had promoted themselves to something different these days and it seemed as if there were no secretaries any more. Mma Ramotswe was not one of those people who believed in holding people back—anything but—yet she felt that there was a role for secretaries, and it was a good and honourable one, and she did not see why people should be so keen to stop being a secretary and become something else.

"We've expanded," went on Mma Makutsi. "To begin with it was just me and the other lady, but we were so busy that I thought we needed a bit of help. So we have a very charming man—a Mr. Polopetsi—who is a very scientific man, Mma, and he brought all those skills. And we have an office boy, Charlie, who is off on some errand at present . . ."

Office boy! Mma Ramotswe bit her lip. Charlie would be incensed by that description. He was, of course, very junior, but he still regarded himself as being a sort of apprentice detective, and to hear Mma Makutsi refer to him as an office boy would cause him immense distress. And as for describing her as "the other lady," that was going just a little bit too far.

Mma Ramotswe reached for the door handle once more but again was stopped by what she heard.

"So you see, Mma," Mma Makutsi was saying, "I am just the person to take on this enquiry of yours."

She pushed the door open to see Mma Makutsi seated at her desk, with the client, a tall woman with long blonde hair, seated in the client's chair in front of her. Each had a cup of tea in front of her.

"Ah," said Mma Ramotswe, as briskly as she could. "You are already here. And I see that Mma Makutsi has been—"

Mma Makutsi did not let her finish. "This is Mma Ramotswe, Mma," she said. "She is back now."

The woman turned in her seat to greet Mma Ramotswe. Mma Ramotswe lowered her gaze in politeness; it was rude to stare, something that people from other cultures simply did not understand. They told their young children to look at old people when they spoke to them, but they did not do this in order to be rude—they simply did not know that a young person should not stare at a more senior person as if to issue a challenge.

Her initial glance had enabled her to form an impression of their client, who now introduced herself as Susan Peters. She noticed the pleasant, open expression—a face devoid of guile or suspicion; she noticed the carefully ironed blouse and the thin-banded gold watch on her wrist; she noticed the small lines around the eyes, which were lines, she thought, of sadness, of sorrow.

Mma Makutsi was getting up from Mma Ramotswe's desk. "You sit down at your desk, Mma," Mma Makutsi said. "I will get you some tea."

It was a peace offering, an apology for the unlawful occupation of the desk, and Mma Ramotswe smiled graciously as she took her rightful place. Perhaps she had been hard on Mma Makutsi; perhaps she should not resent her assistant claiming a bit of glory in her account of the agency's history. After all, every one of us wanted to feel important in some sense, and if we occasionally overstated the significance of the role we played in this life, then that, surely, was understandable and should not be held too much against us.

Mma Ramotswe decided to make everything clear. "I am the manager," she told the blonde lady. "But Mma Makutsi and I work very closely together."

Susan looked at her hands. "I see."

"So perhaps you might tell me what it is that brings you to Botswana, Miss Peters."

Susan looked up. "Please call me Susan."

"If you wish, Mma. It is a fine name, that one."

Susan smiled. "It started a long time ago, Mma."

"Most problems start a long time ago," said Mma Ramotswe. "There are hardly any that began yesterday."

"I'm not saying I have a problem," said Susan. "It's more of . . ."

They waited.

"A doubt?" suggested Mma Ramotswe.

"It is a doubt, or an . . . an area of ignorance. It's to do with piecing together bits of the past."

"So that you know what happened?" suggested Mma Makutsi.

"Maybe," said Susan.

"You should tell us, Mma," said Mma Ramotswe. "Starting at the beginning."

"The beginning," said Susan, "was thirty-five years ago. That, *Bomma,* was when I was born."

Mma Ramotswe and Mma Makutsi exchanged a glance. The use of the correct Setswana plural, *bomma,* for two women was a sign that this was a woman with more than a passing knowledge of Botswana. Few outsiders spoke the language, and even those who spent years in the country might never progress much beyond the basic greetings.

"You see, I was born here."

Mma Ramotswe smiled. "You are a Motswana, then, Mma."

It was a compliment, and Susan responded warmly. "You're very kind, Mma." She knew, though, that it was impossible; one might be a *paper* Motswana—there were plenty of people who were eligible for various African nationalities, but one could never become the real thing. It simply did not work that way. Citizenship and membership were different things, whatever the law might say. Mma Ramotswe understood that; she did not like it, but she understood it.

Susan continued. "I was never a citizen, though, Mma. I didn't have the right, as my parents were foreigners—working in the country when I was born. They were Canadians, you see. My father was a doctor and my mother was a teacher. He worked out at Molepolole for five years and then they came into Gaborone. He worked for the people who run those medical planes—you know the ones, Mma, the ones that go out to the very remote clinics—that set-up."

"I know the people," said Mma Ramotswe. "They were like Dr. Merriweather's mission, but different."

"That's right, Mma. He worked with them and my mother taught at a small school near the old prison."

Mma Ramotswe waited for her to continue. She was remembering what Gaborone had been like in those days of greater intimacy. She thought of it as the *quiet time;* the time before the world suddenly became busier and noisier. The time of cattle; the time of bicycles rather than cars; the time when the arrival of the day's single plane was an event; the time of politeness and courtesy.

It was as if Susan had heard her thoughts. "Gaborone was a different place then," she said wistfully.

This was the signal for Mma Makutsi to join in; she had said very little since Mma Ramotswe had returned. "The whole world was different in those days, Mma. Up in Bobonong it was different. Down here it was different. None of this rush, rush, rush."

Mma Ramotswe saw the flashing light from Mma Makutsi's spectacles. "No, people walked more slowly in those days."

"They certainly did," said Mma Makutsi. "If you look at people today, their legs go fast, fast—just like a pair of scissors. We did not walk like that in the old days."

Susan nodded. "I'm not sure why people are in such a hurry. I live in Toronto now and—"

"Oh, they must walk very fast in Toronto," interjected Mma Makutsi. "That will be one of the worst places for walking fast. That and Johannesburg, where they are always running to get from one place to another." She paused, and then shook her head. "But Toronto . . ."

She did not finish, and Susan looked at her with some puzzlement. "Toronto is a nice place in other respects, of course . . ."

"I am not saying it is not a nice place," said Mma Makutsi. "I am just saying that they walk very fast there. I have seen a film of that. They were walking very fast in the film."

"I think you should continue," said Mma Ramotswe. "So you were born out in Molepolole, Mma?"

"Yes. I actually don't remember Molepolole very well because I was only four when we left and came into town. I think I have a memory or two of the place; I remember a garden with a tall rubber hedge—you know those hedges with the white sap that comes out if you break off a piece? I think I remember that. And I remember sitting on a verandah, which must have been at my parents' house out there. Apart from that, my early memories are of this place—of Gaborone."

Mma Ramotswe made a note on the pad of paper before her. *Early life,* she wrote. *Gaborone.*

"We stayed here until I was eight. Then we left."

"Why was that, Mma?" asked Mma Ramotswe.

"My father was paid by the Canadian government," said Susan. "It was a funded project and the money was given to something else. Aid people are always doing that—they support something for a while, and then it's somebody else's turn. It's fair enough, I suppose. And anyway, his work was to do with tuberculosis, and they had made such good progress with treating TB that they probably wanted to spend their funds on something else. So it was time for us to go back to Canada—except in my case I hardly knew Canada. I had been there twice, I think—just for holidays on my grandmother's farm in Ontario. I didn't know the place otherwise. It was meant to be home, but it wasn't really.

"So leaving Botswana was like leaving my real home—the place I'd grown up in, the first place I knew, the place that was so familiar to me." She paused. "I remember it very well—the day we left. We had to drive over the border to get the plane from Johannesburg. I remember being in floods of tears because I was leaving my friends. It's like that for children, isn't it? Leaving friends is a very big wrench for them. It seems that you're losing everything. You don't believe your parents when they say you'll make new friends—you will never make any more friends, you think. It's like saying goodbye to the whole world."

Mma Makutsi made a sympathetic noise. "Oh, I know what that's like, Mma. I know that very well."

"I'm sure you do," said Susan.

"I remember when I left Bobonong," Mma Makutsi went on. "I came down here to go to the Botswana Secretarial College, you know, Mma—I graduated from that place, you see."

Mma Makutsi's eyes went to the wall where her framed certificate from the Botswana Secretarial College hung in pride of place.

Susan followed her gaze. "That's your certificate up there, Mma?" she asked politely.

"As a matter of fact, it is," said Mma Makutsi, her voice dropping in modesty.

"Ninety-seven per cent," said Mma Ramotswe. "Mma Makutsi was their most distinguished graduate, you see. Ninety-seven per cent. That grade has never been . . ." She stopped. There had been that talk of somebody since then getting ninety-eight per cent, but now was not the time to mention that.

Mma Ramotswe decided to steer the conversation back to the client. Mma Makutsi, she had noticed, had a tendency to introduce her own agenda into a discussion, and although this was sometimes interesting, it could make it difficult for the business in hand to be transacted.

"So, Mma," she said. "You went off to live in Canada?"

Susan nodded. "Yes, we went to a place called Saskatoon. My father had trained with a person who ran a hospital there, and she offered him a job. My mother was not too keen, as she did not know that part of Canada and thought that it was too far away from anywhere else. It's a very big country, Canada, and the distances can be—"

"Very big," interjected Mma Makutsi. "Canada is a very big place."

"That's what the lady has just said," observed Mma Ramotswe.

Mma Makutsi seemed indifferent to the censure. "I've looked at maps," she went on, "and, oh my, there is so much space there. It goes on and on, just like the Kalahari, but even bigger. No lions, of course."

Susan laughed. "No lions. At least not the sort of lions you have here."

Mma Makutsi looked interested. "You have other lions in Canada, Mma?"

"There are mountain lions in the Rockies," said Susan. "They're big cats, all right. They're called cougars."

"That is very interesting, Mma," said Mma Makutsi. "Are they smaller than the lions we get here? More like leopards?"

"They're certainly smaller," said Susan. "I've never actually seen one, as it happens. I believe they're rather secretive creatures."

"And would they attack a person?" asked Mma Makutsi.

"They might. There certainly have been cases of people being killed by mountain lions. Mauled, I suppose."

"That is very bad," said Mma Makutsi.

"Yes," said Susan. "It's very sad."

Mma Ramotswe cleared her throat. "I think perhaps we should—"

"Of course there are many bears in Canada, aren't there?" said Mma Makutsi. "You have that very big sort of bear . . ."

"The grizzly. Yes, we have those. Once again, those tend to be up in the mountains. You won't get those down where most people live."

Mma Makutsi had more to say. "They say that most of these cases where people are attacked by bears—and other animals—happen when the person has surprised the animal, when they have given it a shock." She paused, but not long enough for Mma Ramotswe to get the conversation back on track. "That is often the case with snakes, you know, Mma Susan."

"I can well believe it," said Susan. "We used to get snakes coming into the house sometimes when we lived here in Gaborone. I distinctly remember it."

"Oh, that is very common, Mma," said Mma Makutsi. "But when you meet a snake in the bush—when you're walking, for instance—it's often because you are walking too softly. You have to take firm footsteps so that the snake feels the vibration in the ground. That way it has a warning and it gets out of your way."

Mma Ramotswe tried again. "I think we should talk about snakes some other time, Mma Makutsi. Mma Susan was telling us—"

"I was not the one who raised this subject," protested Mma Makutsi.

Mma Ramotswe was placatory. "It's not a question of who started what," she said. "It's just that we need to hear what Mma Susan has to tell us."

Mma Makutsi sniffed. "I am listening, Mma Ramotswe. I have been listening all along."

Susan made light of it. "I'm happy to talk about snakes," she said. "I love talking about anything to do with Botswana—even snakes."

"There," said Mma Makutsi, glancing at Mma Ramotswe.

There was a brief silence before Susan continued. "You can imagine what a shock it was for me," she said. "We went straight up to

Saskatoon after we came back to Canada—and it was the beginning of winter. My visits to Canada before that had all been in the summer and I had never seen snow before. I couldn't believe that such cold could exist—that unremitting, merciless cold of the Canadian winter. My parents told me that I would get used to it and that there were all sorts of things you could do in the winter—skating, snowshoeing, and so on. But I think I must have been in a state of shock—I just sat at the window and gazed out on the white landscape, wondering how it could ever be warm again.

"And it wasn't just the cold. I felt that all the colour had been drained from my world: I felt surrounded by people who were somehow lonely—quiet people who were frightened to smile and laugh. I felt as if I was in the presence of ghosts. Botswana—Africa—had been full of life; now my life seemed to be full of silence. A silent sky; silent people; a sense of emptiness. You do know, *Bomma,* that people in Canada talk about feeling solitude? They sometimes call it a country of solitudes."

Mma Makutsi removed her glasses and polished them. "People in Botswana can be lonely too," she said. "And quiet as well. We aren't noisy people like some of those people over the border. Those Zulu people, for instance . . ."

"I know that," said Susan. "Canada is not really like the way I felt it was. The problem was inside me, not in Canada. The Canadians are good people; in fact, I think there are many similarities between Batswana and Canadians . . . but there are many differences too, and it was the differences that I felt when I went to live there as a young girl."

"Your heart had been left behind," said Mma Ramotswe. "It is not uncommon—many people who leave Africa feel that way."

"Yes," said Susan simply. "My heart stayed here. I went off with my parents, but my heart stayed here."

"But it would not have lasted forever, surely," said Mma Ramotswe.

Susan looked up; she held Mma Ramotswe's gaze. "It did last," she said slowly. "I never got over it. Never."

"You felt homesick for Africa?" asked Mma Makutsi.

Susan nodded. "I did. I expected to forget it, but I didn't. Even when . . ."

She broke off. Mma Ramotswe waited.

"Yes, Mma? Even when?"

Susan did not answer directly. "I had something happen to me, Mma."

Mma Ramotswe caught her breath. She had been in this exact place before—and on more than one occasion. She had sat with a client, with Mma Makutsi at her desk behind her, and been told about some dark thing that had happened, and that could ruin the life of the one to whom it had happened. It was horribly, painfully familiar.

"I am very sorry, my sister," she whispered. "You do not need to talk about it. Not now. You can tell me later, if you wish."

Susan looked up, seemingly surprised by the gravity of Mma Ramotswe's words. "But it happens to most people, Mma," she said. "Most people fall in love, don't they?"

Mma Ramotswe stared at Susan uncomprehendingly. "But, Mma, I don't see . . ."

Susan smiled. "I'm sorry, Mma, I've confused matters. You see, all I meant was that my . . . well, I call it my Africa sickness, was very strong, and lasted even when something very important took over my life. That was all."

"I see . . . and that other thing was falling in love with somebody?"

Mma Makutsi's spectacles caught the light. "Hah!" she said. "That is something that can turn you upside down. Upside down. Like that."

"Well it did for me," said Susan. "As I told you, I wasn't very happy when we went off to Saskatoon. And I wasn't happy all through high school there. I didn't fit in, you see—the others had all grown up together, so I was the outsider. And so I was quite happy to go away to college, which I did when I was eighteen. I thought that would be a new beginning and it was, I suppose. I met new people. I made friends. My whole world opened out."

Mma Makutsi nodded. "When I came to the Botswana Secretarial College . . . ," she began. But Mma Ramotswe looked at her, and she stopped.

"I went to university in a place called Kingston," said Susan. "And I was happy there. Then I met a young man and I fell in love with him. I had never imagined what it was like to fall in love, Mma; I had no idea. I could only think of him, just of him, all the time. Nothing else mattered."

"That is what it is like," muttered Mma Makutsi. "It is a very strange feeling."

"You were lucky," said Mma Ramotswe. She hesitated. "As long as . . . as long as he loved you back."

"That is very important," said Mma Makutsi. "If you fall in love and the other person does not notice you, you can feel very, very sad."

"He did," said Susan. "He felt the same way. He told me that. We were very happy."

Mma Ramotswe shifted in her seat. She was beginning to feel anxious about this story. Was Susan expecting her to find this young man who had disappeared from her life? If so, how did Botswana come into it? Had the young man come here for some reason?

"You were very fortunate, Mma," said Mma Makutsi.

"I was," said Susan. "But I'm afraid it did not work out as I hoped it would. We went to Toronto together and we lived there for a few years and then . . . well, then, I'm afraid he went off with somebody else. And that was that."

"I'm very sorry," said Mma Ramotswe.

"And I'm sorry too," said Mma Makutsi.

Susan turned to smile at Mma Makutsi. "You're very kind. Thank you. But that is not what I've come to see you about. I haven't come here to tell you about that."

They waited. Through the wall, from the garage, there came the sound of metal striking metal.

"There is a garage next door," explained Mma Ramotswe. "It is my husband's. Sometimes they make a noise."

"Sometimes a very big noise," added Mma Makutsi. "This is not much of a noise."

The metallic sound stopped.

"There," said Mma Ramotswe. "We can talk again."

Susan took her cue. "I decided to come back to Botswana," she said, "because I'd been so happy here. I wanted to see the place I loved so much. I wanted to see some of the people."

Mma Ramotswe wrote on her pad: *Place. People.*

"May I show you a photograph, Mma Ramotswe?"

Susan dug into the handbag she was carrying and extracted a black-and-white photograph. It was a large print, the size of a paperback book, and its edges were scuffed. As she passed it to Mma Ramotswe, Mma Makutsi rose from her chair and came to look over her shoulder.

"That is me when I was about seven," said Susan. "And that lady was the nurse my parents engaged to help look after me. She was called Rosie. She had a Setswana name, but I'm afraid I don't know what it was." She looked apologetic. "I wish I could ask my parents— they might have known, but my mother died, you see, a few years back and my father . . . well, his memory is very weak now—he's in a home. He can't remember much about Botswana."

Mma Ramotswe nodded sympathetically. "It is very sad to lose your world."

Susan pointed to the photograph. "You see her face?"

Mma Ramotswe peered at the photograph. A young girl wearing a faded frock, barefoot, stood beside a woman somewhere in her late twenties—or so it seemed; it was difficult enough, even in the flesh, to tell ages with faces that did not line; harder yet with a photograph such as this, which was blurred. It was as if a filter had been placed across it, softening the edges, draining definition. Mma Ramotswe could tell that the woman was a Motswana—there was something familiar about the face, the bone structure, that enabled her to recognise a kinswoman.

The woman was smiling—not in the strained way in which people may smile in photographs, told to do so by the photographer, but in the natural way of one who wants to smile; who is happy; who is with somebody she loves.

"You were fond of that woman?" asked Mma Makutsi.

"Very," said Susan. "Very, very fond. She was like a second mother to me."

"That can happen," said Mma Ramotswe. "That is why it is a fortunate thing to have a nursemaid. You have one mother, and then you have another mother."

Susan reached out to touch the photograph. Mma Ramotswe noticed the gentleness—the reverence—with which she did this. And she thought of the photograph that she kept in the living room at Zebra Drive—the photograph of her late father, Obed Ramotswe, and of what it meant to her. The photographs of late people had a power beyond that of the photographs of those who were still with us . . . She stopped. This woman, this Rosie, was not necessarily late; and that, Mma Ramotswe realised, was why Susan was here.

"You want me to find this lady?" she asked, tapping the photograph. "That is why you are here, Mma?"

Susan reached out to reclaim the photograph. "If you can, Mma. But I also want you to find out other things. There was a girl I was at school with—I have her full name. And the house we lived in— I don't have an address for it, and when I went to look for it I couldn't work out which one it was. I'd like you to find that. And a few other things too."

"Your life in Botswana?" said Mma Makutsi. "You want us to find the life you lost? Is that it, Mma?"

Susan took a few moments to answer. Then she said, "I suppose it is. I suppose that's exactly what I want." She paused, and looked anxiously first at Mma Ramotswe and then at Mma Makutsi. "You don't think that foolish, do you? You don't think it ridiculous to come here and try to find a past that took place a long time ago? Thirty years, in fact."

Mma Ramotswe shook her head. "Not at all, Mma. You should hear some of the things we are asked to do—then you'd realise that your request is not at all foolish."

"Yes," said Mma Makutsi. "We have been asked to do far stranger things than this. There was this man who came in, Mma, and he asked us—"

There was a warning glance from Mma Ramotswe.

"We must be careful of confidentiality, Mma Makutsi." And to Susan she said, "You can be assured, Mma, that we will not talk about your case to anybody."

"Except when necessary," interjected Mma Makutsi. "There may be circumstances in which we have to reveal something in order to get further information. There was a case once where this man had asked us to watch his wife because she was taking so many lovers, and we—"

"Exactly," Mma Ramotswe cut in. "Confidentiality is very important, Mma."

"I have nothing to hide, anyway," said Susan.

"That is good," said Mma Makutsi. "We have had clients in here with a lot to hide, Mma—I can tell you. In fact, there was—"

"Mma Makutsi!" said Mma Ramotswe.

"In fact, there was a case I cannot tell you about," concluded Mma Makutsi. "But it was definitely a case of that sort."

Susan leaned forward in her chair. "So you'll be able to help me, Mma Ramotswe?"

Mma Ramotswe did not hesitate. "Of course, I shall try, Mma."

Susan expressed her gratitude. "You have made me very happy," she said.

But Mma Ramotswe was cautious. "Try to help you, Mma . . . try to help you. I cannot guarantee anything. Thirty years, you see, is a long time."

"I know that," said Susan. "But we can try, can't we?"

"Of course we can, Mma," said Mma Ramotswe. "If we didn't try, then we would get nothing done."

"That is very true," said Susan.

"Mma Ramotswe often says things that are true," said Mma Makutsi. "She is a very truthful lady, you see." And then she added, "That is well known."

"That is why I came here," said Susan quietly. "For the truth."

CHAPTER FOUR

MR. POLOPETSI'S GREAT IDEA

THEIR CONVERSATION WITH SUSAN lasted until shortly after twelve. At that point, with instructions taken and having agreed to see her again in two days' time, Mma Ramotswe left Mma Makutsi in charge of the office. She was to meet Mma Potokwane for lunch, out at the Orphan Farm—an engagement that the two of them had every few weeks. The meeting always took the same form, with the two of them visiting one of the housemothers to have lunch with the children, and, after that, sharing a cup of tea in Mma Potokwane's office. That involved an exchange of information; Mma Potokwane was always keen to hear of the latest cases—always anonymised, of course, to preserve the client's confidence. She also liked to hear the latest observations from Mma Makutsi and news of Fanwell, of Charlie, and of the garage. In return she brought Mma Ramotswe up to date on orphanage affairs, on the activities of the Tlokweng council, and on the bulletins Mma Potokwane received from her extensive network of friends and relatives throughout Botswana. Had anybody ever compared Mma Potokwane's briefings of Mma Ramotswe with those that the government of Botswana received from its intelligence services, there may have been little to distinguish the two in terms of reach, complexity, and accuracy.

"So, Mma Ramotswe," Mma Potokwane announced as her friend knocked on her office door. "I have been sitting here thinking *When will my good friend Mma Ramotswe arrive for lunch?* and even as I think that, I hear your knock on the door."

"And I have been thinking, *What good things will my friend Mma Potokwane have arranged for us to have for lunch?*"

"I've spoken to one of the housemothers," said Mma Potokwane. "She will be cooking goat. And there will be plenty."

They left the office and made their way to one of the cottages behind the main buildings. Each of these cottages, neat red-roofed buildings, was home to eight children looked after by a housemother. She cooked for the children, ironed their clothes, bathed them, dealt with their nightmares, wiped away tears, and made up, as far as was humanly possible, for the loss that each of the children had suffered.

Mma Kentse, the housemother, greeted them at the entrance and led them into the living room. A table had been laid for six, three places for the adults and three at the end for the older children, the younger children having already been fed. Once they were seated, one of the children, a girl of ten, fetched a pot from the kitchen and placed it on the table. Mma Ramotswe sniffed appreciatively at the aroma of the stew. Goat was one of her favourites, but it was not a dish that they had very often at Zebra Drive, as Mr. J.L.B. Matekoni was indifferent to it, preferring chicken, even if it were served every day for an entire week.

They joined hands as Mma Potokwane said grace, their eyes lowered.

"This good food is given to us by the land," she said. "There are many who do not have this and we think of them now. And we think, too, of the mothers and fathers of these children who are gathered to the Lord and who are at his table today. They are looking down on their children here, and they are pleased that their children have a full plate. So we give thanks."

Mma Ramotswe glanced at the girl who had brought the pot

to the table. She was seated next to her and she saw that she was wearing a thin bracelet of knotted wool, home-made. Her heart went out to her. She knew what it was not to have a mother, but she, at least, had had her father; how could any child bear the loss of both? The girl was staring at her plate; now, she raised her eyes, and for a moment looked directly at Mma Ramotswe, who smiled and gently took her hand under the table, squeezing it in encouragement.

The three children at the table had been told to speak to Mma Ramotswe about their schoolwork. She heard of how they were drawing a map of Botswana with all the roads outlined in red and with contour lines to show the heights of hills. They were learning cookery and carpentry; they had been taught all about birds and their habitats.

"You are learning all the things you need to know," said Mma Ramotswe. "You will know a lot by this time next year."

"There is always more to learn," said Mma Potokwane. "I am still learning things."

"But you must know everything, Mma," said one of the children.

"I wish that were true," said Mma Potokwane, smiling. "I shall be happy if I eventually know as much as Mma Ramotswe."

The goat was every bit as delicious as Mma Ramotswe had expected; pressed to do so by the combined forces of Mma Potokwane and Mma Kentse, she had three helpings before the pot was carried back to the kitchen.

"Three helpings is not too much," said Mma Potokwane. "It is a vote of confidence in the cook. It is a compliment."

The children left to do the washing-up and then, after a short discussion with Mma Kentse about one of the children who was new to the house and who was having difficulty settling, Mma Potokwane and Mma Ramotswe returned to the office for the post-lunch cup of tea.

"She is a good housemother, that one," said Mma Ramotswe.

Mma Potokwane agreed. "Whenever I hear people say that the

country is going to the dogs—and there are such people, you know, Mma . . ."

"Oh, I know that," agreed Mma Ramotswe. "There are always people who say that things are getting worse and that the old ways are disappearing . . ." She paused. She was one of those people, she realised; not that she said that all the time, but she did occasionally say that, because it was so obviously true. Things *were* changing; she had noticed that a long time ago, and other people had noticed it too. People were less concerned about other people, less prepared to help them, not so ready to listen to them. Did that mean that things were getting worse? Well, in her view it did—at least as far as those matters were concerned; in other respects, things were undoubtedly getting better. People had more of a chance in life no matter where they came from; those who worked for other people had more rights, were protected against the cruelty that employers could show in the past. That was an improvement. And the hospitals were better, and school bullies found it a bit harder to bully people; and there were fewer cruel nicknames; and fewer power cuts just when you wanted to cook the evening meal.

She looked at Mma Potokwane. The matron was staring up at the ceiling, and Mma Ramotswe realised that her friend was probably thinking exactly the same thoughts that she was, even if she had made the original comment about people saying that things were getting worse.

"Of course," mused Mma Potokwane, "you might say . . ."

Mma Ramotswe waited, but the sentence remained unfinished, hanging in the air like an immense question mark over the state of the world.

"You might say," Mma Ramotswe suggested, "that in some ways—just in some ways, Mma—things are going to the dogs."

"Maybe the dogs don't want it that way," said Mma Potokwane. "Maybe the dogs say: Why are they giving all this to us, when we are just dogs and we have enough to do scratching ourselves for fleas and looking for things to eat? Maybe that is what the dogs are thinking, Mma."

They both laughed.

"What I was going to say, Mma Ramotswe," continued Mma Potokwane, "is that even if some people say that things are becoming worse—and I'm not saying they don't have their reasons for thinking that—there are some things that are not changing." She paused to take a sip of her tea. "And one of those things is the women of this country. We are still making women like that housemother—like Mma Kentse. Those ladies are still here, Mma."

"I am very glad," said Mma Ramotswe.

"So when I put an advertisement in the paper for a housemother, I am overwhelmed by the replies, Mma. Thirty, forty ladies apply—sometimes as many as fifty. And when I interview them, almost every single one of them has what it takes to be a housemother. Would you believe that, Mma Ramotswe?"

Mma Ramotswe had heard of the large numbers of people who applied for jobs, and she wondered how employers managed to select from such a wide field. Was everyone interviewed? And even if that happened, how did one distinguish one applicant from another when they all probably had roughly the same qualifications?

She asked Mma Potokwane how she made her selection.

"It is very difficult," replied the matron. "You have thirty ladies—all wanting an interview. You cannot speak to them for very long."

"No, you cannot do that. That would take days."

"Weeks," said Mma Potokwane. "Because they all like talking in an interview. And they want to show you how well they can cook. They go on and on about their recipes. And their children. They tell you about their children so that you will know what a good mother they are. Some of them bring the children to the interview and the child starts telling you why her mother should get the job. That is a very difficult situation, Mma."

Mma Ramotswe could imagine that. She felt glad that she had

never had to interview anybody for a job. When Mma Makutsi was appointed, it was she—Mma Ramotswe—who had been interviewed by Mma Makutsi, not the other way round. And other people who had worked for the agency—such as Mr. Polopetsi—had been taken on without an interview because she felt sorry for them.

"So do you look at references?" she asked.

Mma Potokwane looked thoughtful. "Sometimes references are useful, but only if they tell the truth. Most references, I'm afraid, are not very truthful."

"And why is that, Mma?"

"Because people are too kind," said Mma Potokwane. "People do not like to write unkind things about other people. So they say that this person is very good at her job and shows plenty of initiative, and so on. They say that she is a quick learner and has been a great asset to the company. They say that everybody in the office likes her. They say all these things, Mma, because a person who works for you is often like your child—you feel you have a duty to say nice things."

She paused, and then raised an admonitory finger. "Or, if the person has been a very hopeless employee and the employer then wants to get rid of him, then they write a glowing reference. This is to make sure that they get the job and go. What do they say, Mma? Don't they say: 'Make sure that the road is always clear for your enemy to leave'? There is a lot of truth in these sayings, Mma—a lot of truth."

Mma Ramotswe shook her head. "It must be very difficult for you, Mma. Because you don't want to choose somebody just because she is a distant relative or something like that . . ."

Had Mma Ramotswe been looking at Mma Potokwane at the time, she would have noticed her friend squirming slightly at this; it was only a brief reaction, though, and there might have been nothing to it. A squirm may really be a shifting of weight, a momentary compromise with the gravity that eventually defeats us all.

"No," said Mma Potokwane, perhaps more firmly than might have been necessary, "one would not want to make an appointment on that basis. You should not give people a job just because you know their parents or because they are from the same village as you. No, you must not do that."

"No," said Mma Ramotswe. "You must not."

They were silent for a moment. Then Mma Ramotswe said, "So how did you choose that lady, Mma? How did you choose Mma Kentse?"

Mma Potokwane drained her cup and reached out for the teapot. "It was very difficult, Mma," she said. "I had a shortlist of five ladies—all of them with the right experience. Three had worked in the hospital, and two had worked in a school. They all had their school-leaving certificate and they all had brought up their own children. They were all members—or had been members—of a choir too; it is a good thing, I find, if the housemother can sing to the children."

Mma Ramotswe agreed. Singing to children was one of the traditions that she most wanted preserved. It was what the grandmothers had always done, and it lay, she felt, at the heart of what it was to be brought up in Botswana. It was the blanket, in a sense, in which a child was wrapped—that blanket of love that a nation should provide. It might seem to be a small matter, but it was in reality a very big thing indeed.

"So how did you choose?"

Mma Potokwane hesitated before replying. "You are a traditionally built lady, Mma," she said. "As am I. We are both traditionally built. So . . ."

Mma Ramotswe leaned forward in anticipation. "So you . . ."

"So I chose the most traditionally built lady of the five," said Mma Potokwane.

Mma Ramotswe let out a whoop of delight. "You didn't, Mma!"

Mma Potokwane nodded. She was smiling now. "I did, Mma. And I did so because I felt that the most traditionally built lady would be the happiest. And the happiest lady would make the children happy, which is what the job of housemother is all about. The children love a traditionally built housemother—such a lady has more acreage, so to speak, Mma, for the children to climb on. Her lap will be big enough for many children to sit on at the same time, and . . ." She searched for additional reasons.

"And her heart will be traditionally built," said Mma Ramotswe. "She will have a large heart."

"There you are," concluded Mma Potokwane. She looked at Mma Ramotswe enquiringly. "Do you think I did the right thing, Mma?"

"Of course you did," said Mma Ramotswe, who was sure of her response. It was not just that she was a traditionally built person speaking on behalf of the ranks of traditionally built people; it seemed to her that any reasonable person would agree with Mma Potokwane's reasoning. So she repeated her reassurance to her friend that she had done the right thing, and they moved on to the next subject, which was a conversation that Mma Potokwane had had with Mr. Polopetsi. This gave rise to a rather different issue altogether.

"I had a visit from Mr. Polopetsi," said Mma Potokwane. "It was a bit of a surprise, as I don't really know him all that well."

Mma Ramotswe raised an eyebrow. "Nothing official, Mma? Nothing to do with his work for the agency?"

Mma Potokwane shook her head. "No, nothing to do with business—or not your agency's business. It was more personal."

Mma Ramotswe wondered what personal business Mr. Polopetsi might have with Mma Potokwane. Mma Makutsi had always hinted that there was a side to Mr. Polopetsi that they knew nothing about, and she was right: they knew little about Mr. Polopetsi's personal life, about his friends, about the place he originally came from.

"He stopped by a couple of weeks ago," continued Mma Potokwane. "He sat there—in the chair you're on—and asked me whether I was financially secure."

Mma Ramotswe frowned. "How strange."

"Yes, I thought so. So I told him that I got a good salary here and that my husband was doing reasonably well. I said that we were far from being rich, but we did not want for anything." She paused. "Mind you, I wish we could afford a more reliable car, but then who doesn't wish for that? Can you name one single person who doesn't want a more reliable car?"

Mma Ramotswe laughed. "I'm happy with my van. It is very old . . ."

"But very reliable, Mma. I have never seen it break down—ever."

"No, it does not break down. It just goes on and on. Mr. J.L.B. Matekoni would like me to get rid of it."

"You couldn't do that. It would be like getting rid of your aunt. You cannot get rid of these important things just like that."

"So what was Mr. Polopetsi driving at?" asked Mma Ramotswe.

Mma Potokwane stared out of the window. Somewhere outside a child was crying, and her matron's antennae had responded. But then the child stopped, and she moved her gaze to Mma Ramotswe.

"He told me that he had become a member of some sort of investment club," she said. "He said that it was called the Fat Cattle Club and it offered very good returns. He said that the returns were, in fact, better than anything you could get from the banks or the insurance companies. He said that if I had a spare ten thousand pula he could arrange for me to join this club and get—and this was the part that astonished me—twenty-five per cent return on the money I put in."

Mma Ramotswe's astonishment showed. "Twenty-five per cent! That's impossible, Mma."

"Not with this scheme," said Mma Potokwane. "At least, not according to Mr. Polopetsi. He said that he's already drawn his twenty-five per cent profit—and he's only been in the club for a few months. He said that an early pay-out was the reward you got for recruiting new members."

Mma Ramotswe asked what the Fat Cattle Club did. She imagined that it was something to do with the buying and selling of cattle—a popular activity in Botswana and one that her own father, Obed Ramotswe, had excelled in.

"This Fat Cattle Club," Mma Potokwane explained, "buys cattle from the drought areas in the north. Then it brings them down to a place near Lobatse and feeds them up until they are ready to sell. That's how it makes its profits."

"But twenty-five per cent?" said Mma Ramotswe. "You can't make twenty-five per cent just by fattening cattle. You have the cost of the feed—cattle don't get fat on air."

"He said that's all taken into account," said Mma Potokwane. "The real return is twenty-five per cent. That's what he said."

Mma Ramotswe hardly dared ask the next question. But she had to know. "And did you join the club, Mma?"

The answer was the one she wanted. "Certainly not," said Mma Potokwane. "To begin with, I don't have a spare ten thousand pula. And then, even if I did, I don't think I would invest it with Mr. Polopetsi. It's not that I have anything against him, it's just that he doesn't strike me as being the business type. You know how some people have 'business type' written all over them, Mma? Well, I don't think that Mr. Polopetsi is like that. He's a chemist and occasional private detective. He's not a business type."

Mma Ramotswe agreed with that evaluation of Mr. Polopetsi, but she knew that Mr. Polopetsi himself might see things differently. "Was he upset, Mma?"

Mma Potokwane shook her head. "Not in the slightest. But he did ask me whether I could recommend other people to him. So I thought and thought and eventually I came up with a cousin of my husband's. This is a person who has quite a bit of money—he used to own a factory that made ladders—and likes to invest in good ideas."

"I'm not sure that this is such a good idea."

"Perhaps not. But there we are. I hope that it continues to do well—this Fat Cattle Club. It's certainly doing a community service."

Mma Ramotswe looked dubious. "By growing people's money by twenty-five per cent?"

Mma Potokwane explained what she meant. "No, not by doing that. You see, he told me that they buy the cattle from the drought areas . . ."

"You said that."

"Yes, but they give the poor farmers ten per cent more than they'd get from the Meat Commission. So they are doing them a favour in their hour of need. Isn't that good, Mma?"

Mma Ramotswe knew what it was to have to sell your cattle because of drought. It was a last resort, a shameful thing, brought about by sheer desperation. There was something worse, of course, and that was when the cattle were in such poor condition through lack of grazing that they had no value and had to be slaughtered. That was the end of everything for some; to see the poor beasts so debilitated they could barely walk, standing there passively, awaiting their fate.

She very much approved of the idea of giving people more money for their cattle, but she was puzzled as to how this could be done. The price of cattle was ultimately determined by the market, and the market took all sorts of factors into consideration in deciding what to pay. Alongside supply—the more cattle, the lower the price—there was the cost of feed to be considered, and that was a major influence on price. Ideally, cattle would be left to fend for themselves, finding in grass and leaves all the sustenance they needed. Even in a dry land, such as Botswana, cattle could find enough in what seemed unpromising surroundings, but when drought struck and the last of the vegetation withered, they needed feeding to remain alive. That was expensive, as animal feed had to be brought in from over the border, and if the desiccated fingers of drought stretched out into the rich grasslands, the veld of Gauteng, then the price of foodstuff would soar.

If the Fat Cattle Club bought thin cattle for fattening, then that would only come at a cost. It was possible that they could move them to areas where there was still grazing to be had, but such areas were already under pressure because of the drought further north. And if the cattle were not to be given good grazing, then how was their condition to be improved—other than through the purchase of feed and salt licks? One did not have to be an economist to understand that this would eat into any profit on the eventual sale of the cattle, particularly if you had paid ten per cent above the going rate in the first place.

Mma Ramotswe raised these concerns with Mma Potokwane, who shrugged. "I don't know much about these things, Mma," said the matron. "All I know, though, from running this place, is that everything costs money, and there's no easy way round that. You can't grow money in the fields, no matter how hard you try."

"Exactly, Mma. So how does Mr. Polopetsi imagine he'll get twenty-five per cent?"

Again Mma Potokwane shrugged. "But he says he's already had twenty-five per cent return on his original investment." She paused. "Maybe the cattle were very good beasts, Mma. Maybe they were already quite fat."

That was impossible, and Mma Ramotswe told her friend that. "Those poor cattle from up north are skin and bone these days. They would need to eat and eat to get into good condition."

"Then it is a mystery," concluded Mma Potokwane. She was losing interest in Mr. Polopetsi's scheme, and wanted to talk about Mma Makutsi's baby. "I hear that that baby of hers purrs like a cat, Mma. Is that true?"

"It is true," said Mma Ramotswe. "It is very strange. I believe it is the only purring baby in Botswana."

Mma Potokwane shook her head in wonderment. "There is more to Mma Makutsi than meets the eye," she said. "Is it true that she talks to her shoes?"

Mma Ramotswe smiled. "Or they talk to her. Yes, I believe that something like that is going on, although I cannot believe that shoes would ever talk. That's just nonsense, Mma."

The practical side of Mma Potokwane was in firm agreement. "Of course it is. I suppose that it's a question of her imagination. She imagines that her shoes are talking to her, but it's really all in her mind. You see a lot of that with children, you know. They imagine things."

"Oh yes, Mma. They do that all right."

Mma Potokwane pointed in the direction of one of the cottages. "There's a child in that cottage over there—a very imaginative child. She told the housemother that she has a friend who comes to visit her—a friend called Dolly. She seems convinced that this friend lives somewhere over in the Kalahari and rides a giraffe. Such nonsense. And yet she insists it's all true. She even made a small cake for this friend the other day and left it out for her. Of course the ants got it first."

"I have heard that children do that, especially if they're lonely."

Mma Potokwane looked thoughtful. "I suppose that if I didn't have a real friend called Mma Ramotswe, I could invent one. I could say that this lady comes out here to see me in a tiny white van and we drink tea and eat fruit cake together. I could make up something like that—if I had to."

Mma Ramotswe looked pointedly at the saucer beneath her teacup. That saucer was often used for a piece of Mma Potokwane's fruit cake, but for some reason none had been offered that day.

"Oh, my goodness!" exclaimed Mma Potokwane. "What a thoughtless person I am—I have forgotten to offer you a piece of fruit cake, Mma. I thought after three helpings of goat stew you might not . . ."

"That was some time ago, Mma," said Mma Ramotswe politely. "A piece of fruit cake would be most welcome, now that you mention it."

Cake was produced, and their conversation continued for another ten minutes before Mma Ramotswe looked at her watch and said that she would have to leave. Although it was mid-afternoon, she wanted to call in at the agency and deal with one or two matters before going home. So she said goodbye to Mma Potokwane and began the drive back to town, thinking, as she did, of the story Mma Potokwane had told her of Mr. Polopetsi and the Fat Cattle Club. It was none of her business what Mr. Polopetsi did in his spare time, but she was fond of him and she felt a certain responsibility towards him. He was, after all, an employee—even if only a very part-time one, and a volunteer at that. More importantly, though, he was a friend, and Mma Ramotswe would never allow a friend to do anything stupid without at least issuing some sort of warning. Was that what she needed to do here? Was Mr. Polopetsi being stupid, or, on the contrary, astute? He was an intelligent man, with his degree in chemistry from the university, but intelligence and judgement were two different things—as her work had shown her on so many occasions and as Clovis Andersen, she seemed to remember, said at some point in *The Principles of Private Detection.* The great Clovis Andersen, from Muncie, Indiana— what would he say about the Fat Cattle Club if he were told about it? She thought for a moment, and then she heard his voice: *Be very careful of anything that looks too good to be true. Because if it looks too good to be true, that's probably because that's exactly what it is!*

CHAPTER FIVE

THE DOG REALLY LOVED THAT SMALL MAN

SHE COULD TELL from Mma Makutsi's expression that something had happened. It was not her *Something dreadful's happened* expression; it was more her *You'll never guess what's happened* look, and it involved a wry, rather coy smile.

"So you are back," said Mma Makutsi. "And how was my friend Mma Potokwane?"

"She was very well, Mma. She sends you her good wishes. She was asking after you."

Mma Makutsi's smile broadened. "I'm glad to hear that, Mma. I haven't seen her for some time—I should go out and visit her, perhaps." She paused. "Fruit cake?"

Mma Ramotswe nodded. "It was as delicious as usual."

"How many pieces?" asked Mma Makutsi, adding hurriedly, "I would never blame you for having more than one, Mma. Her fruit cake really is special."

Mma Ramotswe was able to be strictly honest; the question had been about fruit cake, not goat stew. "Just one piece, Mma." She added, "Since you ask."

Mma Makutsi shuffled a small pile of papers on her desk. "I must do some filing," she said. "These papers are getting on top of me."

Mma Ramotswe knew what was expected of her. "Did anything happen round here, Mma?"

She had read the situation correctly. Mma Makutsi did not wait long to reply, and her tone was triumphant. "Have you been round the back?" she asked.

"Round the back?"

"Yes, outside. The back of the garage. Go and take a look."

The back of the garage was part of Mr. J.L.B. Matekoni's domain and Mma Ramotswe rarely ventured round there. It was a place for the storage of oil drums, old tyres, empty wooden crates, and the sundry detritus of a small garage business. It was a place where Charlie and Fanwell liked to sit, perched on empty oil drums, and eat their lunchtime sandwiches. It was a male rather than a female place, one devoted to bits and pieces of old garage equipment, to things that were not currently useful but that may come in handy at some point; a place where men would feel at home.

She left the office by its front door and began to walk round the building. She had no idea what would await her, and her surprise was complete when she saw the dog tied to an old engine block. It was the dog that Fanwell had run over and that she had taken back to Old Naledi. It was back, and it greeted her with a frantic wagging of the tail and a combination of barks and howls. There was no sign of Fanwell, but as she stood there she saw him emerge from the back of the garage, hesitate when he saw her, but then come up to her. His expression was apologetic.

"The dog came back, Mma," he said, pointing at the excited creature at his feet. "It was while you were over at Mma Potokwane's place. He came back."

"So I see," said Mma Ramotswe.

"I don't know how he did it," Fanwell continued. "They say that dogs are very good at finding their way. Do you think it's to do with their very strong sense of smell? Do you think that's how they do it, Mma? Don't you think he's clever, Mma?"

His eagerness betrayed his anxiety, and when Mma Ramotswe looked at him, he winced.

"I didn't encourage him to come back," he muttered. "I promise you, Mma."

Mma Ramotswe made a gesture of acceptance. "I know you didn't, Fanwell. This is not your fault."

"I didn't know what to do, Mma. So I tied him up here."

"That's all right, Fanwell," she said. "You mustn't blame yourself."

His relief was obvious.

"Has Mr. J.L.B. Matekoni said anything?" she asked.

Fanwell sighed. "He said that I would have to take him back again. He said we cannot keep a dog in the garage."

"I'm not surprised," said Mma Ramotswe. "We couldn't leave a dog here overnight. He would be miserable. He'd just howl."

"I know," said Fanwell. "But I can't take him home. My uncle has said that he will not have a dog about the place. He says there isn't even enough room for the people already in the house."

Mma Ramotswe had seen the house that Fanwell lived in; she knew that what he said was true: it was a very small house, not much more than a shack, really, and there were at least three people in every room. She thought, too, that there was probably not much spare food in the house, and that even the few scraps that a dog needed would be hard to come by.

She scratched her head. "I will have to think about this," she said. "We can't leave him here."

She made her way back into the office, where Mma Makutsi greeted her with an inquisitive look.

"I've seen the dog," said Mma Ramotswe. "And I'm not surprised. These creatures have maps in their heads. I'm not surprised he came back."

Her calm acceptance caught Mma Makutsi unawares.

"But I never thought . . ."

"Well," said Mma Ramotswe. "As I said, I'm not all that surprised."

She crossed the room to switch on the kettle. "Tea helps in these situations," she said. "It clears the mind. It helps you think of possible solutions."

"I can see none," said Mma Makutsi.

Mma Ramotswe returned to her desk. She stared up at the ceiling with its criss-cross of fly tracks. For flies, the ceiling board must have been a great white Kalahari, featureless and limitless.

"Mma Makutsi," she began. "You have a lot of room at that new place of yours. You have a very big yard. You have that man who works in the garden for you. You have all that space."

Mma Makutsi looked suspicious. "Yes, Mma, all of that is true, but . . ."

"I just wondered whether you wouldn't find a dog useful. You don't have one at the moment, do you?"

Mma Makutsi took off her glasses and polished them energetically. "You're not suggesting, are you, Mma, that I should take Fanwell's dog? That it should come and live with Phuti and me?"

"The thought had crossed my mind," said Mma Ramotswe.

"Well, it's out of the question," said Mma Makutsi firmly. "Phuti does not want another dog. He had one, and it was a lot of trouble. It bit people. He does not want history to repeat itself."

"So I take it that means no?"

Mma Makutsi nodded. "I'm sorry, Mma. I'd like to help, but I can't take Fanwell's dog."

Mma Ramotswe felt that she had to correct her. "It's not Fanwell's dog," she said. "Not really."

"It thinks it is," said Mma Makutsi. "It has adopted him, I think. That's what's happened, Mma. Dogs can sometimes do that. They see somebody and think, *That's a good person who will give me a lot to eat,* and that's that—as far as the dog's concerned." She rose to her feet. The kettle was beginning to boil and she usually made the tea. As she prepared the teapot and cups, she continued: "We had a case like that in Bobonong, you know. It was a long time ago. There was a very small man—really small, Mma; about half the size of Mr. Polo-petsi, although he had a very big nose—and this big dog came into the village and sat outside this small man's house. It was a very large dog, Mma—I'm not exaggerating when I say that when people first saw it they thought it was a donkey, but then it began to bark and they realised that it was a dog."

Mma Ramotswe sat back in her seat. She had never visited Bo-bonong, and felt that her idea of the place, as depicted in Mma Makutsi's stories, was an unlikely one; dogs as large as donkeys, very small men with outsized noses . . . it all sounded rather improbable.

"Anyway," Mma Makutsi went on, "this dog just sat outside the small man's house, and when the man came out of the house he licked him and almost knocked him over. He really loved that small man, and nothing would keep him away from him. The dog moved in and ate most of the small man's food. He also took over the bedroom, and made the small man sleep outside on some sacking. I'm not mak-ing this up, Mma—it all happened."

Mma Ramotswe watched as Mma Makutsi poured the tea. She hoped that the story would have a proper ending; often Mma Makutsi's stories ended in doubt: she would say, "And I don't know what happened after that, Mma, but it can't have been good." Or she might conclude, "Nobody knows what became of these people but I think they are late, or maybe not late yet—who knows?"

"So what happened to the dog?" she asked.

"That small man died," said Mma Makutsi. "Somebody reversed a tractor over him. They didn't see him, because he was so small; it was nobody's fault."

"And the dog?"

"Oh, that dog was very sad after his owner became late. He sat there and howled and howled, Mma—looking up at the sky and howling. Dogs think that their people will last forever, Mma—they do not understand about becoming late."

"No, I suppose they do not." And that made it easier for them—

or, perhaps, harder. Mma Ramotswe felt that she would have to think more about that.

"One of the small man's relatives came," Mma Makutsi continued. "He was also very small—they all were, those people. Same nose too—these things run in families, you know, Mma. We saw that up in Bobonong; we saw that a lot. There was a family there that had only four toes: grandmother, mother, children—four toes. On each foot, of course: eight toes altogether. It was as if God had said, 'You people are going to get four toes only. No argument. Four toes, so shut up.'" She paused. "Anyway, this relative of the small man took the dog off somewhere and he was never seen again. It is not a very happy story, Mma, but Fanwell's dog has brought it all back to me."

Mma Ramotswe took the teacup Mma Makutsi passed her. "Thank you, Mma," she said. "Tea always helps clear the mind. And as for your story about that small man—I'm very sorry to hear about the tractor."

"These things happen," said Mma Makutsi. "And I think those small people—that man's relatives—were used to things like that. That is how their life is, you see. They start off underfoot, so to speak, and they remain there."

Mma Ramotswe imagined the small family, with their prominent noses, putting up with the indignities heaped upon them by larger people. Mma Makutsi could sometimes simplify things, but she was often very good at seeing the world from another perspective. Tall people could forget that the world might look quite different if you were short; and of course well-off people had a marked tendency to forget how things might look if you were poor. We have to remind ourselves, she thought. We have to remind ourselves how the world looked when viewed from elsewhere.

Mma Makutsi took off her spectacles. She began to polish the lenses, thoughtfully, as one might do when contemplating some great truth. "We would like the world to be different," she said gravely.

"We would like things like that not to happen—but they can't be avoided, Mma—particularly if you're very small."

"No," said Mma Ramotswe. "You're right. They can't be avoided."

Yes, she thought, no amount of wishful thinking could obliterate the hard facts of existence. There were those who prospered, and those who did not. There were those for whom life was easy, not a struggle at all, and those to whom daily existence was painful and humiliating. That was the pain of the world, and it was all around us, washing at the shores of whatever refuges we created for ourselves. She thought of Fanwell, a young man who had very little in this life, and of his dog, who had even less. She could turn away and say that they had nothing to do with her, or she could accept that they had somehow touched her skirt. For that was how she viewed it: we all had a skirt, and those who touched our skirt became our concern.

After a few sips of tea, Mma Ramotswe had reached her conclusion. "Mma Makutsi," she said, "you're nearer the door. Could you call Fanwell in, please?"

Fanwell came in, wiping his hands. He looked timidly at Mma Ramotswe, expecting further reproach. But that was not what Mma Ramotswe had in mind.

"Fanwell," she said. "That dog can come to Zebra Drive this evening. It can stay there until we work something out. You needn't worry."

Fanwell clapped his hands together, dropping the paper towel as he did so. "Oh, Mma . . . Oh, Mma, you are the kindest lady in Botswana—in the whole of Africa. That is one hundred per cent true, Mma—I'm not just saying it. You are the best lady there is . . ." He glanced at Mma Makutsi. "And you too, Mma Makutsi, you are a very good lady too. You are both very kind."

Mma Ramotswe explained that she would need his help to create a run for the dog. "We'll need a long wire pegged out so that we can attach his lead—you know the sort of thing. That will mean that the dog can run backwards and forwards when we are not there."

"I'll make that myself, Mma," promised Fanwell. "The dog will be very safe there, at your place. And he will keep burglars away too, Mma. They'll see the dog and think, *I'm not going to steal from that place—not with that dog there.*"

"No burglar would dare to steal from Mma Ramotswe anyway, Fanwell," said Mma Makutsi.

"No, maybe not," said Fanwell.

"Why?" asked Mma Ramotswe.

Fanwell looked at the floor. "Because . . . because . . ." It was to do with traditional build, but he could not say that. He had never witnessed Mma Ramotswe engaged in a physical struggle—not surprisingly, since she abjured violence of any sort—but he had heard that when absolutely pressed, she had been known to sit on people, crushing the resistance out of them remarkably quickly and efficiently. A well-informed burglar might know that, and give the house on Zebra Drive a wide berth for that reason.

Mma Makutsi took over. "Because burglars aren't stupid, Mma. They know that you're a detective. What burglar would steal from a detective's house? Only a very stupid one, Mma."

"Yes," said Fanwell hurriedly. "That's what I meant, Mma. That's exactly what I meant."

Mma Ramotswe looked at her watch. "Get your dog ready, Fanwell," she said. Then, to Mma Makutsi, she said, "Mma, have you talked to Mr. Polopetsi recently? He hasn't been in for a while."

Mma Makutsi made a vague gesture. "He's been teaching, I think. You know what he's like—he never tells anybody what he's doing. The school calls him up at short notice."

"But have you spoken to him?"

Mma Makutsi replied that she had seen him the previous week. "He was very excited. He came to my place."

Mma Ramotswe was interested. "Specially to see you?"

Mma Makutsi smiled. "Yes. You know about his scheme? You know he has a business scheme, Mma?"

Mma Ramotswe caught her breath. "Yes," she said hesitantly. "I've heard about it."

"It's a very good scheme, apparently," said Mma Makutsi.

Mma Ramotswe hardly dared ask. "And did you . . ."

She did not finish. Mma Makutsi looked pleased. "You know something, Mma? He let me in on very preferential terms."

Mma Ramotswe sighed. "He did, did he?"

"Yes. Phuti gives me a bit of money now and then for my own savings—you know how kind he is. Well, I put some of that into Mr. Polopetsi's scheme. He wanted ten thousand, but I didn't give him that. I put in three thousand pula, though, and I believe that I shall be getting—"

"Twenty-five per cent return," supplied Mma Ramotswe.

"Exactly. How did you know, Mma? Are you in on it too?"

Mma Ramotswe sighed again. "I heard about it," she said.

"Word gets out," mused Mma Makutsi. "Have a good idea, and word gets out. It always does."

CHAPTER SIX

MR. TWENTY-FIVE PER CENT

MA RAMOTSWE had been confronted with cases like this before, where the client wanted to find out something but could provide very little information. The fallibility of human memory, its vague and impressionistic nature, meant that the details that would enable a reconstruction of the past were simply not there. Sometimes the vagueness was extreme, as where a woman searching for the father of her child, conceived twenty-five years previously, remembered only the nickname by which she and his friends knew him. As if this were not difficult enough, she had then produced a photograph of him in which his face had been cut out, leaving only torso and limbs for identification.

"I was cross with him," she said, "and so I cut out his face and threw it down the toilet."

Mma Ramotswe had been understanding. Men who sired children and then failed to accept responsibility for them were anathema to her, and she reserved particular disapproval for those who then completely disappeared. She wondered how they managed it; was there some sort of secret organisation, known only to men, that spirited them away, perhaps giving them a new identity under which they could continue their irresponsible ways? In that case she had eventually managed to find him through a trick, mentioned by Clovis Andersen in *The Principles of Private Detection*, that she had thought would never work, but did. *If all else fails,* wrote Mr. Andersen, *you can try to trace people by asking them to step forward! Yes, believe it or not, that works. Place an ad in the press asking for—and here insert the name of the person (you have, at least, to know that)—to reply to a box number about a possible legacy. That may work. Of course there is the familiar ethical issue, but remember you are only talking about a possible legacy and it's always possible that anybody will get a legacy one of these days.*

Mma Ramotswe had been very doubtful but had eventually put in a small advertisement saying, *"If the person known as Fancy Harry, resident in Gaborone twenty-five years ago, contacts the undermentioned, he will learn something of great interest to himself."* That wording, she decided, was completely honest. Fancy Harry, if he responded, would imagine that it was financial interest to which the advertisement was referring, but learning that your child and her mother were keen to contact you was undoubtedly of interest too, even if it was not exactly welcome information.

To her astonishment it worked. Fancy Harry responded, giving his current address and his real name, and adding that he could provide details of his bank account if required. She did not know what happened after she had provided this information to her client, but if Fancy Harry had an unwelcome shock, it was thoroughly deserved, as far as Mma Ramotswe was concerned; not that she expressed the same delight in this outcome as did Mma Makutsi. She had danced a small jig round the office when the reply was received, chanting, "That will teach men to have their fun and then disappear."

Mma Ramotswe wondered whether a similar approach might bear fruit in Susan's case. She asked Mma Makutsi for her views, and was told that there would be no harm in trying. "People read the small ads in the *Botswana Daily News*," she said. "There are many people who find them more interesting than the main news. If you put in something like *'Are you called Rosie and did you work a long time ago for a Canadian family?'* then there may be people who knew her even if she herself does not read it."

"But what about impostors?" asked Mma Ramotswe. "There will be many people who will sniff out some financial gain and will claim to be that Rosie. What will we do about them?"

Mma Makutsi clearly had not thought about that, and looked disappointed. But then she brightened. "We have the photograph, Mma," she said. "We could publish that. We could say: *'Are you this woman?'* That will discourage those people because they will not look like the real Rosie." She paused. "I know the photograph is very indistinct, Mma, but at least it gives us some idea of the lady's build—and of the shape of her head."

Mma Ramotswe considered this. It was a good idea, she thought, and it would not cost a great deal. They might even get the newspaper to make a news story of it, in which case it would be completely free. She raised this possibility with Mma Makutsi, who agreed.

"I can telephone that journalist woman," she said. "Phuti gave her a big discount on her dining-room furniture a couple of months ago. I will enquire how her table is doing and then ask her."

The telephone call was made that morning. The journalist required no persuasion. "Our readers are always interested in these human interest stories," she said. "I shall come and interview you this morning, Mma Makutsi, and perhaps we can have your photograph in the paper as well. Shall I bring our photographer?"

The arrangements were made. Mma Ramotswe was pleased because she now had something to report to the client; Mma Makutsi, who had only been mentioned in the papers once before—when she graduated from the Botswana Secretarial College—was excited at the prospect of being interviewed and photographed. She was concerned that Mma Ramotswe might feel that she was stealing the limelight, but there was no sign of that. Mma Ramotswe, in fact, was happier being in the background. Everybody knew who she was, anyway, and she did not need any further exposure. And Clovis

Andersen, it seemed, agreed with her. *Always remember the case is not about you,* he wrote. *The case is about the client. The more invisible you are, the better. Keep a low profile. Don't tell the press anything you don't need to tell them. Quietly does it—every time.*

The journalist and the photographer arrived together, barely an hour after Mma Makutsi had made her telephone call. The journalist was called Bandie Mokwena, and she was known not only for her feature articles but also for her recent marriage to Quicktime Tsabong, a jaunty and well-liked sports commentator on Radio Botswana. They were the perfect media couple, much photographed themselves at charity events and public occasions. Quicktime had accompanied the Botswana team to the last Olympic Games, and wore the Olympic rings symbol on his blazer to remind people of the fact. Bandie, although quieter than her colourful husband, had a natural charm that set her interview subjects at ease and elicited facts that a less friendly manner would simply fail to uncover.

The photographer was a young man with a rather effusive manner. He looked at Mma Makutsi critically, asking her to move around the office until she was in the right light before he started to photograph her.

"I think I should stand over here," said Mma Makutsi, positioning herself in front of her certificate from the Botswana Secretarial College. "Do you think this would do?"

"Okay, that's good," said the photographer. "Now smile, honey. Show those teeth to the readers. That's perfect; snap, snap. Perfect."

The interview was conducted over a cup of tea prepared by Mma Ramotswe. Bandie addressed all her questions to Mma Makutsi. "It complicates matters to have too many names in a piece," she said. "So we'll stick to you, Mma, if Mma Ramotswe doesn't mind."

She did not mind, and listened, bemused at times, to Mma Makutsi's telling of the story.

"This lady had a broken heart," Mma Makutsi explained. "All the time she was in Canada she was pining, pining for Botswana. And now she wants to come back and see all her old friends. That quest brought her to our door, and it will be our pleasure to help her. I shall not rest until I bring these two ladies together so that they can talk about those old times.

"The place where you are born, you see, is very special. If you are born in Botswana, you are very lucky, as from your very first day you will have the sun of Botswana on your face. You will have the sounds of Botswana in your ears. You will have the smell of Botswana in your nose."

That was a lot for a small baby to deal with, thought Mma Ramotswe, but she agreed with the general sentiment. There were blessings to be counted, and Mma Makutsi was right to list them. She would have added the sound of cattle coming home in the evening and the smell of their sweet breath. She knew that these were the things that her father said he would miss as he lay on his bed of illness.

"This lady has been thinking of these things for many years," continued Mma Makutsi. "Now she has come to the No. 1 Ladies' Detective Agency to help her find the people she knew as a child, in particular a lady who looked after her. Please look at the picture and ask yourself: Am I this lady?"

It all came out in a flood, and it surprised not only her audience, but Mma Makutsi herself.

"That was very moving," said Bandie, as she transcribed the words in her notebook. "The readers will all hope that Rosie steps forward."

Mma Ramotswe had been thinking. "I'm not sure whether the readers all need to ask themselves whether they are that lady," she said. "They will know, surely, what their name is. So if you are called Alice, for instance, you will know that it cannot be you."

Mma Makutsi looked to Bandie for support, but the journalist, after a few moments' thought, agreed with Mma Ramotswe. "That's a good point, Mma," she said. "I think you should say: If you are called Rosie, are you the Rosie this lady is looking for?"

Mma Makutsi pouted. "But that lady may not be called Rosie any longer," she said. "People change their names. So perhaps I should say: If you have at any time been called Rosie, then are you the Rosie this lady is looking for?"

"That is even better," said Bandie. She looked impressed. "You ladies are very exact. Perhaps that comes from being detectives."

"That is true," said Mma Makutsi. "We are very careful with our words."

Mma Ramotswe smiled.

"And one other thing," said Mma Makutsi. "When you print my photograph, could you please refer to me as a graduate of the Botswana Secretarial College?"

Bandie looked up at the certificate on the wall.

"Ninety-seven per cent, Mma," said the photographer. "Did you see it?"

"That's an amazing mark," said Bandie.

"Thank you," said Mma Makutsi.

"I must tell Quicktime about it," Bandie went on. "He's interested in all sorts of records—not just sporting ones. He told me once about a boy in his class at school who got one hundred per cent in all his Cambridge exams." She waited for a reaction, but none was forthcoming. "One hundred per cent, Mma!"

Mma Makutsi sniffed. "School is one thing; college is another."

"Oh, of course," said Bandie quickly. "I'm not saying that one is equal to the other. But it was nonetheless quite an achievement for that boy—one hundred per cent in everything." She paused. "He was called Brainbox Tefolo, Quicktime said. A very suitable name for a boy like that."

MMA RAMOTSWE KNEW that the newspaper article might help and could, if they were lucky, bring an immediate result—at least in the search for Rosie. But there was more to the request that Susan had made of them. A reunion with Rosie might be her main ambition, but she had been at pains to stress that she was keen to find her old house and some of the children with whom she had been at school at Thornhill. These would not be easy things to discover, thought Mma Ramotswe, but she could at least make a start on the task while they were waiting for the outcome of the article.

They agreed on a division of labour. Mma Makutsi would handle any responses they had to the article, which would appear, Bandie assured them, in the following day's edition of the newspaper. While she was doing this, Mma Ramotswe and Charlie, who was due back the following day from a family funeral, would set about the task of finding the house in which Susan's family had lived. That done, they might be able to trace some of the neighbours from those days, and in this way start piecing together Susan's cherished past. She was not optimistic, though; thirty years was a long time in human affairs anywhere, but it was a particularly long time in a city like Gaborone, which had grown so quickly. A sleepy small town, no more than a handful of streets, had become a city, with all that this entailed. It was still recognisably the same place, though, and its character had remained intact. So whatever they were able to serve up to Susan, even if it was only a few fragments, would, she imagined, ring true and bring back to her at least some of the childhood she was so keen to re-create.

That evening when she went home, Mma Ramotswe found Motholeli and Puso busy with Fanwell's dog. Puso had resurrected an ancient floor brush and was grooming the dog, while his sister had refilled his water bowl and was feeding him scraps of bread spread with beef dripping.

Mma Ramotswe was touched by the sight. There was something particularly appealing, she thought, about children lavishing care on an animal. They were repaying, in a way, the love and care given to them; showing that the message that we should look after one another had not fallen on stony ground. A child who loved a pet was showing the love that would in due course be given to another, and that was a reassurance. Love was like rain; there could be periods of drought when it seemed that love would never return, would never make its presence felt again. In such times, the heart could harden, but then, just as droughts broke, so too could love suddenly appear, and heal just as quickly and completely as rain can heal the parched land.

"Fanwell's dog is very happy here," said Puso. "Look at him, Mma. He is smiling."

Mma Ramotswe looked at the dog. Puso was right: its mouth seemed fixed in a wide, gum-revealing grin.

"We should give him a name," she said. "We cannot call him Fanwell's dog."

"We could call him Zebra," said Motholeli. "This is Zebra Drive and he lives here now. Zebra would be a good name for him."

Puso agreed. "Is that all right with you, Mma?" he asked. "Can we call him Zebra?"

She had been more concerned with Motholeli's saying the dog now lived here. It is too late, she thought; Zebra is no longer temporary—he is permanent.

She left the children and went inside. Mr. J.L.B. Matekoni had arrived back from the garage a few minutes before her, and had put on the kettle.

"You go and sit on the verandah, Mma," he said. "I will bring you your tea. We can talk there."

She imagined that he would want to talk about Zebra, and about the dog's precise status. She rehearsed in her mind what she would say. *Permanent.* Perhaps that single-word answer would be best. Or she might say, "The children have decided the matter for us." That had the merit of truth, but it seemed, in a way, to be transferring responsibility for the decision to them rather than accepting it herself. Perhaps she might say, "What alternative do we have?" And then she would wait to see if he could come up with something, which she doubted he would be able to do.

She need not have worried.

"That dog seems to have settled quite well," said Mr. J.L.B. Matekoni as he took his first sip of tea. "He'll be a useful guard dog."

"Yes," she said. She had not anticipated he would be that accepting. Mr. J.L.B. Matekoni liked dogs well enough, but had expressed concern about the responsibility of keeping one. But then there had been a spate of break-ins recently—small thefts of garden tools and the like, but it was enough for him to be concerned. Cautiously, she asked, "You don't mind, do you?"

He shrugged. "Not really—these break-ins, you see . . . It's the one thing that will deter a burglar. You can build fences as high as you like, you can put big locks on your gates, but it is always dogs that look after your property."

She looked into her teacup. There had been a time when locks had been virtually unknown in Botswana, when you could leave your possessions anywhere with the confidence that they would be there when you returned, when there was no point in stealing because people would see you with some item that they knew you did not own and would draw their own conclusions. That had changed, at least in the towns; it was different in the country, where the old ways still prevailed.

What would her father, the late Obed Ramotswe, make of high, locked gates? She gazed out into the yard; dusk was settling on the town, covering the trees and buildings with its gentle, cooling mantle; there was the smell of wood-smoke, of cooking somewhere. She could hear his voice: *What are these gates for, Precious? Why do these people want to close themselves off from their brothers and their sisters?* It would be hard to explain that people no longer thought of others as their brothers and sisters, although she did; she would never abandon the presumption that we were bound one to another in that way.

She moved on from the subject of the dog. She had been thinking of Mr. Polopetsi and his scheme. It seemed to her that everybody to whom she had spoken knew about it and that she was the only one who had not been approached. Had Mr. Polopetsi also confided in Mr. J.L.B. Matekoni?

"Mr. Polopetsi, Rra," she began.

He laughed. "Mr. Twenty-Five Per Cent, you mean."

For a moment she was unable to say anything.

Mr. J.L.B. Matekoni smiled. "He will have spoken to you about it, Mma?"

She shook her head. "No, Rra. It looks as if he's spoken to everybody else, though."

She wondered whether Mr. J.L.B. Matekoni had invested anything. Surely he would have told her about it—they kept most of their money in a joint account, but they both had separate savings accounts for the occasional individual treat. She did not think, though, that his savings account had more than a couple of thousand pula in it at present; there had been the new roof for the garage and a needy aunt up in Francistown—these were exactly the sorts of things that drained a bank account.

"You didn't . . ."

His laughter cut her short. "Invest in Mr. Polopetsi's great scheme? Certainly not. To begin with, he actually asked for ten thousand pula, Mma. Ten thousand pula? We don't have that at the moment and, if we did, I'm afraid I would never entrust it to Polopetsi Enterprises, or whatever it's called."

"The Fat Cattle Club," said Mma Ramotswe. "That's what he calls it."

"Fat Cattle indeed," muttered Mr. J.L.B. Matekoni. "Does Mr. Polopetsi know anything about cattle? I know that he's very good at chemistry, but cattle . . ." He paused. "The trouble, Mma Ramotswe, is that everybody in this country thinks that he or she is a big cattle expert. Speak to anybody and they'll start going on about cattle. They'll tell you what's best for cattle; they'll explain to you all about the different sorts of salt licks; they'll talk for ages about breeding and horns and diseases that cattle get in their hooves, and ticks too . . . There's no limit to the knowledge that people have about cattle, Mma."

Mma Ramotswe knew what he meant. Cattle were at the heart of Botswana society, the ultimate unit of wealth, the form of property that people appreciated above all else. It did not matter if you had money in the bank; what really counted was the cattle, and many people measured themselves, and others, by how many they had. People were odd about cattle.

"Well," she said, "he's already made his own twenty-five per cent. He told Mma Potokwane about it."

Mr. J.L.B. Matekoni shook his head. "I don't believe it, Mma. Fattening cattle at the moment is a loss-making business—look at the price of feed. I had that man from Molepolole in the garage the other day. He deals in animal feeds, and he says that farmers are finding it difficult to pay him these days. He asked me for credit because his truck repair was going to be so expensive . . . A new differential, new suspension, and other things too." He shook his head at the litany of cost. "An engine is not a cheap thing, Mma." She had heard him say that so often—sometimes to his garage clients, as he broke bad news; sometimes to her; sometimes to friends. He spoke from experience, but always with sympathy.

"No, Rra, you are right: an engine is not a cheap thing." Nothing was cheap, she thought—even the things that were said to be free. Love itself was not cheap—it came with a price tag of its own, a price tag that, at the extreme end, was a broken heart. Freedom was not cheap—its price tag was watchfulness and courage. Even fresh air, the air we breathed each day, had its price tag, it seemed— one we were only now beginning to understand and was all about not destroying the things that gave us that fresh air—the trees, the greenery.

She looked at him; she knew that she did not have to ask whether he agreed to give credit. He always did. "You helped him, Rra, I suppose."

"Yes. How could I not?"

"No, you had to help him." She frowned. "I am worried about Mr. Polopetsi, Rra. I'm afraid that he's going to end up in . . ." She had been going to say "in difficulty," but Mr. J.L.B. Matekoni said "in prison."

And that made her reach her decision. Her already lengthy list of things to do had just grown by one item: *Speak to Mr. Polopetsi.*

CHAPTER SEVEN

THEY LIKE THIS PLACE VERY MUCH

CHARLIE CAME BACK from the funeral in his grandfather's village the following morning. He was full of village news—the sorts of stories that always emanated from such places: whose house had been attacked by termites; who had married whom; who had gone off to Lobatse and who had come back, and why. Mma Ramotswe listened patiently. She knew the appeal of such matters, and she was pleased that Charlie, belonging as he did to a generation brought up outside the villages, should be enthusiastic about what happened in such places. This was the spirit of the country being passed on—it was as simple, and important, as that. But there was business to be done, and she gently reminded him of that.

"Very interesting, Charlie," she said. "But we have work to do. We have a pressing case: a foreign client."

Charlie's attention was immediately engaged. "I am ready, Mma Ramotswe. I am fresh and ready to go. Whatever needs to be done— I am the one, Mma. Tell me, Mma."

He sat before her in the client's chair, leaning forward eagerly to hear every detail. She told him about Susan's visit and the account she had given of her childhood in Botswana. Charlie nodded as she spoke; he understood.

"There are many people like that," he said. "They come to Botswana and they fall in love—not with a person, Mma, but with a country. They like this place very much."

"She was born here, of course."

"Yes," said Charlie. "That is different. But it is also the same."

She did not press him on the distinction, but continued by telling him of Susan's specific requests. "These are not the usual sorts of things a detective agency has to look into, Charlie."

Charlie grinned. "No, Mma, this is not about bad husbands, or wives who become too friendly with other men. It is not that sort of thing."

From behind him, Mma Makutsi, who had been busy filing, joined in. "There is more to our work than that, Charlie." She paused amidst a shuffling of paper. "Even if that's the only sort of thing that some people seem to think about."

Mma Ramotswe's expression told Charlie that she did not want him to engage with Mma Makutsi. He closed his eyes briefly, as if struggling with something. "Go on, Mma. Tell me more."

She reached for the envelope into which she had slipped Susan's photograph. "There is this," she said, laying it on the desk between them. "This is the photo of Mma Susan as a small girl. This lady is her nursemaid."

Charlie leaned over to examine the picture. "Then we can find her," he said quickly. "We will show people this photo and say: 'Who is this lady?'"

He sat back, looking at Mma Ramotswe with the satisfaction of one who has made a brilliant suggestion. From behind him, though, came Mma Makutsi's voice.

"Done. Already done."

Mma Ramotswe nodded. "Mma Makutsi arranged an interview with her friend at the *Botswana Daily News*."

"And it will be in today's edition," said Mma Makutsi. "Phuti is going to buy a copy a bit later and drop it round."

Charlie looked crestfallen. Mma Ramotswe gave him a glance that conveyed a complicated message, the gist of which was that for all sorts of reasons he should congratulate Mma Makutsi on her fast footwork. Charlie, for all his young man's impetuosity, was good at interpreting looks, and he complied.

"That is very good, Mma Makutsi," he said. "That will bring very good results—I'm sure of it."

Mma Makutsi basked in the compliment. "Thank you, Charlie. I hope so." She paused, before adding, "And I am sure that you'll be able to find that house. You're good at those things, I think."

There, thought Mma Ramotswe. There. A kind word, a word of encouragement or admiration, could shift the heaviest, most recalcitrant baggage.

"That photograph," she continued, "shows a bit of the house, as you'll see. There is its verandah, with its fly gauze, you see, and there are the drainpipes round the side leading to a water tank."

Charlie looked at the photo again. "That is one of those BHC houses," he said.

"It was built in the late nineteen-sixties or the early nineteen-seventies, then," said Mma Ramotswe. The Botswana Housing Commission had done much of the building of Gaborone after independence in 1966, using designs that were common in early post-colonial Africa. These houses were for the new class of senior civil servants, local or expatriate, who guided the new state through its early years. They were also for the engineers and doctors, and others who brought their skills to the task of making a country out of a large slice of land that had, for the most part, lain relatively untouched.

"So it would have been over near the old Mall," said Charlie. "Or the Village."

The Village was the area that lay just across the Tlokweng Road from the agency's office. Mma Ramotswe drove through it every day on her way to Zebra Drive and if the house were there, then she would expect to find it quickly. The problem, though, was that many of those earlier houses had been knocked down to make way for newer buildings—for blocks of flats in some cases, or for more prosperous homes. A number of the BHC houses remained, though, and with luck this would be one of them.

"If it's further in," said Charlie, "then there's less chance of it still being there. Those new parts of the hospital have taken up lots of land and those new flats too, the ones on Nyerere Drive, must have been built over places like that."

"That's right."

He looked puzzled. "Doesn't she remember roughly where it was? She would have known where the airstrip was in those days. She would have seen the planes. Was it near there?"

"She thinks it was not far from the university," said Mma Ramotswe. "But she can't be sure which side of the university. She says that when she drove round the other day everything seemed to have shifted."

"There are many new roads," said Charlie. "New roads can make a place look very different."

"So we start from scratch," said Mma Ramotswe. "We go down every road. Unless . . ." She looked at the photograph once more. "Unless there's something here that we're missing."

"You mean some clue, Mma?"

Mma Ramotswe picked up the photograph and scrutinised it. "What have we got? The lady herself? There's nothing in her clothing that tells us anything."

Charlie, who had now left his chair to peer over her shoulder, agreed. "Nothing. Just ordinary clothes."

"And the verandah," continued Mma Ramotswe. "Nothing there either. Just those fly screens."

Mma Ramotswe transferred her attention to the small area of yard that appeared in the photograph. There were aloes round the side of the verandah and then, in the background, the spreading branches of a large tree. Such trees were common in gardens in the older parts of town; where new building had been erected, they were sparser.

"What sort of tree is that?" asked Charlie, touching the photograph with a forefinger.

Mma Ramotswe saw that the leaves were just distinguishable. "Jacaranda," she said.

"There are lots of those," said Charlie.

Mma Ramotswe sighed. "I'm afraid so," she said. "So we shall have to start driving round and round."

"I am very good at that, Mma. I can drive your van for you, if you like."

Mma Ramotswe hesitated. She normally drove herself, but she knew how much Charlie liked driving. He had no car of his own, of course, and so his only opportunities to drive had come with his work in the garage—now brought to an end for financial reasons—or his work with the agency.

"Will you drive slowly?" she asked. "I know what you young men like to do."

"I will drive at walking pace, Mma. Slow, slow. We will be overtaken by bicycles."

Mma Ramotswe laughed. "Perhaps not that slowly," she said. "All I ask is that you stick to the speed limits."

"I always do, Mma."

She looked at him incredulously, but he held her gaze.

"Right, Charlie," she said, rising from her chair. "Off we go. The investigation begins."

"And I think it will be over very soon," said Charlie. "We will find this place, Mma. I have a feeling."

Mma Ramotswe was about to warn him about trusting feelings, but then she remembered two things. The first was that Clovis Andersen said that there were circumstances in which feelings were a useful pointer to certain information that could not be obtained through proper investigation, and the second, perhaps more persuasive, thing was that she herself trusted her feelings all the time. So instead of challenging Charlie's hunch, she simply said, "Well, we'll see," which was incontrovertibly true, whichever way one looked at things.

They set off in the white van, with Charlie driving in an exaggeratedly careful manner, slowing down at intersections to allow for thorough assessment of any approaching vehicles, frequently looking into the driver's mirror to check for overtaking cars, and every so often glancing at Mma Ramotswe beside him to satisfy himself that she had noticed his caution.

Mma Ramotswe suppressed a smile. "There's such a thing as being overcautious, Charlie," she said after a while. "A driver who goes too slowly can cause as many accidents as a driver who goes too fast, you know."

"I'm doing my best, Mma," he muttered.

"So you are, Charlie," she said, reaching out to touch him lightly on the shoulder. "You're a very thoughtful person, Rra."

Charlie beamed with delight. "You know, Mma Ramotswe, I'm not sure that I've said thank you to you—or said thank you enough. You are my mother, Mma. You are the lady who has saved everything for me. I will be your number one, big-time fan for my whole life, Mma—right up to the time that you become late."

"That is very reassuring, Charlie. I hope that I do not become late too soon."

He gasped. "Oh, I would not want that, Mma. I hope that you live to just over one hundred years. Maybe one hundred and one—something like that."

She had known several centenarians, and they had struck her as markedly content. One lived just outside Mochudi, and could be seen every morning, sitting in front of her daughter's house, enjoying the sun, still exchanging good-natured banter with passers-by. Another was a man who had served in the Second World War with the troops who had gone from the Bechuanaland Protectorate, as Botswana then was, to serve alongside the British in Italy, who had done so without question and without complaint, out of loyalty that today some might find naïve or misplaced, but had been for them something not to be questioned. People forgot about them, the African troops who had contributed to the defeat of evil, and that seemed to her to be so unjust, but then where would one end if one started to compose a list of the wrongs that this world had seen? Better perhaps, thought Mma Ramotswe, to make a list of those things that were right with the world, of people who had made life better for other people, or who had done what they had been called to do with honour and without complaint. Her list would start with the late Seretse Khama and would include Nelson Mandela and Bishop Tutu and Queen Elizabeth and President Carter, whom Mma Ramotswe had always admired. Then there was David Livingstone, and Moffat, his father-in-law, who had been such a friend of the Batswana and their language, and Mr. Gandhi . . . There were so many of these people, and one day she would update her list and see what new names should be added to it.

"I'm not sure that I'll live to one hundred," she said. "But if I do, you'll be over eighty, Charlie."

Charlie whistled. "I can't see myself being that old, Mma."

"Neither can I, Charlie." But for a moment she saw him in her mind's eye, an eighty-year-old, relying on a walking stick, chasing an elderly woman along a road, amorous to the last.

"Why are you smiling, Mma?" Charlie asked.

"Oh, no reason, Charlie." She pointed to a turning in the road ahead. "We should start there, Charlie. There are some old houses down there. We could look at them."

IN THE OFFICE of the No. 1 Ladies' Detective Agency, Mma Makutsi had just received a copy of that day's *Botswana Daily News,* delivered by Phuti's driver from the Double Comfort Furniture Store. Pinned to the front was a note in Phuti's handwriting drawing her attention to page six. *A very good photograph, Grace!* Phuti had written. *And a first-class article.*

Fanwell looked over her shoulder as she opened the paper. Then, as she reached page six, he emitted a cry of delight. It was utterly unforced—a shout of joy.

"There you are, Mma! The whole page, or almost." They had both noticed the small news item beneath the main article, but now was not the time to bother with that.

"What do you think of the photograph, Fanwell?" asked Mma Makutsi.

"I think it is A1 excellent, Mma," enthused Fanwell. "And look, your certificate comes out very well. You can see the ninety-seven per cent very clearly. See, you can read it without looking up close. Ninety-seven per cent."

"I'm very glad," said Mma Makutsi. "For the college's sake, of course—not for mine."

"And you look very beautiful, Mma. Any man reading the paper will be saying to himself, 'This is a very beautiful lady, this detective lady.' That's what they'll be saying, Mma—I'm not making it up."

Mma Makutsi giggled modestly. "Oh, I don't think so, Fanwell."

She read out the entire article to Fanwell, who listened gravely. At the end, as she put the paper down on her desk, he said, "That will bring results, Mma."

"I hope so," said Mma Makutsi. "I think that Mma Susan is rather a sad lady, you know. I think that it is very important for her to find what she is looking for."

Fanwell picked up the paper again. For a moment he was silent, and then he let out another cry.

"Mma! Mma! Look at this other article. Same page as you. Oh, Mma . . ."

He passed the newspaper to Mma Makutsi, who adjusted her glasses to read the smaller article at the bottom of the page. She read it out to Fanwell, who listened open-mouthed.

Woman of the Year Nominations ran the headline. *Five nominations have been received with the necessary number of signatures for the Woman of the Year Award. The two top-runners are both from Gaborone and both have successful business careers behind—and before— them. They are Ms. Gloria Poeteng, a senior client manager with the Standard Bank, a lady going places in the banking world, and Ms. Violet Sephotho, a business consultant, who has featured widely on radio and television and who is well known in Gaborone business and social circles. Don't forget to cast your votes in this popular contest for the lady who will be chosen to represent the best in Botswana and southern Africa.*

Mma Makutsi dropped the paper. "Violet Sephotho!" she exclaimed.

"I can't believe it," said Fanwell. "What will Mma Ramotswe say?"

"She will have a heart attack," said Mma Makutsi.

"Oh, Mma, that will be very serious . . ."

"Not a real one, Fanwell. There are heart attacks that are real and make you late, and heart attacks that are not real heart attacks but are big, big shocks. She'll have that sort of heart attack, I think."

For Mma Makutsi, it was a blow on more than one level. It was bad enough hearing of Violet's shortlisting, but what made it particularly hard to bear was the fact that it was on *her* page, right underneath *her* photograph. It spoiled everything and made it hard to imagine how she could show her article, as she had planned to do, to her friends.

Fanwell sensed the problem. "Cut the other article out," he said. "That way you won't have to look at it."

Mma Makutsi approved of this suggestion, and reached for the scissors she kept in her top drawer. As she did so, the telephone rang, and she looked at it with annoyance. Abandoning her task, she picked up the receiver and answered, her irritation showing in her tone of voice. But that soon changed: it was Rosie—the first of the three Rosies who were to call the agency over the next hour.

THEIR PROGRESS WAS SLOW. As they drove down the roads that divided the Village into its fenced plots, scrutinising each for possible investigation, Mma Ramotswe realised just how much must have changed over the past few decades. Older houses were still there—shady bungalows tucked away among now well-established growths of shrubs and trees—but in many cases the generous yards that had surrounded these houses had been sub-divided, and newer houses been erected cheek by jowl with the older. The process had been a discreet one, like that of a river moving stones and mud banks, placing one here and one there, and then, with the next high water, moving a larger rock to rest among the smaller ones. You would not notice this going on if you saw it every day, but, after a while, the shape of things could be quite different from what it had been when you first walked by. That, thought Mma Ramotswe, was why Susan had been unable to find the place where she had lived. The house might still be there, exactly where it had been all those years ago, but the things around it could all be these new things, shifted about by the river of human activity.

Charlie was impatient. "Maybe around this corner, Mma," he said. "There are some old houses there. I have been past that way—I remember them."

She had explained to him about the patience required for investigative work, but she was not sure that he had understood.

"You know what a painting is like, Charlie? You look at a painting and you see there are many strokes of the brush—tiny strokes. These little things make up the whole picture, but you need every one of those little strokes."

He had looked at her blankly, and she realised that he might never have looked at a picture. He saw photographs, of course—he understood those, but had he ever looked at a picture that some human hand had painstakingly painted?

"A building, Charlie," she had said. "Think of bricks. You need lots and lots of bricks to make a building."

Charlie's blank expression turned into a wry smile. "Oh, I know that, Mma. You need a lot of bricks to make a building. But what's that got to do with investigations?"

"It's the same thing, Charlie. You have to make the whole thing with lots of small things. So when you want to know the whole story of whatever it is you want to know about . . ."

"The whole story? What happened in the beginning?"

"Yes. And why it happened, and what happened next—then you need to know all the facts. And these facts might be very small. And they might seem to have nothing to do with the main question, but they can be very important." She paused. "And all of that, Charlie, requires patience."

"I know that, Mma. You don't need to tell me."

And now, sitting in the van with Charlie, who was looking ahead of them and not really paying much attention to where they currently were, she reflected on the possibility that young men were a completely alien breed, and that however much you tried to get them to see things the way you saw them, you were destined to fail. And that perhaps part of the secret of leading a life in which you would not always be worrying about things, or complaining about them, was to accept that there were people who just saw things differently from you and always would. Once you understood that, then you could accept the people themselves as they were and not try to change them. What was even more important, perhaps, was that you could love those people who looked at things so differently, because you realised that they were not trying to make life hard for you by being what they were, but were simply doing their best. Then, when you started to love them, love would do the work that it always did and it would begin to transform them and then they would end up seeing things in the same way that you did.

She told Charlie to stop.

"Where, Mma?" he asked as he pulled over. "That place over there?"

She pointed to a gate off the road a few yards ahead of them. "Look at that house, Charlie. See it?"

The short driveway behind the gate was largely obscured by trees that had been allowed to grow unrestrained. There were a couple of acacia trees, a bottlebrush tree with its red, feathery flowers, and a number of flame trees, with their elongated seed pods like desiccated flat loaves. Beyond that, only its roof visible from the road, was a house. From the style of the roof, which was of corrugated tin, it was clear that the house was an older one.

"Do you see the big tree?" asked Mma Ramotswe.

Charlie nodded. "And it's a jacaranda, Mma?"

"It is," answered Mma Ramotswe.

Charlie was excited. "We have found the place, Mma. This must be the place. The old house. The jacaranda tree. Everything's right."

Mma Ramotswe made a calming gesture. "Don't reach conclusions too quickly, Charlie," she said. "Some things might be right—other things might be wrong. We cannot tell yet."

They left the van by the side of the road and walked up to the gate. Somewhere inside the house a dog barked, but became silent. A door slammed.

"*Ko! Ko!*" called Mma Ramotswe.

Behind the square white pillars of the verandah, a door opened and a woman appeared. She was carrying a broom, which she propped against the wall as she approached the front steps. She uttered polite greetings, glanced at Charlie, and then looked again at Mma Ramotswe.

"You're Mma Ramotswe, aren't you? You're that lady from that . . ." She waved a hand in the direction of the Tlokweng Road.

"The No. 1 Ladies' Detective Agency," said Mma Ramotswe. "And this is my assistant, Charlie."

Charlie looked pleased. It was the first time he had been called her assistant.

"I am called Mma Bothoko," said the woman. She pointed to a group of seats on the verandah. They were white-painted metal, and shabby. They did not look comfortable.

"Please sit down," Mma Bothoko said. "I will fetch you water."

It was the polite, old-fashioned thing to do. The offer of water signalled to visitors that they were welcome.

"I'm sure this must be the place," whispered Charlie as Mma Bothoko went back into the house to fetch water. "Look at that tree, Mma. It is just like the tree in the photograph."

"There are many houses with jacaranda trees beside them," said Mma Ramotswe.

"But this one is a very old one, Mma," said Charlie. "Look at it. That big branch is just like the branch in the picture."

"And the verandah?" asked Mma Ramotswe. "Are the pillars the same?"

She had the photograph in her bag and she brought it out. Charlie pointed at it exuberantly. "See," he said. "Same pillars. Square—just like this place."

"All verandahs were like that in those days," said Mma Ramotswe. "It was the style."

Mma Bothoko returned, carrying a tray with three glasses and a large green jug. Mma Ramotswe glanced at her as she sat down, noticing the lines around the eyes and the dry, cracked skin of the hands. She was, she thought, at least seventy, possibly slightly older.

"Are you the grandmother here, Mma?" she asked, as the water was poured out.

Mma Bothoko shook her head. "No, this house belongs to us. It is my husband and I who live here. He is . . ."

Before she could finish, Mma Ramotswe realised who they were.

"Of course," she said. "He is the chairman of the Law Board."

"That is right, Mma. But you know that, don't you?"

Mma Ramotswe smiled. "This city is a village still, Mma. You knew who I was."

"Everybody knows who you are," said Mma Bothoko. "They see your sign when they drive down the Tlokweng Road. It is a very unusual business. A ladies' detective agency—there are not many of those, Mma."

Mma Ramotswe noticed that as she raised the glass to her lips, Mma Bothoko's hand shook. That could be nervousness, or it could be the onset of an illness. Clovis Andersen said *watch the body language,* but he very specifically warned against judging people's nervousness. *Innocent people can be very nervous,* he wrote. *A shaking hand may mean nothing. Once again, the rule is: don't jump to conclusions!*

There was a polite silence. Then Mma Ramotswe said, "You'll be wondering why I'm here, Mma."

Mma Bothoko put down her glass. As she looked at Mma Ramotswe, her lower lip trembled.

"You want to speak to me, I suppose," she said.

Mma Ramotswe nodded. "Yes, I want to speak to you about a long time ago."

Mma Bothoko said nothing. She reached for her glass. Her hand shook more noticeably as she took another sip of water. Charlie saw it now and threw Mma Ramotswe a glance.

"Have you lived here for a long time, Mma?" asked Mma Ramotswe.

The question seemed to distract Mma Bothoko, who asked Mma Ramotswe to repeat it before she answered.

"We have been here for a very long time, Mma. This house belonged to my father-in-law before my husband took it over. He—my husband's father—had it from the time it was built in 1968."

"So nobody else has lived here?"

"No. Just us."

Mma Ramotswe put down her glass. "Then in that case . . ."

She had intended to say that they would not keep her, but before she could do so Mma Bothoko had begun to wail.

"Oh, Mma, it was a long time ago. It was very long. And nobody knew the pressure he had been under. Nobody knew what it was like for him in those days."

Mma Ramotswe held up her hands. "Mma, I didn't—"

But Mma Bothoko was not for stopping. "Things were different then, Mma. It was not easy to tell what was what—maybe you're too young, Mma, maybe you don't know about how it was—but speak to anybody my age, Mma, and they'll tell you. Thomas was no different from anybody else. If anything, he was better than the rest of them."

Mma Ramotswe tried again. "I didn't come here," she began, "to talk about—"

Once more she was interrupted—this time by a further wail, an incoherent jumble of words and half-words, intermixed with sobs. Charlie, astonished and embarrassed, looked to Mma Ramotswe for guidance, but she was at a loss.

But then she rose to her feet and moved over to stand next to the distraught woman. Putting an arm about her shoulder, she said, "I didn't come here, Mma, to talk about your husband."

Somehow her words penetrated the haze of distress enwrapping Mma Bothoko. After a few moments, the sobbing stopped.

Mma Bothoko struggled to speak. "Why are you here, then, Mma?"

"I wanted to know who used to live in this house, Mma—that is all."

Mma Bothoko glanced at Charlie, as if he might have a different, more sinister purpose.

"And this young man was helping me with that," Mma Ramotswe went on. "You have answered that question for us, and we need not trouble you further."

Mma Bothoko sniffed loudly. Mma Ramotswe had handed her a handkerchief, and now she used this to wipe her eyes. Her voice was now under control, although there was an edge of fear to it. "I've been talking nonsense," she said. "You mustn't listen to me, Mma

Ramotswe. I have been very upset and when I'm upset I just speak nonsense—nonsense, nonsense."

Mma Ramotswe noticed that as she spoke, Mma Bothoko's eyes were fixed on her, appraising her reaction. "Of course you were upset, Mma," she reassured her. "That can happen to all of us. It's only natural."

There was relief in Mma Bothoko's expression. Now she was the conscientious hostess. "I have only given you water," she said. "I must give you something to eat."

Mma Ramotswe shook her head. "You're very kind, Mma, but my assistant and I must be on our way. We still have to look for this house, you see."

Mma Bothoko did not seek to persuade them but ushered them out onto the driveway. Her conversation now seemed focused on restoring normality.

"Our garden needs the rain," she said. "I have been trying to keep these plants going, but every year it gets harder, doesn't it, Mma? More and more of a battle."

"Yes," agreed Mma Ramotswe. "My husband grows beans and he is complaining too."

"Beans need water," said Mma Bothoko.

Mma Ramotswe nodded. "A drip system is best. You waste very little water that way."

Charlie felt that he had to say something. "We mustn't waste water," he said.

Mma Bothoko said that this was absolutely true, and Mma Ramotswe took the same view. By that time, though, they had reached the gate and were able to make their farewells.

"You must forgive me for being so silly," said Mma Bothoko. "Talking all that nonsense."

"Of course," said Mma Ramotswe. "I have forgotten all about it, Mma. You mustn't worry."

They walked to the van in silence and it was not until they were well down the road that Mma Ramotswe spoke.

"That was very sad," she said.

"She thought you'd come about something else?" said Charlie.

"Yes. About her husband—obviously."

Charlie asked her whether she knew who he was, and she told him. "One of the most important people in the country," said Mma Ramotswe. "Chairman of this and chairman of that. Mr. Chairman, really."

Charlie whistled. "But he must have done something bad, Mma."

Mma Ramotswe thought for a moment before she replied. "Who hasn't, Charlie?"

"Not me, Mma."

She looked at him and smiled. "Perhaps you should think again, Charlie."

Charlie frowned. "I haven't been really bad, Mma Ramotswe. Not *really* . . ."

Mma Ramotswe laughed. "Charlie, you're one of these people who are easily forgiven." She paused. "Not for everything, of course, but for most things."

MMA MAKUTSI WAS WAITING at the office. She greeted Mma Ramotswe and Charlie with a grave look—one in which concern and outrage both played a part. Mma Ramotswe realised immediately that something serious had happened, and she listened in silence as the story of Violet's nomination was related.

"I would not be surprised if you did not believe me," concluded Mma Makutsi. "It's truly unbelievable, Mma—truly unbelievable."

Mma Ramotswe sighed. "Sometimes I realise that I'd believe anything," she said. "There are so many things that happen that are, well, truly unbelievable."

Charlie joined in. "Like the story of that woman who ate only soap," he said. "She lived for two years on nothing but bars of soap. That's all she ate—it was in the papers."

The two women looked at him. "That's different, Charlie," said Mma Makutsi. "This is about somebody we actually know—not about some mystery lady in . . . wherever it was."

"She lived in Indonesia," said Charlie. "That's what the papers said. They had a photograph of her. She was . . ." He hesitated. "She was traditionally built."

"Well, that may be," said Mma Ramotswe. "But this is a more serious matter, Charlie."

Charlie frowned. "You know, Mma Makutsi, I think I may know how she survived. They have many coconuts in Indonesia, I think. You get coconut oil from coconuts, don't you? And you can make soap from coconut oil. That must be how she survived."

Mma Ramotswe turned to Mma Makutsi. "I'm very shocked by this, Mma. But I do not think she will win. People will not vote for her—they just won't."

"Are you sure, Mma?" asked Mma Makutsi.

"I am very sure, Mma. I do not believe that our fellow citizens would be so foolish—not in Botswana."

Mma Makutsi was silent. She wanted to believe Mma Ramotswe, but it was difficult. Violet Sephotho was ruthless and would do anything to get her hands on a title such as Woman of the Year; she would do anything that was necessary.

"I hope you're right, Mma Ramotswe," she said, trying to convince herself that Mma Ramotswe, who was right in so many other respects, would be right in this.

CHAPTER EIGHT

THREE LIARS ALL GETTING IN TOUCH

MMA MAKUTSI was shocked. Three women had dared to contact her claiming to be the woman who had looked after Susan. Three Rosies! And there would be more, she thought, as word got round and every opportunist sensed the prospect of gain. People did not come all the way from Canada empty-handed, after all—there had to be something in the offing.

"I cannot believe it, Mma," she said to Mma Ramotswe. "Three liars all getting in touch one after the other—just like that. Liar Number One, Liar Number Two, and then Liar Number Three."

She looked at Mma Ramotswe in a way that expressed outrage. Her glasses flashed in the shaft of sunlight from the office window. This was a band of gold in which flecks of dust floated, weightless, barely moving.

"The country must be full of liars," she continued. "There must be liars around every corner. Liars hiding behind every bush. Liars just waiting to tell lies about something. Unrepentant liars. Old liars, young liars; perhaps even babies whose first word is a lie. Perhaps even that, Mma."

"Oh, I don't think so," said Mma Ramotswe. "By and large, people are truthful, don't you think?"

Mma Makutsi shook her head. "No, Mma, I don't. I think that there are more and more liars. Soon it will be impossible to believe anything that anybody tells you. You'll ask somebody on the street the time and the answer will be a lie. The person will say that it's four o'clock when it's really only three. You'll ask somebody the way to some place, and what directions will you get? The wrong ones, Mma. They'll say go that way when you should go the other way. All lies, Mma."

Mma Ramotswe smiled.

"It's not an amusing matter, Mma," said Mma Makutsi reproachfully. "It's very serious. You start with a small trickle of lies, and then the trickle becomes a river—a river of lies. And the river becomes a dam, and then you drown in all the lies, Mma, you drown."

Mma Ramotswe defended herself. "I'm not saying that lying is not a serious matter, Mma Makutsi," she said. "All I'd say is that you can't assume that somebody is lying just because they make a claim that may not be true."

Mma Makutsi thought for a moment. "But it's not a question of *may not be true,* Mma—it can't be true." She looked intently at Mma Ramotswe, eager to drive home her point. "Let me put it this way, Mma Ramotswe: There is one Mma Potokwane, is that correct?"

Mma Ramotswe nodded. "Yes, although there are other people with that name."

"But I'm talking about Mma Potokwane, the matron of the Orphan Farm. There is just one such lady—is that right?"

"I believe that to be true," said Mma Ramotswe. "There is only one Mma Potokwane in that sense."

Mma Makutsi clearly thought she was getting somewhere. "So if somebody comes along and says, 'I am Mma Potokwane' and she is not the Mma Potokwane we know, then what are we to conclude, Mma?"

Mma Ramotswe shrugged. "We would conclude that this is not the Mma Potokwane we have known for a long time."

"But would we conclude more than that?"

"I'm not sure."

"Well, I am, Mma," said Mma Makutsi forcefully. "I would conclude that the person who says, 'I am Mma Potokwane' is a liar. That is what I'd conclude."

"Unless this person was very confused," said Mma Ramotswe. "If the person were ill, for example, and not thinking straight. Such a person might claim to be Mma Potokwane but would not necessarily be a liar."

Mma Makutsi grudgingly accepted that there could be such delusions. "But leaving aside such cases, Mma, what if a person who is not ill says, 'I am Mma Potokwane'? Such a person would have to be a liar."

"Maybe . . ."

"Not maybe, Mma. Definitely."

Mma Ramotswe looked up at the ceiling. They were sitting in the office when this conversation took place and she felt hot and uncomfortable. The rains had to come soon; there had to be relief from this severe heat that was like a hammer on the land, and the dryness that came with it. She was not sure that she wanted to have a hair-splitting argument with Mma Makutsi, but there were issues here that had to be addressed. If she allowed Mma Makutsi to win every argument, then she would be giving up on a duty that Clovis Andersen identified as one of the real threats to successful and principled detective work. *Don't make any false assumptions,* he wrote. *Don't jump to conclusions. Explore every possibility.*

"It's possible," Mma Ramotswe began, "that these Rosies might not be liars."

Mma Makutsi was quick to retort. "Two of them must be," she said, "even if all three aren't."

"But what if one—or more—of them *thinks* that she is Rosie?"

Mma Makutsi scoffed at this. "How could she, Mma. You know who you are; I know who I am. How can you think that you're somebody you aren't? It's impossible."

"Unless your name *is* Rosie."

Mma Makutsi was disconcerted by this answer. "If your name . . ."

"Rosie is a common enough name, Mma Makutsi. So there might be many Rosies in Gaborone—there probably are, in fact. Just as there are many Graces, I think, and quite a few ladies called Precious too."

"But even if they are Rosies," objected Mma Makutsi, "they will know that they are not *this* Rosie—the one who looked after Mma Susan."

Mma Ramotswe inclined her head; it was a reasonable point. "Yet Susan is also a common enough name, Mma. So what if there were many Susans at the time—and many Rosies? Would it not be possible that one of these Rosies might have looked after a Susan—but a different Susan?"

Mma Makutsi gave her a doubtful look. "I do not think so, Mma. Oh no, I do not think so at all."

"Well . . . ," began Mma Ramotswe.

But she did not finish. The first of the Rosies had made an appointment and there was a hesitant knock on the door.

"The first of the liars," mouthed Mma Makutsi.

Mma Ramotswe gave her a discouraging look, but said nothing. It would have been too late to do so, anyway, as the office door was now being pushed gently and she saw, peering into the room, a tall woman in a green dress.

"This is the No. 1 Ladies' Detective Agency?" asked the woman. She spoke with a rather strange, guttural accent, as if she were not a native speaker of Setswana, or of English.

"It is," said Mma Ramotswe. "And you must be Rosie."

She gave the woman a considered look. Did she resemble the woman in the photograph? It was hard to tell, because of the image's lack of definition, but it was just possible that this woman's head was the same shape as that of the woman in that blurry photograph.

The woman seemed to hesitate before she replied. Only for a

moment or two, but it was long enough for Mma Makutsi to notice and to flash a warning glance in Mma Ramotswe's direction. The meaning of this glance was clear enough—at least to Mma Ramotswe. It was: *she had to remind herself that she was claiming to be Rosie.*

Mma Ramotswe was less ready to jump to that bleak conclusion. People can be hesitant for all sorts of reasons, she felt—unfamiliar surroundings, social awkwardness, lack of confidence: all of these could explain a brief hesitation in answering.

"Yes," she said. "I am Rosie."

Mma Ramotswe invited her to sit down. She offered to make tea, but Rosie declined. As she settled herself in the client chair, Mma Makutsi started to quiz her.

"You read the article?" Mma Makutsi asked.

"I did," said the woman. "That is why I am here." She paused, and then continued, "I'm sorry, Mma, but could you tell me who you are?"

The effect of this question on Mma Makutsi was dramatic. Straightening her back, Mma Makutsi sat bolt upright, her lips pursed, her fingers intertwined. "You're asking my name, Mma?" she said. "Is that what you're asking me?"

"If you don't mind, Mma."

Mma Ramotswe was puzzled—not by the question, but by Mma Makutsi's intense reaction to it. "This is Mma Makutsi," she offered. "She is my assist—" She stopped herself. Mma Makutsi was no longer her assistant, but her co-director. It could have been worse, of course; she might have referred to her as her secretary, something she had almost done a few days earlier, but had fortunately avoided just in time. "She is the co-director here, Mma."

Mma Ramotswe caught Mma Makutsi's eye. A signal was being sent in her direction—a signal of great and urgent importance—but she could not work out what it was. Why should Mma Makutsi be so agitated simply because their visitor had asked who she was? She would no doubt find out later, but for the moment she had other questions to ask.

"Now," Mma Ramotswe began, "you say, Mma, that you are the person who looked after that child all those years ago. May I ask how old you are, Mma?"

The woman nodded, as if she had been expecting the question. "I am fifty-three now, Mma. I was in my early twenties when that child was here."

Mma Ramotswe jotted 53 on her pad of paper. The woman's eyes followed the movement of the pencil.

Mma Ramotswe looked up from her note, her pencil poised. "And where were you born, Mma?"

"Mahalapye."

Mma Ramotswe wrote this down.

Now Mma Makutsi asked a question. "Mahalapye, Mma? I have cousins there."

The woman said nothing.

"They are called Makutsi, like me."

The woman shrugged. "I do not know those people, Mma."

"No," mused Mma Makutsi. "I'm sure you wouldn't. You must have left a long time ago."

The woman looked at her. "I was eighteen, Mma. I came to Gaborone then. That's over thirty years ago."

"Of course," said Mma Makutsi. "Thirty years ago is not yesterday. But . . ." She hesitated. "These cousins of mine lived fairly close to the railway line—right in the middle of town. What was that place called? The area in the middle? Leretlwa? It was Leretlwa, wasn't it, Mma?"

Mma Ramotswe sensed what was happening, but did not say anything.

"Yes," said the woman. "That is right. There is Leretlwa. I know it."

Mma Makutsi sat back in her chair, her expression one of scarcely disguised triumph.

Mma Ramotswe looked away. She was taken aback by Mma Makutsi's questioning, but did not show it. "Tell me, Mma," she said evenly. "How many years did you look after that girl? Two, three years?"

The answer came back quickly. "Eight," she said. "From when she was a little baby—I helped the mummy even then—until the time those people went back to Canada. I was looking after her all that time."

"Always in Gaborone?"

"No. In Molepolole to begin with. Then in Gaborone."

Mma Ramotswe scribbled a note on her pad. "You must have been sad when they left."

"I was very sad, Mma. I cried and cried. It was like losing my own child."

Mma Ramotswe inclined her head briefly and then looked up again. "I can imagine how you felt, Mma." She gazed out of the window at the slice of sky that could be seen from this angle. Blue—almost white with heat. No cloud. No rain. Just dry air all the way up to the heavens. Dry, hot air.

"The house?" Mma Makutsi said. "Do you remember where it was?"

The woman replied immediately. "Of course, Mma."

Mma Ramotswe drew in her breath. "Where was it, Mma?"

The woman pointed over her shoulder. "That way."

"In the Village? In the old part?"

The woman shook her head. "No, more towards town. You know where the Sun Hotel is? You know that place where the ladies sell their lace tablecloths? You know that place?"

"Of course."

"On one of those roads that go off the main road right there. On one of them. Round a corner."

Mma Ramotswe made a further note. "Could you show us, Mma? If I took you in my van—could you show us?"

The woman thought for a moment. "I suppose so."

"Right now, Mma?"

"If you want me to."

Mma Ramotswe saw Mma Makutsi make some sort of sign, but she could not make out what it was. She threw her an enquiring glance, but all that Mma Makutsi did was to shake her head slightly.

"My van is very small, Mma," said Mma Ramotswe. "There would not be room for the three of us, but I can borrow my husband's car. He runs that garage through there."

The woman made to stand up. "I'm ready, Mma. I can show you where the place is."

Mma Ramotswe slipped her notepad into a drawer and rose from her chair. "Mma Makutsi and I will go and fetch the car," she said, looking purposefully towards Mma Makutsi. "We will only be five minutes or so."

The woman sat down again. "I can wait, Mma," she said. Then she added, "Tell me, Mma: Is this Mma Susan wanting to say something to me?"

Mma Ramotswe stood still. "What do you mean, Mma?"

"I mean: Why is she wanting to see me? Is she wanting to . . ." She did not finish the sentence, but Mma Ramotswe knew what lay behind the question. Avarice, she thought, always shows in the eyes. Avarice could shine, could shine forth like a searchlight.

"I think she wants to thank you," she said. "That is all I know."

It was true, and she saw the effect of her reply. The woman smiled, and in an attempt at modesty said, "Oh, I do not need to be thanked."

"But she would like to do so," said Mma Makutsi. "Sometimes that is important for people."

The woman said nothing.

"We shall fetch the car," said Mma Ramotswe.

MR. J.L.B. MATEKONI'S CAR was parked on the other side of the garage. It would take only a minute or so to start the engine and drive round the building to the other side, but Mma Ramotswe realised they would need to talk. And she was right; the moment they were out of the door and out of earshot of the office, Mma Makutsi seized Mma Ramotswe's elbow and whispered urgently into her ear.

"She is a very big liar, that woman. A very big liar. One of the biggest in the country, probably."

Mma Ramotswe turned to face her. "I saw that you were very upset when she asked your name. Why was that, Mma?"

Mma Makutsi's eyes widened. "Don't you see, Mma?" she exclaimed. "Don't you see?"

Mma Ramotswe frowned. "Why should she not ask your name?"

"Because of what she said, Mma. That's why."

Mma Ramotswe's puzzlement deepened. "I'm sorry, Mma Makutsi," she said. "I just don't see what you're trying to tell me."

Mma Makutsi did not look impatient; rather, she looked understanding. "Now listen, Mma Ramotswe," she said quietly. "She said that she had read about all this in the newspaper. Remember that?"

Mma Ramotswe nodded. "I think so."

Now came the disclosure, the revealing of the clue. "Well, who was in that article? I was, Mma—it was me. And whose photograph was on that page? Mine, Mma—mine!"

It became clear. "So she should have recognised you if she had read the paper? Is that what you're suggesting?"

"Of course. If she had seen the article, she would have seen me. But she didn't know who I was—that's why she had to ask my name. Strange, isn't it, Mma? A lie, you see. Somebody has put her up to this; she knows nothing—somebody is *behind* her, Mma."

Mma Ramotswe was far from convinced, pointing out to Mma Makutsi that one might easily ignore the photograph accompanying an article—or forget the details. "Look at these articles about politicians saying this, that, and the next thing. We may read all about it in the newspapers, and there will be a photograph of the politician—they love that, those people—but do we remember what they look like? I don't think I do."

Mma Makutsi raised an admonishing finger. "But, Mma," she said, "there is another thing—another thing altogether."

Mma Ramotswe waited. There was a gleam of revelation in Mma Makutsi's eye. "She mentioned Mahalapye."

"Ah," said Mma Ramotswe. "And you found her out with that reference to . . . where was the place, Mma?"

Mma Makutsi seemed disappointed that her trap had been detected, but continued, "Leretlwa."

Mma Ramotswe waited. "And?"

"That place is not in the middle of town—it is not near the railway line, Mma. Yet when I said it was, she did not correct me." She shook a finger for emphasis. "She did not correct me, Mma, and if you had really been born in Mahalapye, then you would not let a mistake like that go unremarked upon. You would not let people say Tlokweng is in the middle of Gaborone, would you? You would not, Mma. You would say, 'Hold on, Tlokweng is miles away.' That's what you'd say, I think."

Mma Ramotswe took Mma Makutsi's wrist and led her gently round the side of the building. "We must get into the car," she said. "We cannot stand outside talking about this."

"There is more than enough evidence to prove this woman is an impostor," muttered Mma Makutsi.

"Possibly," said Mma Ramotswe. "Possibly, but not definitely, Mma. And there is a difference, you know."

THEY DROVE IN SILENCE. Mma Ramotswe could not converse because she had to concentrate on driving Mr. J.L.B. Matekoni's car, which, although slightly familiar to her, felt far too powerful. Her tiny white van had very little power—just enough to keep the wheels turning, she thought—and it would never run away with her, as this car seemed to be keen to do. For her part, Mma Makutsi had no desire to talk to the person whom she now thought of as the "so-called Rosie"—so she was silent too. And as for the woman, seated in the back, she simply stared out of the window, rather vaguely, as if she were thinking of something else altogether.

They drew near to the Sun Hotel. There, sitting on the verge of the road, their wares spread out beside them, were the ladies who made the crochet tablecloths. The woman had mentioned these in their discussion, and they were the signal for her to lean forward and tap Mma Ramotswe on the shoulder. "Turn left here, Mma," she said. "This is the road."

Mma Makutsi glanced at Mma Ramotswe. "Zebra Drive," she said. And then, craning her neck to address the woman behind them, she asked, "Are you sure this is the road, Mma? Are you quite sure?"

The woman nodded. "I wouldn't tell you it was if it wasn't," she said sullenly.

"I will go down here," said Mma Ramotswe, and added, "I know this road well, Mma."

"Well, the house is further down here—on the left."

Mma Ramotswe drove slowly now, but she was not prepared for the sudden instruction that came from the back seat. "There it is, Mma. That is the place. That was the house those people lived in."

Mma Makutsi gasped. "You see, Mma Ramotswe," she muttered.

"That is the house," repeated the woman. "I remember it well."

Mma Ramotswe pulled in and brought the car to a halt, leaving the engine running. Turning to face their passenger, she said, "That is my house, Mma. That is where I live with my husband, Mr. J.L.B. Matekoni."

The woman's expression did not change. She now looked bored, shrugging her shoulders at this information. "So you live here now, Mma," she said. "I'm not talking about now—I'm talking about then."

Mma Ramotswe hesitated, but Mma Makutsi had already made

up her mind. "Mma Ramotswe, I think we should go back to the office now," she said. "We can drop this lady off near Riverwalk so that she can get a minibus home." She turned to address the woman. Her tone was gruff. "Will that suit you, Mma?"

The woman shrugged. "If that's what you want. But when will I see this Canadian lady?"

"Leave us your address," said Mma Makutsi briskly. "We'll be in touch."

The woman became animated. "I am very keen to see her, Mma Ramotswe. I have been missing her so much, so much. My heart is very sore, you know."

Mma Makutsi rolled her eyes. She had not intended this to be seen, but it was, and the woman turned on her angrily.

"You do not believe me, Mma—I can tell that. You think I am making this up, don't you?"

Mma Makutsi turned round to face the back seat. Her spectacles flashed dangerously. Then came her reply, each word delivered with the gravity that comes from complete conviction. "I do not believe one word you've said, Mma—not one word." Her judgement delivered with defiance, she turned back to Mma Ramotswe.

"I think you should drive on, Mma," she said.

Mma Ramotswe did not like conflict. She was unfailingly polite to others, and she could not condone this rudeness on Mma Makutsi's part.

"I'm sorry, Mma," she said over her shoulder. "We have to be very careful, you see."

The woman was staring ahead fixedly. "I did not hear any of this," she said suddenly. "I cannot hear what you're saying."

They drove back up Zebra Drive and out onto the main road. *Perhaps I'm in the wrong job,* Mma Ramotswe thought. What is that saying about not staying in the kitchen if you don't like the heat? Should she give a bit more thought to that? After all, these old sayings were often right. Mind you, she said to herself, it's not just the kitchen that's hot—the whole country is too hot at the moment, this baking heat that wraps Botswana until suddenly the summer rains arrive and cool everything down. She might think differently then, she imagined; and Mma Makutsi might be a little less confrontational. Cool weather brings cool tempers. Was that a saying? she wondered. If it was not, then it could well become one, and she, Mma Ramotswe, would be the author of it. She might even write to Clovis Andersen and tell him about it. He would appreciate it, she thought. But then does he remember me? What am I, who is just Mma Ramotswe of Botswana, to that important man who lives so far away in Muncie, Indiana? Can I really call him my friend?

The woman in the back started to mutter.

"You don't know anything," she said. "You don't know that I was like a mother to that girl. When she cried I was there; I was the one who comforted her. You don't know that, do you? And when her little dog became sick and died I was the one who helped her bury it at the end of the garden and put the stones around its grave. I was the one who wiped away her tears. I was. And I was the one who nursed her when she was ill because the real mother was always working or playing tennis. I was the one, and you people don't know that—and you don't care, do you? You don't care because all you think about is money and being paid by these people who come to see you. And having your picture in the newspapers too. That's what you think about."

Mma Ramotswe felt that she had to reply to this. Slowing down, she spoke into the driving mirror. "No, Mma, you are wrong. We do care. And I'm sorry if you think that we do not."

"Can you please stop the car," the woman said. "Stop the car and let me get out."

Mma Ramotswe pulled over to the side of the road. With their passenger out, Mma Ramotswe turned to Mma Makutsi. "Well," she said, "that was a bit of a mess, Mma."

"Not at all," said Mma Makutsi. "That woman was a fraudster, Mma."

"Maybe," said Mma Ramotswe. "But fraudsters can have feelings, Mma."

"But what about the feelings of the people they defraud? Don't you think we have to consider those?"

"Yes," said Mma Ramotswe. "But—"

"No buts, Mma," said Mma Makutsi. "Some people are just *skellums*. That's the way it is, Mma. That's just the way it is."

Mma Ramotswe smiled. It was some time since she had heard the word *skellum,* as it seemed to have passed out of favour. Yet it was such a fine word, that so effectively described a rogue or a rascal; a word that her father had used eloquently, picked up from the Boers, when describing dealers who paid poor farmers too little for their cattle, or traders who doctored their scales so that they could give short shrift to buyers of sorghum or maize meal. Obed Ramotswe had seen these as *skellums* and would call them that to their face; now, perhaps, the *skellums* could get away with it because people were afraid to stand up to them, or were no longer sure what was right or wrong, or were afraid to identify wickedness or sleaze when they saw it. Mma Makutsi may be a bit extreme at times, she thought, but at least she speaks up against bad behaviour. She was probably right about this woman, who had made some bad mistakes in her story and probably was what Obed, once again, would have called a *chancer,* if not a *skellum.* And if she was right, then Mma Makutsi's unmasking of her was probably the right thing to do, and yet, and yet . . . life was rarely as simple as Mma Makutsi thought it was. *Subtlety,* wrote Clovis Andersen, *is the best aid to the understanding of human complexity.* That was rather too long a pronouncement to use too often, but it had its place, and should be remembered, as she was doing now, from time to time.

CHAPTER NINE

TRUST YOUR NOSE

MR. J.L.B. MATEKONI sniffed at the air. There was no doubt about it—Mma Ramotswe was making his favourite stew. The aroma, detected even as he set foot on the stoep, was unmistakable, and enough to get the gastric juices going in anticipation. Onions were the key to that: the recipe, developed specially for him by Mma Ramotswe, advised by Mma Potokwane, involved onions chosen for their smallness and sweetness—"not these football-sized onions they try to sell us," warned Mma Potokwane. These were gently softened in sunflower oil flavoured with a pinch of chilli flakes, and then the beef, fine Botswana grass-fed beef—"none better anywhere in the world," claimed Mma Potokwane—was added in small pieces. This was then sealed before the addition of stock and a small quantity of chopped ostrich *biltong,* the dried and salted meat that people considered such a delicacy.

He went into the kitchen, where the children were sitting at the table, a plate of macaroni cheese in front of them. If the stew was his own favourite, then macaroni cheese was theirs. They liked to add quantities of tomato sauce—something of which Mr. J.L.B. Matekoni did not approve but that he tolerated. He had eaten strange things as a boy—things that would turn his stomach today but had seemed delicious then—raw bacon sandwiches with added sugar; pineapple dipped in golden syrup; fried bread with a thick spreading of lard; flying ants, caught on the wing, that tasted like butter and could be popped into the mouth with a satisfying crunch. It was best not to think too much of what one ate—or had as a child—thought Mr. J.L.B. Matekoni; memory blotted things out for a reason, he believed.

"So what is the mummy cooking for the daddy today?" he asked, as he slipped out of the pair of greasy suede shoes that Mma Ramotswe had been trying unsuccessfully—for years, it seemed—to replace.

Motholeli looked up from her macaroni cheese. "The mummy is cooking the daddy that special stew he likes," she said.

"And we're eating macaroni cheese," chimed in Puso. "With ice cream for afters."

Mr. J.L.B. Matekoni smiled. "So it looks like everybody is happy," he said. "Did you say grace, Motholeli?"

She shook her head. "It's Puso's turn."

He sat down at the table and looked at the young boy. "Well then, young man. Let's hear grace before you start on your macaroni cheese."

They lowered their heads, as did Mma Ramotswe, who laid down her stirring spoon.

"Bless this macaroni cheese," said Puso quickly. "Amen."

Without delay, the two children began to tackle their dinner. Mr. J.L.B. Matekoni caught Mma Ramotswe's eye, and they exchanged a grin.

"Sometimes only a few words are needed," remarked Mma Ramotswe.

Motholeli looked up from her plate. "Least said, soonest mended."

Mma Ramotswe looked at her encouragingly. "Where did you learn that?" she asked. "At school?"

Her mouth half full of macaroni cheese, Motholeli replied, "You said it, Mma."

"Don't speak with your mouth full," muttered Puso, swallowing as he spoke.

"Don't throw the first stone yourself," retorted Motholeli mildly.

Mma Ramotswe chuckled. "So you heard me say it? Well, I suppose I might have done. It's true, after all."

She thought of the day's events, and of the awkward journey with the woman whom Mma Makutsi had begun to refer to as Mma Not Rosie. It was a handy description, and she understood why Mma Makutsi might reach such a conclusion, but there was something about it that made her feel uncomfortable. Even if there were doubtful aspects to the woman's story, inconsistencies could occur in even the truest of tales: people told the truth not as it necessarily was, but as they saw it. And of course that could lead to things not sounding quite right. It was the watertight story that often needed closest examination, thought Mma Ramotswe; stories that looked unassailable could be the result of careful planning—and careful invention.

And there was something rather sad about Mma Not Rosie. Her little outburst in the car had a tragic feel to it. It sounded contrived—and she could see why Mma Makutsi had rolled her eyes—but pain, when exposed to others, could sometimes sound false. Mma Makutsi could be a bit brisk; she had a good instinct for people, but it was not infallible, and there had been occasions in the past when her instinct had misled her. *Trust your nose, but make sure it's pointing in the right direction.* Who had said that? Mma Ramotswe realised that it was she herself. And I am right, she thought, modestly at first, but then with a tinge of self-satisfaction. *Trust your nose, but make sure it's pointing in the right direction.* She would try that out on Mma Makutsi the following day and see how she reacted. It could give her something to think about—but on the other hand, it might not; you never knew with Mma Makutsi.

She resumed her stirring of the stew. The oddest thing about the whole day had been that journey in which they had been led to Zebra Drive and her very own house. That had been a moment of utter astonishment, enough to make one laugh, although she had resisted the temptation to do so. Of course she had entertained the possibility that her house had previously been occupied by the Canadian doctor and his family, only to dismiss the proposition immediately. She knew that her house had belonged to the Public Works Department from its first construction in the mid-sixties, and that it had been the official residence of the deputy head of the Public Works right up to the point at which it had been sold off as surplus to requirements. That was when she had bought it, using her legacy from her father— the legacy of fine cattle that had so prospered out at the cattle post. It had never been a medical house, or a missionary house for that matter, and what was more, there was no large jacaranda tree in the yard. There were acacias and that favourite mopipi tree of hers, but no jacaranda. No, that claim by Mma Not Rosie must have been entirely made up.

Once the children had finished their meal they settled in their bedrooms—Motholeli to read and Puso to complete his arithmetic homework. Mma Ramotswe and Mr. J.L.B. Matekoni went out onto the verandah; night had fallen with the suddenness of those latitudes, a curtain of darkness that came down after only a few minutes of dusk, heralding a world of dark shapes, of night-time sounds, of mystery, and, at times, of fear. They sat in their customary chairs and looked out beyond the small circle of light that the window behind them threw into the yard. Mr. J.L.B. Matekoni had poured himself a cold beer; Mma Ramotswe had the half-glass of lemonade that she had saved from the day before. The effervescence of the lemonade had all but disappeared, but enough of the taste remained to make the drink palatable. She sipped at it slowly; the acidity made her teeth tingle. Red bush tea never did that, she thought.

He told her about his day. Fanwell had succeeded in finding the cause of an engine fault that had flummoxed him for two days. "I couldn't work out what was going on," he said. "It was not one of these cars that have all the computers in them—it was a good, honest car. But I couldn't for the life of me see why it was overheating—and then Fanwell found the problem. It took him half an hour."

"That means he has become a good mechanic," said Mma Ramotswe.

"Or I'm becoming a bad one," remarked Mr. J.L.B. Matekoni, taking a sip of his beer.

Mma Ramotswe shook her head. "Oh no, Rra. Nobody could ever say that. In fact, they say exactly the opposite—I've heard them. They say, 'That Mr. J.L.B. Matekoni is the best mechanic in all Botswana.' I have heard at least three people say that—all in the last couple of years."

"Perhaps they know you're married to me, Mma. Perhaps they are trying to be kind."

She denied this vigorously. "They mean it, Rra. You can tell when somebody means a compliment and when it's just empty words. You can tell . . ."

"How? How exactly can you tell?"

She looked out into the darkness. His question was a good one; how could you tell something like that? Instinct? A sixth sense? That was all very well, but how could you explain what instinct or a sixth sense meant? Or did they both boil down, when all was said and done, to nothing more than a hunch?

She thought of what had happened that day with Mma Not Rosie. She was sure that Mma Makutsi had been acting on some sort of hunch about that woman when she first met her, and then had tried to find grounds for dismissing her as a fraud. By contrast, Mma Ramotswe was now beginning to feel that whatever the flaws in her story might be, she was genuine. This feeling had been building up ever since she'd started to cook the stew, and now it was quite strong. That poor woman had been telling the truth and all she had encountered was a wall of suspicion from Mma Makutsi, and from herself something not much better—a bit politer, perhaps, but still not much better.

She turned to Mr. J.L.B. Matekoni. "What do you think it's like, Rra, to be telling the truth and then to find that nobody believes you?"

He thought for a moment. "Horrible," he said with conviction. "It is a very horrible feeling, Mma."

The forcefulness of his answer surprised her. "Has it happened to you, Mr. J.L.B. Matekoni?"

He took his time to answer. "Once," he said. "And it was very, very bad."

She glanced at him. Marriage was all about honesty, and being open, but she had always felt that just about every married person had something, some sorrow or secret, that was not shared, that was a private area of their lives that might not be shared with a spouse. It could be something sad or painful, or it could be something just mildly embarrassing, some tiny failing or silliness, some moment of mild shame, but it was no reflection on the marriage that this thing should be kept tucked away. We are the people we want ourselves to be, and then there are the people we actually are: sometimes it is easier to be the people we want ourselves to be if we keep at least some things to ourselves. That, thought Mma Ramotswe, is only human.

And she thought of what Note Mokoti, her first, abusive husband, had done to her. She had never told anybody—not her father, to whom she had run for protection, not her friend Mma Potokwane, not even Mr. J.L.B. Matekoni. Note had beaten her; he had hurt her. She did not talk about it because she felt ashamed, and she wanted to forget it. There was a time for talking about things that distressed us, but there was also a time for not talking about them. These days people seemed to suggest that you should talk about everything, even those things that people never talked about in the past, but did this make life any easier? She was not sure. In fact, she thought there were occasions on which talking about distressing things merely kept those things alive, whereas not talking about them, consigning them to the past, forgetting them, allowed one to think about things that were positive, things that made the world a bit better.

She was unsure whether to ask him about it. But he continued anyway.

"You know I did my service in the brigades?" he said.

She nodded. The brigades had been part of the national service that Botswana had required of young people. Some of the brigades still survived as training organisations, especially in the rural areas; others were now merely a memory of the time when the country was just emerging, when Botswana was learning to walk.

"I was in a brigade that did mechanical training," he went on. "We were based up at Serowe. I enjoyed myself—and learned a lot."

"Many people did," she said. "And it was good work."

"It helped us grow up," said Mr. J.L.B. Matekoni. "We went in as teenagers—rather aimless teenagers, perhaps—and came out as adults."

She waited. In some respects, even after years of marriage, they were strangers to one another. He had never talked about his time in the brigades before.

"It was after I had been in the brigade for five or six months," he continued. "I had been given extra responsibility—I was in charge of organising extra transport for those occasions when we had too many people for our own vehicles. We would hire a minibus from one of the taxi people, and I paid them. I had a float for that—money that was kept in a tin and then locked away in a drawer in the office. I was the only person with a key to that drawer—or so I thought."

Mma Ramotswe put down her glass. It was obvious which way this was going—and it was clear that the story would be one of major injustice. Mr. J.L.B. Matekoni was a person of the utmost probity— she had known that right from the beginning. He was scrupulously honest in all his dealings, but particularly where money was involved. On one occasion he had driven twenty miles to hand over an inadvertent overpayment made by a client: a fifty-pula note had been stuck to the back of another note and had not been counted.

"I can imagine what's coming, Rra," she said.

He sounded sad. "Yes, that's what happened. I went to open the drawer and found that exactly half the money had gone from the tin. Thieves don't always take the full amount, I believe—if they leave some, then the person they've robbed might think that he had made a mistake about how much was there in the first place. It's a common trick.

"But I knew I hadn't made a mistake," he continued. "I knew that there had been exactly six hundred pula in that tin—I was certain of it. And so I decided that I would tell the director about it and start looking into the question of who else might have got hold of a key to the drawer."

"That was the right thing to do," said Mma Ramotswe. "Go straight to the relevant authorities. That's what I always advise—then you're protected."

Mr. J.L.B. Matekoni shook his head sadly. "I wish I had gone straightaway. I didn't. I was going to go first thing the following morning, but . . ."

Mma Ramotswe's heart sank. "Oh no, Rra!"

"Yes. That afternoon the accountant and the director carried out an on-the-spot check. The director asked me for the key to the drawer and before I could say anything he had opened it and discovered the shortfall. I said to him that I was just about to tell him about the missing three hundred pula, but he just looked at me as if to say, 'That's a likely story!' I felt awful. I knew that I was telling the truth, but I also knew that if I were in the director's position I would probably think exactly the same thing. So I could do nothing but protest my innocence, knowing that I was not believed."

Mma Ramotswe groaned. "An awful situation, Rra. A nightmare."

"Yes. And no matter how much I tried, I could not convince him that I was telling the truth. So he said to me that I had one week to pay the money back, or he would report the matter to the police. He said that he was giving me a chance because, apart from this incident, he had been impressed with my work."

"And did you?"

"Yes, of course, I borrowed it from my uncle and I handed it over to the director. When I did that, he looked at me sternly and said, 'Don't ever be dishonest again. Never, ever take money that does not belong to you—even if you think you can repay it.' I felt so wronged, Mma. I felt that I was being judged to be dishonest when I was not. I felt dirtied by the whole matter."

Mma Ramotswe wondered whether the real culprit had ever been found.

"We never found out who it was," said Mr. J.L.B. Matekoni. "But here's a thing, Mma: there were several thefts after I had left the brigade—after the end of my time there. They were the same sort of thing, and I heard that the director then realised that I had, in fact, been innocent. But do you know what? I saw him about six months after that—I met him in the street—and he did not say sorry to me. He did not say, 'I was wrong to accuse you of theft.' He said nothing, in fact. He just asked me what I was doing and left it at that. He could have said sorry. He could have said that they had found the real thief, but he did not. What do you think of that, Mma?"

"Not very much," said Mma Ramotswe. "But then I've noticed it, Rra: people are very slow to say sorry. I don't know why this should be, but they do not say sorry easily."

"Perhaps it's because they think that saying sorry means that they were wrong. Perhaps it makes them feel small. Or look small."

Mma Ramotswe was quick to propose the exact opposite. "Saying sorry does not make you look small—it makes you look big."

"I think so too," said Mr. J.L.B. Matekoni. "But some people are small inside, and if you're small inside, you can't be big outside. It just won't come to you."

"Perhaps not," said Mma Ramotswe. She looked at her watch. "I think it is time for dinner. Shall we go inside, Mr. J.L.B. Matekoni?"

They left the verandah and went back into the kitchen. The smell of the stew was rich on the air. Mr. J.L.B. Matekoni closed his eyes in delighted anticipation of the treat ahead. It was the onions, he decided; they had to be small and sweet—they just had to be.

MR. J.L.B. MATEKONI LAY under a sheet, there being no need for a blanket in this warm weather. He was already dead to the world when Mma Ramotswe went to bed that night; she slipped into bed, being careful not to wake him up, although she knew that he was a sound sleeper and would not be disturbed by her coming to bed, as she often did, an hour or so after him.

She settled herself, turned out the light, and composed herself for sleep. Normally this involved deliberately putting out of her mind the affairs of the office. It was always tempting to think about what had happened in the working day, but it could be fatal for the onset of sleep. What she should have done, what she had done, what she might do the following morning—these were all matters that did not belong in the bedroom. But that night, as she lay there in the dark, she found herself staring up at the darkened, all but invisible ceiling, thinking about what had been said on that curious, unsatisfactory car journey. She could no longer think of the woman as Mma Not Rosie and now thought of her as Rosie; nor could she get out of her mind the glimpse she had been afforded—in the rear-view mirror—of the expression on Rosie's face as she vented her anger. *When she cried I was there; I was the one who comforted her.* That was exactly what a nurse might say . . . *And when her little dog became sick and died I was the one who helped her bury it at the end of the garden and put the stones around its grave.* You would not make that up; that had the ring of the heartfelt about it. *And I was the one who nursed her when she was ill because the real mother was always working or playing tennis.* The reference to tennis did not sound like part of a prepared script; that, again, had a genuine feel. *I was the one, and you people don't know that—and you don't care, do you?* The final accusation, voiced with all the feeling of one who had been discourteously treated. By me, she thought; by me and my assistant—co-director, or whatever Mma Makutsi now was; in my husband's car . . .

She sat up in bed, staring directly ahead of her. Her neighbour had a jacaranda tree in his garden. What if . . . She swung her legs out of bed, stood up, and put on her dressing gown. She felt with her toes for her old felt house-shoes, found them, and slipped into them. A thought had come to her, and it had elbowed everything else out of her mind: her neighbour had a large jacaranda tree to the side of his house, in roughly the position that the tree in the photograph would have been. And his house was one of those old BHC houses, very similar to hers, with a verandah in the right place. It had been staring her in the face, and it had not even occurred to her that when Rosie brought them to Zebra Drive she was looking for her neighbour's house and had mistakenly identified hers. His was set back further from the road and was largely obscured by the shrubs and trees that he never bothered to control. Of course, of course . . .

The obvious, wrote Clovis Andersen, *is often very obvious—not just a little bit obvious, but glaringly obvious. Yet we fail to notice it and, when we do, we are astonished that we did not see it much earlier . . .*

She made her way along the corridor and into the kitchen. The glowing red light on the cooker flashed out the time: 12:02. It was already tomorrow, and here she was proposing to go outside into the yard at the very time that was the preserve of snakes, out hunting for rats and mice and other prey, because this hot time of the year was exactly when snakes liked to move about at night. Mr. J.L.B. Matekoni had seen a cobra only a few days before, when he had come home later than usual and had gone to inspect his beans. It had been curiously oblivious of his presence, and had glided across the vegetable beds with all the confidence of ownership. Snakes did that; most of the time they kept out of your way but when it was very hot and they had business to attend to, the ground over which they moved was theirs, not yours, and you had to watch out for them.

She went outside. She had with her a flashlight, but the batteries were coming to the end of their life and gave out only the faintest beam, which on the ground ahead of her was not much more than a half-hearted glow. The night was particularly dark, as there was just the faintest sliver of moon, a curved wisp of silver, and there were no lights in the surrounding houses. Only the stars shone, those constellations hanging over the Kalahari to the west, field upon field of pulsing white, the stars she had never really learned to name but one day hoped she would. But she could pick out the Southern Cross, which she saw above the dark treeline of the horizon, and felt somehow comforted by it.

There was a noise, and she gave a start before she recognised that it was, of course, Fanwell's dog, Zebra, for whom Mr. J.L.B. Matekoni and the children had prepared a kennel of sorts—an old packing case upended at the end of his wire run. The children had accepted responsibility for Zebra, for the time being at least, feeding and replenishing his bowl with water. He was appreciative, and licked them from head to toe with his protruding pink tongue. "Not on your face," she said. "Not on your face." But the dog had ignored her, as had the children, who delighted in the dog's moist displays of affection.

She crossed the yard to where Zebra was half in his kennel and half out. In the dim light of the flashlight she noticed that one of his legs was sticking out at an awkward angle. Crouching down, she saw that the leg had become entangled in the cord that linked his collar to the running wire. She fumbled with this, trying to extricate him—he licked her hand as she did so—but the cord had wound round too tightly and had become a knot. The dog whimpered; he was not in pain, but he could not be left like this. They would have to make different arrangements and she would speak to Mr. J.L.B. Matekoni about it later this morning. A pen of chicken wire could be the answer—a pen in which he could be untethered and could patrol in relative freedom.

She attempted to disentangle the cord, but failed. She would need to release the dog before she could do this, and so she began to undo his collar. He licked her as she set about the task, as if to endorse her decision.

"There," she said, removing the thick leather collar. "Now we can—"

She did not finish. Springing to his feet, the dog gave a yelp, shook himself vigorously, and then bounded away into the darkness. Mma Ramotswe had been bending down for the task; now she stood up and felt light-headed as the blood drained from her head.

"Zebra!"

Her voice was swallowed in the night. She thought she heard a bark, but already he was far enough away for it to be almost indiscernible. She dropped the collar. There was enough to think about without having to chase after an exuberant dog. He might return, or he might not; these creatures were headstrong and unpredictable.

She sighed. The children would reproach her for losing him. She would have to reassure them that he would turn up, tail between his legs, when he became hungry. He might, or he might not; on balance, she thought that he was gone. He was a restless dog, one who was not quite sure where he lived, and he might not want to stay at Zebra Drive.

She moved away from the kennel. She had come outside with a search in mind, and she was going to carry it out, dog or no dog. She started to cross the vegetable patch, heading for the fence that ran between her neighbour's property and hers. The sticks that supported Mr. J.L.B. Matekoni's beans made a small forest in the night; she stepped round them, playing the light on the ground before her, for what it was worth. It illuminated very little, but it was something. Without it, each step would be an act of faith that there was nothing waiting for her to step on it—no scorpion or snake, none of the small, scuttling creatures that had no name but that might sting or nip those who disturbed their nocturnal business.

The fence consisted of four strands of wire, strung carelessly and sagging through neglect. Her neighbour, Mr. Vain Kwele, had declined to do anything about it when she and Mr. J.L.B. Matekoni had offered to bear half the cost of new posts to replace the ones that had suffered the ravages of termites. "No need," he said. "I've got nothing to keep out or in. And we both know where the boundary is, so we do not really need a fence."

He was mean, Vain Kwele: he owned a bottle store on the Francistown Road, and everybody knew that people who owned bottle stores made money. Although he could have afforded something newer, he drove an ancient car that he expected Mr. J.L.B. Matekoni to fix at little or no charge. In spite of the undoubted profits of a bottle store, his wife was dressed in dowdy clothes and had no help in the house. His two children, though, were clearly overindulged. They sat at the window watching Puso and Motholeli working in the vegetable garden, and as they sat there they ate fat cakes and other delicacies prepared by their dowdy mother in her dirty kitchen.

"They will explode one day," said Motholeli. "Those fat ones next door will explode from eating too many fat cakes."

"Bang!" said Puso. "There will be a big noise and bits of them will be all over the place. That will be the end of them."

That will be the end of them. She had noticed that this was an expression that Puso used quite frequently, and in all sorts of situations. Usually there was an element of justice in it: people got their just deserts, and that would be the end of them. Or they would lose an argument, and that would be the end of them too. It was catching, and she found herself using it herself, telling Mma Makutsi that somebody she suspected of dishonesty would run into trouble one day, and that would be the end of him. Mma Makutsi had agreed, and added, "And not before time, Mma."

She hesitated at the fence, but only briefly. Bending down, she pulled two strands sufficiently apart to squeeze herself through. *Am I really doing this?* she asked herself. *Is this really Mma Ramotswe, respectable citizen, climbing through a fence in the middle of the night?*

Is this what a traditionally built woman should be doing? She almost laughed at the thought—it was that absurd. But she had committed herself; she was now in her neighbour's garden and had her task ahead of her.

That task was clear enough. It had been a long time ago—over thirty years—but Rosie had said that she had laid stones around the grave of Susan's pet dog. Well, if these stones were sufficiently large—the sorts of stones used to mark the boundaries of flower beds—then there was a possibility that they would still be there. Her neighbour's garden had been untended for years, with beds left uncultivated and plants allowed to grow unrestrained. There was even a clump of prickly pears that other neighbours had begged Vain Kwele to remove: once those got onto the land they could run rife. But he had done nothing, with the result that the prickly pears had colonised a whole section of his yard, making for an ugly and impenetrable corner. Down at the end of the garden, though, running along the front fence, was a line of random shrubs, self-seeded for the most part, that was less inhospitable than the rest. It was here that she would find what she was looking for—if it was to be found at all.

Playing the steadily weakening beam of the flashlight on the ground in front of her, she made her way along the front of the garden. Something caught the light at her feet—an empty beer bottle, tossed across the fence by some passer-by; and something small and dark that moved—a dung beetle labouring with its trophy towards its home. She stepped sideways to avoid disturbing it and held the flashlight closer to the ground in the hope of getting a better view of where she was putting her feet.

And there, not far ahead of her, to be made out in the fading beam, but only just, was a small rectangle of stones embedded in the soil. It looked like a flower bed, but was too small for that, and she knew at once that this was the place where all those years ago Rosie had made a grave for her charge's dog. She bent down and examined the stones. One or two of them had become almost completely covered with sand, but were revealed when she brushed this aside with her hand. In a dry country, the bones of the land often remain visible for years—there is no mulch, no covering loam to obliterate the marks that people leave on the earth; they simply remain there. Nor is there the rain to wash those bones away—just the wind, which will eventually erode what lies on the surface, although that will take many years.

Yes, she thought. Yes. This is exactly what Rosie meant. This was the proof that Mma Ramotswe needed to establish that what Rosie had said was true, and that however much she might have been motivated by the prospect of reward, this woman had been who she claimed to be, and, what was more, she had loved that child.

She looked down at the earth. We cry over bits of earth; we fight over it; we take our monuments and place them upon the land to assert our claims; we make small patches sacred in some way, as happened here over thirty years ago when a much-loved animal was buried amidst a child's tears.

The beam of the flashlight now flickered and then failed altogether, the batteries finally drained of their weakening amps. She turned away; this was not the time to feel bad about how Rosie had been treated. She could rectify that over the next day or two when she would seek her out and apologise. Then she would bring Susan and Rosie together, and let them talk about whatever it was they would wish to talk about. She suspected that Susan wanted to say thank you, but she may wish to say other things too. In all of it there would be tears, she thought, but then tears had their place in the reliving of the past.

She began to walk back towards the fence. Without any light to guide her, she trod carefully, making sure that her footfall was firm enough to give warning to any snakes that might be abroad. The steps of a traditionally built woman, she thought, would deter any snake except . . . except the puff adder, the sluggish, traditionally built snake that could hardly be bothered to get out of anybody's way, and one of them was moving slowly across her path as she neared the fence. She felt it underfoot—a soft, giving feeling—and she heard the sound of its hiss. And then she felt something hit her ankle, as if she had trodden on a branch that had whipped up and struck her.

She knew immediately what had happened, and although she jumped back instinctively, she realised that it was too late and that the snake, now retreating into the cover of vegetation, had struck her.

She thought of her father, of Obed Ramotswe, and wanted to cry out to him, which she did. She screamed for him, as a child will scream for its parent. "Oh Daddy, Daddy!" . . . There was silence. Then she screamed again.

A light came on in Vain Kwele's house. There was a voice, thick with sleep: "Who is that? Who is that out there?"

She called out, "Me! Me!"

"Which me?"

She started to cry, and hobbled towards the neighbour's door, which was now opening to allow a square of light to fall outside.

"Mma Ramotswe! What are you doing, Mma? Is something wrong?"

She stuttered out what had happened, and her neighbour gasped.

"I will drive you to the hospital," he said. "I will take you there right now."

She nodded. It would be quicker going with him than going back to wake up Mr. J.L.B. Matekoni. With a snake bite, she knew, time was of the essence. If it was a mamba that had bitten her, then she might only have a few minutes. What did people say about the bite of that snake? That you had four minutes at the most? In which case, she was now down to three.

In the light from the door she looked down at her leg. There was no blood, no sign of a wound, and all she saw was a small scratch. Yet the skin could be broken and some poison may easily have entered her system—in which case she would soon feel the symptoms.

"I'm sorry to disturb you," she said.

He invited her to sit down. "I shall fetch my car keys," he said.

She closed her eyes. Did she feel any of the symptoms? Did she feel a tightening of the chest as the neurotoxin took effect? That would make breathing difficult. And then it would go to the eyes, and vision would go, and the heart would race as it tried to pump blood about a body that sensed the venom the blood bore with it.

She felt no pain. Nothing. She looked again at her ankle. There was nothing to see beyond the scratch. "I don't think I am going to die," she said, under her breath. And then added, "Yet."

CHAPTER TEN

THE FAT CATTLE CLUB

MMA MAKUTSI AND FANWELL looked at Mma Ramotswe with concern. She was seated on her verandah, her leg freshly bandaged just above the ankle; at her side, on a small, rather rickety table was a pot of red bush tea.

"We were shocked, Mma," said Mma Makutsi. "Very shocked indeed."

"Yes," said Fanwell. "To our foundations, Mma. We were shocked to our foundations."

Mma Ramotswe laughed. They were her fourth set of visitors that morning, and everyone had expressed much the same sentiments of shock; this was flattering, but had made her feel as if she was making a fuss about nothing. She felt completely well and had now decided that the doctor who said she should rest for two days had been far too cautious. After this visit from Mma Makutsi and Fanwell, she would bring her convalescence to an end and resume normal life.

"Tell us what happened," said Mma Makutsi. "You were in your neighbour's garden at midnight and . . ."

Fanwell frowned. "Why were you in your neighbour's garden, Mma—especially at midnight?"

Mma Ramotswe made a gesture that implied that this was not

a question they needed to bother about. "I'll explain in due course," she said. "It's a bit complicated. I was there and my light ran out of power."

"So you were in the dark?" prompted Fanwell.

"Yes, I was in the dark and couldn't really see where I was putting my feet. And I trod on a snake—I think it was a puff adder."

Mma Makutsi's detection instincts came to the fore. "How could you tell in the dark, Mma?"

"I felt it," said Mma Ramotswe. "You know how most snakes are thin and quite lean? Well this was fat and soft. That meant it was a puff adder—that is what they are like."

"She's right," said Fanwell, nodding in agreement. "Those snakes are like that. They are two or three times as fat as ordinary snakes."

Mma Ramotswe continued her account. "It struck, and I thought that I was dead. I thought: this is the end."

Fanwell drew in his breath. "Ow, Mma! I have heard that your whole life flashes before you just before you die. Have you heard that? Did that happen?"

"She did not die," Mma Makutsi pointed out. "So her life would not have flashed before her, Fanwell."

"My neighbour took me to hospital," said Mma Ramotswe. "He drove very fast and we almost went off the road, but we got there in a couple of minutes, I think." She paused. "They put me on a trolley and wheeled me in. I told them what had happened and they fetched a doctor straightaway. He looked at my leg and said that he could not find the puncture wounds of a snake bite. He said that the snake must just have grazed my leg with its fang as it struck. He said this sometimes happens if the snake starts its strike from the wrong angle."

"You were very lucky," said Mma Makutsi. "If a puff adder gets its fangs into you, then it is very serious."

"Your leg dies," said Fanwell. "Then you die. That's what happens, unless they can chop it off in time."

"The doctor said that no venom had been injected," Mma Ramotswe went on. "Although he thought it possible a tiny amount might have got in through the scratch. That's why they said I should sit in my chair at home today and tomorrow—in case I developed any symptoms. But there is nothing. I am feeling one hundred per cent. I do not need to stay here."

Mma Makutsi's face registered a rapidly changing range of emotions as Mma Ramotswe gave this account. *No venom had been injected*—relief; *a tiny amount*—mouth in a tiny O; *sit in my chair*—nodded agreement; *developed any symptoms*—renewed anxiety; *one hundred per cent*—a smile of encouragement, tempered with slight concern over the non-following of medical advice. At the end of it all, she said, "You have been very lucky, Mma. And we are lucky too, aren't we, Fanwell? If that snake had injected its poison then you could be dead by now, and we could have lost our dear friend."

"And colleague," said Fanwell. He thought for a moment, looking at Mma Makutsi. "You would now be the managing director, Mma."

"We do not like to think about that sort of thing," said Mma Makutsi firmly. "Mma Ramotswe has survived this great danger."

"She is still with us," said Fanwell. "That is very clear. She is still with us." He paused before delivering the final verdict. "The head of that snake was turned aside by the hand of God. That is the only conclusion we can reach. God was present in Gaborone last night, and his divine intervention on behalf of the No. 1 Ladies' Detective Agency bore the result we see before us. That is all I can say on this."

Mma Ramotswe felt that enough had now been said. She was aware of how differently things might have turned out, but she did not think there was much to be gained by further dwelling on the whole matter. It was time, she felt, to put what had happened behind her and get on with her day. The bandage, which was anyway quite unnecessary in her view, had slipped, exposing what now seemed to be a quite unharmed ankle. She noticed that both Mma Makutsi and Fanwell had their eyes firmly fixed on the freshly exposed site, and that they seemed surprised, perhaps even disappointed, that there was no more spectacular injury to be seen.

"I think this bandage is not needed," said Mma Ramotswe, bending down to remove it. "Hospitals feel they have to put a bandage on anybody who goes there—just in case. Sometimes you get a bandage even if you are just visiting somebody."

It was a joke, but Fanwell did not see it as such. "I will be careful next time I visit somebody in the hospital. I would not want a bandage."

"Well," said Mma Ramotswe briskly, rising to her feet. "That is the end of all that." She looked at her watch. "I think I shall meet Mma Potokwane for lunch at the President Hotel. She said that she would be in town today. I shall catch her there, and then I shall come into the office, Mma Makutsi, and tell you about some progress I have made in the case of the Canadian lady."

"That is a very difficult case," said Mma Makutsi. "There are now four more ladies who say their name is Rosie. I shall be interviewing two more of them tomorrow."

"I think those interviews can be cancelled," said Mma Ramotswe. "I shall explain why when I come to the office."

Mma Makutsi looked doubtful. "Are you sure, Mma?"

"I am very sure," said Mma Ramotswe. "I think that we have already met our Rosie." She paused, and then added, "And I think that the house in which Mma Susan lived is closer than we think."

THE RAISED VERANDAH of the President Hotel, reached by an open staircase from the public square below, was busy when Mma Ramotswe arrived. The hotel was known for its lunchtime curries, and these had now been laid out on the buffet table for those wanting to fit in an early lunch before the official lunch hour began at one o'clock. Over that hour, the hotel was popular with civil servants from the government departments just a short walk away. The permanent secretaries of various ministries—men and women burdened with responsibility and importance—would meet one another to exchange the gossip that is so important a part of the life of all officials throughout the world: who is next in line for promotion; who has overspent his or her departmental budget; which minister can be given just the right amount of unhelpful advice so as to hasten an inevitable departure from the Cabinet; and which ministerial mouth to put words into, if necessary, in order to thwart the objectives of new ministers who did not recognise just who should run the country, which everybody knew should be permanent secretaries.

At less senior, and less official, tables, the conversation might follow different lines. Here business might be discussed, or children, or affairs of the heart, or any of the day-to-day matters that were the stuff of ordinary life. At such a table, a sought-after one because of the view it commanded over the square below, sat Mma Ramotswe and Mma Potokwane, contemplating, with evident pleasure, the ample helping of curry that each had on the plate in front of her. They had been given the table in the face of stiff competition because of Mma Ramotswe's friendship with the head waiter. His father had known her father—indeed he had bought a bull from him many years ago. That bull had been the founder of a dynasty of particularly fine cattle, and all of his progeny called to reproductive duty had been named Obed in his honour. That was a connection that could hardly be forgotten, and it was a perfectly valid reason for allocating the best table to Mma Ramotswe, even if one or two senior civil servants felt that by rights it should be theirs. It was also grounds for larger helpings of everything and for a complimentary pot of tea at the end of the meal.

Mma Ramotswe told Mma Potokwane about her brush with disaster. Her friend shook her head at the mention of puff adders, and told her own story of finding one on the steps of her office only two months previously. "It was sitting there, Mma—or lying there, should I say . . ." She stopped, and lowered her voice. "There he is, Mma Ramotswe. There's Mr. Polopetsi. See him—helping himself to curry?"

Mr. Polopetsi had his back to them, but when he turned round, holding his plate, he saw them, and waved with his free hand. Mouthing a greeting, he returned to his table, where a companion, a man in a loud checked jacket, was awaiting him.

"Have you seen him here before?" asked Mma Potokwane. "Is this a place he likes to come to?"

"Once or twice," said Mma Ramotswe. "I've seen him eating with his wife here. She's—"

But she did not have to explain. "I know who she is," said Mma Potokwane. "I've seen her photograph in the papers. She's going places, I think."

"She's already there," said Mma Ramotswe.

Mma Potokwane was staring thoughtfully at Mr. Polopetsi on the other side of the verandah. "You know, Mma," she began, "Mr. Polopetsi is such a . . . such a modest man, even perhaps a bit mousy." She transferred her gaze to Mma Ramotswe. "Not that I want to be rude, Mma."

Mma Ramotswe reassured her that she would never imagine her friend being rude. "You're right," she said. "Mr. Polopetsi is a bit on the timid side—in fact, he's very much on the timid side. He's not one to chase the lions away, is he?" She could not help but imagine Mr. Polopetsi encountering a lion, and smiled. The lion would open its mouth to roar and Mr. Polopetsi would quiver with fear. And so would she, come to think of it; so perhaps one should not use that picture to diminish Mr. Polopetsi. Sometimes the most unlikely people could turn out to be brave; and again she brought Mr. Polopetsi to mind for a few moments, although this time he was in hot pursuit of the lion, rather like one of those tall, red-blanketed Masai warriors who killed lions as a rite of passage to manhood. How would

Mr. Polopetsi look in a Masai blanket? How would he look carrying one of those long spears with which Masai warriors armed themselves? Somehow it was hard to envision it.

Mma Potokwane tackled her curry. It was just the right strength, she said. Those people over in India, how did they manage to eat those extremely hot curries? What did they do to their stomachs? Mma Ramotswe was not sure. She covered her curry with butter, which quickly melted and took some of the heat out of it.

They talked easily and without any real interruption. Two old friends having lunch together; what could be more relaxing and therapeutic than that, especially if one of them had recently had a close encounter with a deadly puff adder? Although Mma Potokwane did make one tactless remark, and that was to enquire of Mma Ramotswe whether she had ever made a will. The trigger for this was not so much her friend's recent brush with death as her ambition to ensure that all her friends considered a legacy for the Orphan Farm. The issue, though, was not pursued, and Mma Potokwane remained uncertain whether Mma Ramotswe was testate or intestate.

As the two women were enjoying a cup of tea after their meal, Mr. Polopetsi's lunch came to an end. Mma Ramotswe saw him stand up and shake hands with his lunch companion. Then the other man made his way from the verandah, turning to follow the staircase to the square below. Mr. Polopetsi watched him go before bending, picking up a small briefcase, and making his way over to Mma Ramotswe's table, a broad smile on his face.

"I had not expected to see you ladies here," he said as he approached them. "But I suppose this is a good place for ladies to have lunch."

Mma Potokwane laughed. "And men too, if they behave."

"I never misbehave," said Mr. Polopetsi. "I wouldn't dare—with Mma Ramotswe there to bring me into line."

Mma Potokwane laughed again. "And Mma Makutsi too," she said.

Mma Ramotswe gestured to the empty chair at their table. "I know you have had your lunch, Rra, but there is always room for an extra cup of tea, I think."

Mr. Polopetsi glanced at his watch. "I mustn't stay too long," he said. "I have an appointment with somebody."

Mma Potokwane and Mma Ramotswe exchanged glances.

"A business appointment?" asked Mma Potokwane.

Mr. Polopetsi, now seated, nodded. "It is to do with an enterprise I am involved in," he said. "That man I was having lunch with—that man who has now gone—he is my business partner."

Mma Ramotswe poured Mr. Polopetsi a cup of tea. "Ah yes, your cattle business."

"The Fat Cattle Investment Club," said Mr. Polopetsi, a note of pride in his voice. "Or the Fat Cattle Club, as we call it informally. I think I've spoken to you about it."

"Not to me," said Mma Ramotswe. "You've spoken to others. Not to me. For some reason." She watched to see if Mr. Polopetsi reacted to this, but he seemed unfazed.

"I can tell you all about it," he said. "If you wish to hear."

Mma Potokwane sat back in her chair. "Before you do, Rra," she said, "maybe you could answer a question I have. Do you think you could?"

"If I can," said Mr. Polopetsi confidently. "I do not know everything about the club, but I know a certain amount."

"Enough to persuade people to give you their money," observed Mma Ramotswe.

If Mr. Polopetsi had not picked up a critical note before this, he now did. He looked hurt. "I do not persuade people, Mma Ramotswe. I give them the opportunity. There is a big difference, you know."

Mma Potokwane agreed. "Oh yes, there is a big difference, Mr. Polopetsi. Just as there is a big difference between a thin cow and a fat one. There is a very important difference, I think."

He looked bemused. "But of course there is, Mma Potokwane.

It's the same difference as between a fat child and a thin child—you know that very well, in your line of business, I think."

Mma Potokwane made much of taking this remark lightly. "Hah, yes! Perhaps I need to choose my words more carefully." But then she added, "The difference I was talking about was the *value* of a thin cow and that of a fat cow. Many pula, Rra." She paused. "Mma Ramotswe here knows that only too well, you know. Her father was a big expert on cattle—one of the best in the country. You know that, don't you, Mr. Polopetsi?"

Mr. Polopetsi shot an anxious glance at Mma Ramotswe. "Yes," he said. "I've always known that, Mma."

There was a brief silence before Mma Potokwane continued. "And that difference in value, Rra, is because of the cost of feed. How much does it take to fatten up a cattle beast if the grazing is bad because of the drought? Four hundred pula? Five hundred? Maybe even more. Cattle feed is never cheap, is it?"

Mr. Polopetsi frowned. "I never said it was, Mma. Everything is expensive these days—even lunch at the President Hotel."

Nobody laughed.

"So what interests me," Mma Potokwane continued, "is how it's possible to make much of a profit on fattening up livestock when the cost of feed is high. When it's cheap and plentiful—yes, I can understand it then. But when it's very high and it has to come a long way . . . How can you make a big profit in those conditions, Rra?"

Mma Potokwane turned to Mma Ramotswe. "Do you understand it, Mma Ramotswe? How can this Fat Cattle Club give such good returns when nobody else can make much of a profit on fattened cattle?"

Mma Ramotswe had begun to feel sorry for Mr. Polopetsi, who had started to squirm under Mma Potokwane's gaze. "We're not trying to catch you out, Rra," she said. "It's just that we're concerned—"

"But there are others," interjected Mma Potokwane. "There are plenty of others who will be interested in catching you out. They will ask the same question, but not over a cup of tea in the President Hotel."

Mr. Polopetsi's eyes were fixed on the floor. "But it works, Mma Potokwane. I put in some money and within a few months I had it back, plus twenty-five per cent."

Mma Ramotswe was gentle. "Yes, Mr. Polopetsi, I'm sure you did get all that. And I would never accuse you of dishonesty. But you have to ask yourself: Where did your profit come from?"

"From the sale of the fat cattle."

Mma Potokwane shook her head. "I don't think so, Rra. I think it probably came from the investment of the next person who joined."

Mr. Polopetsi looked at her blankly. "But that money would be used to buy more cattle."

"Some of it might be," said Mma Potokwane. "But the rest of it would be used to repay earlier investors. So at the end of the day, the people at the beginning make money, while those at the end find their money has disappeared and there are no cattle for them—nor any profits." She waited for what seemed like an unduly long time, and then said, "There's a special name for this sort of thing. It's called a pyramid scheme."

Mr. Polopetsi sat quite still. When he spoke, his voice was faltering. "He said that everything was all right. He said there were many people doing these things."

"Who said this?" asked Mma Potokwane.

Mr. Polopetsi gestured towards the table at which he had been sitting. "My business associate."

"That great financial magician," said Mma Potokwane.

Mr. Polopetsi, defeated and crumpled though he was, suddenly seemed to acquire the strength to defend himself. "He is a good man," said Mr. Polopetsi. "He said that he would be helping the farmers from the drought areas. That is a good thing to do, don't you think?"

Mma Ramotswe sighed. "Oh, Mr. Polopetsi! You are a good man, Rra—I've always known that. But you are not the sort to get mixed up in this sort of thing. You may want to help the farmers suffering from the drought, but I really don't think your friend has that in mind. I think he's using you, Rra."

Mma Potokwane nodded her agreement. "Yes, Rra—you are being used."

"So now," went on Mma Ramotswe, "you need to tell us how many people you have persuaded to invest in the Fat Cattle Club."

"Not very many," muttered Mr. Polopetsi.

"How many?" pressed Mma Ramotswe.

Mr. Polopetsi swallowed hard. "Four," he said.

"Including Mma Makutsi?" asked Mma Ramotswe.

"Five," said Mr. Polopetsi.

Mma Ramotswe drew in her breath. "We shall have to make a plan," she said. "Don't approach anybody else. Do you understand? Not one more person—not one."

He lowered his head. "I am a very foolish man," he said.

"I think so too," said Mma Potokwane.

Mma Ramotswe, though, reached out and placed a hand on Mr. Polopetsi's shoulder. "Listen to me, Mr. Polopetsi," she said, her voice lowered. "Who among us has not done something stupid?" Her gaze fell on Mma Potokwane before returning to Mr. Polopetsi. "I have done some very foolish things in my life. Everybody has." She was thinking of her earlier marriage to Note Mokoti, that dangerous, seductive trumpeter; that violent and unpleasant man who thought nothing of breaking hearts one after the other; that wasteful and grasping man who had come back to wheedle money out of her and whom, in spite of everything, she had forgiven even as she told him never to come back into her life.

Her words seemed to cheer Mr. Polopetsi. "Do you think you can sort it out, Mma Ramotswe?" he asked, his voice rising in hope. "Do you really think so?"

Mma Ramotswe pursed her lips. "I shall try," she said. "And we shall start with Mma Makutsi."

At the mention of Mma Makutsi, Mr. Polopetsi gave a nervous start. It was an open secret that he had always been a bit frightened of Mma Makutsi, even if he admired her greatly. "I won't have to speak to her by myself, will I?" he asked.

Mma Ramotswe looked thoughtful. "I think it's best for us to face up to our own mistakes," she said.

His face fell, and seeing this, she added, "Except sometimes. So, yes, Rra, I'll help you. I'm not frightened of Mma Makutsi." She was tempted to add *except sometimes,* but she decided enough had been said and anything further might simply make the situation more difficult than it already was. So she said nothing, which is what Clovis Andersen said is often exactly the right thing to say.

Least said, soonest ended, he had written. Mma Ramotswe had studied this aphorism very closely. Something was not quite right. Had a letter dropped out back in Muncie, Indiana, and did it make any difference?

She looked again at Mr. Polopetsi. He was a good man, she thought, even if he could be rather naïve. But then she reflected on the fact that of all the failings that any of us might have, naïvety was far from being the worst.

There was something she wanted to ask him. "Mr. Polopetsi," she began, "you say that you made twenty-five per cent on your investment in the Fat Cattle Club. Did you actually get the money?"

He looked surprised. "Of course. It was in cash."

Mma Ramotswe absorbed this information. It was clear to her what had happened: Mr. Polopetsi was the innocent recruiter; he would have been paid exactly what he had been promised so that he could bring others into the scheme with the conviction of one who has seen the whole thing work. "And the money?" she asked. "What have you done with it?"

Mr. Polopetsi started to give his answer, but said very little before his voice trailed off. "I re-invested it. My colleague had another . . ."

She saw his face fall.

"Your colleague? The same man?"

Mr. Polopetsi nodded.

"You gave him back the money?" said Mma Potokwane. Her tone was openly incredulous.

Mma Ramotswe winced. "He has another scheme?"

Mr. Polopetsi looked like a schoolboy whose unlikely story has suddenly been questioned. "Yes," he said. "He told me he had the chance to buy a consignment of medicines from Zambia. He said that he could get these at a very low price and he knew people who would be able to sell them here in Gaborone at a much higher price."

Mma Ramotswe heard Mma Potokwane's sharp intake of breath.

"What medicines?" asked the matron. "Aspirin?"

Mr. Polopetsi laughed. "No, nothing like that. Antibiotics, he said. Blood pressure drugs. That sort of thing."

"And why would they be cheap?" asked Mma Ramotswe.

Mr. Polopetsi shrugged. "Over-orders, probably," he said. "Sometimes hospital dispensaries order far too much stuff and then realise they won't be able to use it all. I suspect it will be something like that."

Mma Ramotswe raised an eyebrow. "I see," she said quietly.

"I'm going to help him," he said. "He can't get away and so he asked me if I could collect them from the other side."

"The other side of the border?" asked Mma Ramotswe.

Mr. Polopetsi nodded. "Yes," he said. "I'll go up to Chobe. He's going to hire a car for me. He said that he'd order some chemicals for the school lab and his order could go in with mine. That would be very useful for us, you see—the school is always running out of the things I need for my chemistry lessons." He smiled; people understood—and sympathised with—administrative inefficiency on the part of others. It was a common burden. "These would be a donation from him."

Mma Ramotswe hardly dared meet the intense look Mma Potokwane sent in her direction, but when she did she knew that they both had exactly the same understanding of what Mr. Polopetsi had said. It was so obvious, she thought; so glaringly obvious. She opened her mouth to speak, but Mma Potokwane had beaten her to it. "Oh, Mr. Polopetsi," she exclaimed. "How could you, Rra? How could you be so stu—"

"So unwise," said Mma Ramotswe quickly.

Mr. Polopetsi looked at Mma Potokwane and then at Mma Ramotswe. He seemed confused now, and remained in that state until Mma Potokwane, taking a deep breath, spelled out to him what she thought. Once she had done that, there was complete silence, and nobody said anything for at least five minutes. Then Mma Ramotswe cleared her throat. "I shall deal with this," she said firmly.

Mma Potokwane looked at her as if to say: How can you possibly pick up the pieces here? But Mma Ramotswe chose to ignore this. She signalled to the waiter for their bill. "Did you come here by foot, Mr. Polopetsi?" she asked. There was a Polopetsi car, but it was always being driven by Mrs. Polopetsi, and he was rarely allowed to use it.

He nodded, glancing at Mma Potokwane, as if preparing himself to forestall any further criticism.

"In that case," said Mma Ramotswe, "I'll run you back. My van is parked on the other side of the square—not far away."

"Well, I'm going back to work," said Mma Potokwane. Whether or not she intended it, there was a strong emphasis on the word *work*. The censure this implied—that there were some whose idea of work was the making of risky investments—found its target, and Mr. Polopetsi, already reduced, crumpled further. He was a small man, and now he was even smaller. His jacket, too large for him at any time, seemed to envelop him like some giant sack, his hands disappearing up the sleeves, the fabric around the shoulders without support now, loose and flapping.

Outside in the square, the afternoon sun made shadows under the trees and around the doorways of the buildings, pools of shade where people took languid shelter from the heat of the day. A few traders, those whose stalls were comfortably under the branches of the acacias, continued to offer their wares; others had packed up and left after the morning's business was over.

They walked slowly, as the warmth of the day dictated.

"Rain," said Mr. Polopetsi.

She barely heard the voice emanating from somewhere under the billowing clothes.

"What was that, Mr. Polopetsi?"

"I said: rain, Mma. I hope there will be rain soon."

She glanced up at the sky. "I hope so too, Rra. Some people say we're being punished by this drought. They say that God is expressing his displeasure."

"Nonsense. That's nonsense, Mma."

"Of course it is, Mr. Polopetsi. This is all to do with the direction of sea currents and things like that."

Mr. Polopetsi made a sound that indicated agreement. It was a strange sound, and she was not sure quite where it came from. It seemed to issue from one of the flapping sleeves of his jacket, but that surely was impossible. She looked at him. His mouth was very small, she decided. Did he take a very long time to eat a meal? she wondered; with that small mouth, the consumption of food would be a slow business. It was a strange thought to have, and she pulled herself up; the mind was a peculiar thing, suggesting all sorts of things of little or no consequence.

They drew level with a trader's stall on which clothing was displayed. There was a neat stack of T-shirts on which *Bostwana* was printed in various colours.

"We don't need one of those," said Mma Ramotswe. "We know where we are."

Mr. Polopetsi looked puzzled. "We're in Gaborone, Mma."

"That's what I meant," said Mma Ramotswe. She had stopped, and was looking at some of the other items on display. The woman behind the table had been perched on a small folding stool, and now stood up. She was an ungainly-looking woman, but the eye went to her smile.

"I have many nice things here, Mma," she said to Mma Ramotswe. "Even things for your husband."

Mma Ramotswe chuckled. "Oh, this is not my husband, this is just . . ." She stopped herself. She was not sure that Mr. Polopetsi had noticed, but it was as if she were laughing off the possibility that she could possibly be married to such a . . . to such a small man. And she had not meant that.

"Unfortunately," she said quickly. "I would be a lucky woman to have a nice man like this as my husband."

The woman looked quickly at Mr. Polopetsi—and then at Mma Ramotswe—and she understood. "Yes, my sister," she said. "A man with a nice face is always a very good catch. Many of the sisters would agree with us on that."

Mr. Polopetsi beamed. He said nothing, but somehow he seemed to grow back into his clothes; not entirely, but it was at least noticeable.

Mma Ramotswe watched him. He had picked up a tie and peered at the price tag. Shaking his head, he put it back on its rack. She reached for the tie and examined it herself. It was dark red, with a small eagle motif running across it at an angle. "Eagles," she said. "This is very nice."

"Those are very popular," said the woman. "Everyone is wearing them now."

"The good men are wearing them," replied Mma Ramotswe. "The bad men are wearing ties with vultures on them, maybe."

The other woman laughed. It was a loud, raucous laugh that

seemed to go perfectly with her ungainly appearance. Mr. Polopetsi smiled. "It is a very smart tie," he said. "Very smart. But it is too expensive, Mma."

Mma Ramotswe held the tie against the front of his shirt, obscuring the thin grey tie he was already wearing.

"More colour," said the other woman. "You see what a difference it makes. You see that, Mma?"

"I certainly do, Mma." She looked at the price tag. "It is not all that expensive."

"It's a bargain," said the woman. "Buy cheap, sell cheap, you see. That's the motto of my business."

Mma Ramotswe smiled. She had read in a magazine recently that every business should have a mission statement. She liked the sound of that—a *mission statement* sounded very purposeful. She had discussed the matter with Mma Makutsi, who had been in strong agreement. "At the Botswana Secretarial College," she said, "they told us to set goals. They said: Put your goals into words—you cannot have goals without words. That is when I made my first mission statement, Mma."

"And what is that, Mma Makutsi?"

The reply came quickly. "It's confidential, Mma."

Mma Ramotswe had been surprised. The whole point of a mission statement, she had thought, was that you declared your purpose to the world. You judged yourself by it, yes, but far more importantly you invited others to judge you by the extent to which you lived up to your professed aims. So when the Botswana Power Corporation printed its mission statement on their customers' bills, it was to let everybody know that *Getting Power to You* was what they wanted, above all else, to do. That was a modest enough goal, after all; it was not as if they said *Lighting Up the Whole World* or something of that sort.

But a confidential mission statement? That, surely, would encourage speculation that something underhand, or even threatening, was being planned. *To Get to the Top at Any Cost*—there were people who behaved as if that was their mission statement, and perhaps that was exactly what it was. Did Mma Makutsi have a mission statement like that? No, on balance she thought not. It would be something to do with filing; Mma Makutsi had an intense interest in filing and often talked about its finer points. Perhaps her mission statement, then, was *To Put Things in the Right Place*. But if that was what it was, then why keep it confidential? Nobody was threatened by one who wanted to file documents correctly, unless you were one of those people who wanted things to be in the wrong place—if there were such people. And then she had thought of Violet Sephotho: now there was somebody who would definitely have to keep her mission statement confidential, involving, as it no doubt did, goals far too shameful to be revealed, goals related to the number of husbands stolen, or some such thing.

She became aware that Mr. Polopetsi was addressing her.

"That tie will suit Mr. J.L.B. Matekoni very well, Mma. He'll look very smart."

She handed over a few banknotes to the trader, who counted out her change.

"It's not for him," said Mma Ramotswe. "It's a present for you, Mr. Polopetsi."

She handed the tie to him. His mouth was wide open in astonishment.

"There you are, Rra," said the trader. "This is a very kind lady. I can tell."

Mr. Polopetsi tried to say something, but no words came. He looked at the tie, with its eagle motif, and then, taking off the grey one he was wearing, he began to put the new one round his neck.

"Very smart," said Mma Ramotswe.

"But why me?" asked Mr. Polopetsi.

She thought for a moment. "Because you have helped me in the past, Rra. Because you have given me your company. Because we have worked together. Because you are a good, kind man, and many people take good, kind men for granted and never say thank you to them. Because of all these reasons I'm giving you a tie."

They walked on in silence. She noticed, though, that the shoulders of his jacket seemed less empty now, his walk more confident.

"I think we shall have rain rather sooner than we thought," said Mma Ramotswe as they reached her van.

"Rain," said Mr. Polopetsi, and nodded.

She started the van and drove off. Before she dropped him at the gates of the school where he was a part-time teacher, she said, "You mustn't worry, Rra. I have a very good idea about how to sort out this . . . this mess you've got yourself into."

He looked anxious once more. "I'll do everything I can to help, Mma."

"I think you'll need to," said Mma Ramotswe.

CHAPTER ELEVEN

DOGS DO NOT HAVE A SOUL INSIDE THEM. THEY ARE JUST MEAT

T WAS UNCOMFORTABLY HOT in the offices of the Botswana Housing Corporation.

"They promised us air-conditioning a long time ago," said the clerk who was leading Mma Ramotswe through a narrow, airless corridor. "The senior people are all right—they've got it up in their offices—but down here, not a chance." He shook his head. "It is always like that, isn't it, Mma? Junior staff don't mind the heat, do they? Junior staff don't mind drinking water from the tap rather than from one of those water fountains they have upstairs. Junior staff don't mind having the last choice of holiday dates, do they? They don't mind all of these things."

Mma Ramotswe made a sympathetic clucking noise. "You are right, Rra," she said. "It is hard to be junior staff."

Unless you were Mma Makutsi, she thought. If you were Mma Makutsi, you simply promoted yourself regularly until you ended up as joint co-director, or whatever her current position was—Mma Ramotswe had rather lost track of Mma Makutsi's stellar ascent.

"I have been waiting for promotion to go into one of those offices upstairs," continued the clerk. "I have been told that I don't have the educational qualifications. They said to me: 'You need a degree.' But you know something, Mma? Having a degree has nothing to do with being able to do the job they do up there. A degree doesn't teach you how to add up rental income. A degree doesn't teach you how to deal with contractors. A degree doesn't make you good at dealing with builders when they try to cheat you on a contract. Oh no, Mma, none of that is taught at the university. All they do there is teach you big words and long sentences."

"Ah," said Mma Ramotswe. She felt some sympathy for the clerk; she herself had left school at sixteen and although she would have liked to have had further education, it had not hampered her unduly. Of course, had she wished to get to the level of somebody like Clovis Andersen and write a book on private detection, then she would undoubtedly need a degree. Mr. Andersen, she knew from the biographical details at the back of *The Principles of Private Detection*, had a BA from Ball State University in Muncie, Indiana. She could never aspire to that, but when it came to the work she did, she felt that her education was perfectly satisfactory.

"And then," continued the clerk, "they send those students out at the end of their course and say, 'Go off and use those big words and long sentences to get all the good, high-paying jobs. And once you're in those jobs, always remember to use long sentences to protect your position. If you use long sentences, nobody will dare remove you. That is an important rule that we have worked out.' That is what they say, Mma—I have heard it on very good authority."

"I think promotion should be on merit," said Mma Ramotswe. "Everybody should be judged the same, whether or not they have a whole cupboard full of certificates. The question should be: Can this person do this job? That is all they need to ask themselves."

This pleased the clerk. "Oh, Mma," he said. "It's so good to hear some common sense being talked."

She had not intended to flatter him, and she had spoken out of conviction, but the warmth that her comments had produced would certainly be useful. Clerks and receptionists were, in her opinion, some of the most powerful people in the country, even if they bemoaned their lowly status and their lack of air-conditioning. A clerk could easily deny the very existence of a file if rubbed up the wrong way, and a receptionist could stop you seeing somebody important simply by saying there were no appointments. That had happened to Mma Ramotswe recently when she had sought a meeting with a senior municipal official who could help her in an enquiry. The receptionist, who was in an uncooperative mood for reasons that Mma Ramotswe could not fathom, but she felt might have something to do with the woman's romantic life, had at first told her that the official in question had no free appointments that day. When asked if there was a slot available for the following day, the receptionist had said that day too was completely full. And the following week? Sorry, Mma, nothing available. It's a very busy time. Next month? No, that was very busy too.

Mma Ramotswe had not argued, but had returned to the office to brief Mma Makutsi and suggest that she try the next day.

"You are very good at dealing with these awkward people," said Mma Ramotswe.

"You're kind to say that, Mma," came Mma Makutsi's reply. "I have no time for obstructive people."

The result was that Mma Makutsi was given an appointment immediately—or at least immediately after she had delivered a stern lecture on the subject of managing appointments and suggesting that the receptionist should enroll forthwith in an office administration course at the Botswana Secretarial College. She—Mma Makutsi—could easily facilitate that and would write to the Mayor to follow up her suggestion. The receptionist knew when she was beaten, and surrendered without further resistance, finding an appointment that had fortuitously opened up that very morning—in ten minutes' time, in fact.

There would be no such difficulties with this clerk, who was already voicing views as to where he might find the information she sought.

"Nobody really knows what we have in our archives," he said. "Apart from me, of course. I know where everything is, Mma. I know it in here." He tapped the side of his head.

"There are some people who need to write all these things down in notebooks," he went on. "And then you know what happens, Mma Ramotswe? I will tell you. You know those ants? You know those bad ones? They love notebooks, Mma—it is their biggest treat. Notebooks are like ice cream to them!" He laughed at his witticism.

"You have to be careful of ants," she said.

"Oh yes, you do. The ants are watching us, you see, Mma. They are watching us all the time. If we let down our guard, the ants will make their move and then . . . goodbye Botswana."

They had reached the end of the corridor and were standing outside a door marked *Records*. "This is the place," said the clerk. "This is where we will find what you're looking for, Mma."

The clerk unlocked the door. The room inside was a large one, and lined on all four walls with high shelving. Box files and ledgers took up most of the shelf space, although here and there were stacks of papers neatly bundled and tied with red tape.

"That is the famous red tape," said the clerk, pointing to the bundles of documents. "You have heard the expression 'red tape,' Mma?"

"I have heard it," said Mma Ramotswe. "Red tape is always making things go slower."

"We have big supplies of it here," said the clerk, smiling. "Some people find it very useful. But remind me, Mma, what is the address of this place you are enquiring about?"

She gave him the details. It was Plot 2408 Zebra Drive, and she gave him the dates she was interested in.

The clerk listened attentively. Then he said, "Can you time me, Mma?"

"You want me to time how long it takes you to find what you're looking for?"

He nodded brightly. "That's the idea, Mma. They call that a 'time and motion study.'"

She looked at her watch. "Very well, Rra. I'm timing you."

The clerk stepped sharply forward to one of the higher shelves and took down a box file. Opening it, he ruffled through a sheaf of documents before extracting one of them.

"Stop the clock, Mma," he called.

"That was forty-five seconds, Rra."

He looked at her proudly. "And here is the list of transactions to do with Plot 2408 Zebra Drive. It covers the period from the construction of the house, through its various tenancies, and then finally to its sale when the Commission decided to reduce its housing stock." He handed the document to her. "It is all there, Mma. The whole early history of that place."

She looked at the paper. It was easy to interpret, and the information she was looking for leapt to her eyes immediately.

"I see that there was a lease to the hospital," she said, pointing to the line in question.

The clerk looked over her shoulder. "Yes," he said. "The Commission let the house to the hospital authorities for twelve years in all. And there, you see, just down at the bottom is the list of the sub-tenants that the hospital arranged. We always insisted on knowing who had signed a sub-lease."

She looked at the names. The one she was looking for was there. Handing the paper back to the clerk, she thanked him for his helpfulness.

"I am happy to have been able to help you, Mma Ramotswe," he said. "It's all part of the service."

"But you have been especially helpful," she said.

He shrugged modestly. And then he said, "You're a private detective, aren't you, Mma? You have that place out on the Tlokweng Road—near that garage?"

"I'm that person," she said.

There was a silence. "Do you think you could do me a favour, Mma?"

She had not expected the request quite so soon, and she knew it would be hard to turn him down. She hoped that his request would not be too bizarre; sometimes people wanted to know the strangest things.

He lowered his voice as he revealed his request. "There is a certain young woman, Mma. She is a very beautiful young woman and there are many men who think that she would make a good wife."

"And are you one of those, Rra?"

He looked embarrassed. "You could say that, Mma."

"Well, I wish you success," said Mma Ramotswe. "But I cannot make a woman like a particular man, you know."

"Oh, I wouldn't ask you to do that, Mma. No, I know you couldn't do that."

"So what would you like me to do?"

He hesitated. "She has a boyfriend, Mma. He's a useless fellow. You only need to look at him and you think *useless.*"

"I see. But obviously she doesn't think that, does she?"

He sighed. "I don't think she knows her own mind. But I feel that if we could find out some concrete facts about this man—about how useless he is, then the scales would fall from her eyes and she would get rid of him."

She looked at him, bemused. "I'm sorry, Rra. I can't do that."

She had expected more of a reaction, but his response was muted. "Oh well, I thought I'd ask."

"I'm sure you'll find another young woman. There are many nice girls around. Many of them would like to marry a handsome young man like you."

"Couldn't you find one for me, Mma?"

"Don't you have any aunts to do this for you?"

He shook his head. "I had two aunts, Mma, but they are late now. That's why I'm asking you."

It came as a sudden, heartfelt plea, and she was taken aback. She was on the point of saying that the No. 1 Ladies' Detective Agency was not a marriage bureau, and then, looking at him, she suddenly relented.

"I could try," she said.

"Oh, Mma, that is all I ask. Find a nice girl who will not be troublesome and who does not have greedy uncles expecting too many cattle. Please could you try that for me?"

"I will, Rra. I'll need a bit of time, but I shall do what I can."

"You can have more than forty-five seconds," he said, and laughed.

Good sense of humour, she thought. You saw that in matrimonial advertisements sometimes, and it seemed important. Well, she could specify that if she had to talk to any prospective brides about him. That, and his speed of approach to any problem. These were both very positive points that she could, in good conscience, bring to the attention of any suitable women. If they existed, of course; presumably they did, and it was just a question of finding them. Well, one favour deserved another—that was how the world worked.

SHE MADE HER WAY back to the office in good spirits. The confirmation that the house she had been looking for was in Zebra Drive— of all places—was a major step forward in what could have been a rather vague and unsatisfactory enquiry, and once she had spoken again to Mma Rosie, she felt that she would be able to present Mma Susan with what she was looking for. *If* she were looking for her past—and Mma Ramotswe was beginning to have her doubts about that. But those doubts could be addressed in due course; for the time being she had achieved what she had set out to find, and that was something to be pleased about. Her leg, too, felt completely normal, and the possibility that venom had entered her system was now discounted. That had been a close thing, and it could have ended very differently, but it had not—and that was another thing to be thankful for. Mma Ramotswe was a bit hazy about statistics, but she imagined that it might be possible to work out the odds of stepping on a puff adder at some point in one's life. Well, she had just done that, and surely this meant that the odds of her doing it again would be infinitesimal, which meant that she was safer now than she had been before that unfortunate night-time encounter—or so she hoped. She might discuss those statistics with Mr. Polopetsi, who, as a chemist, knew a little bit about statistics.

Mr. Polopetsi's problems were, of course, far from over, but at least she had a plan that might extract him from the difficulties he had created for himself. A happy outcome could not be guaranteed, but she could try, and if it worked, she was reasonably confident that he would not do anything quite so foolish again. Her plan would have to be implemented before too long, before more people were sucked into the pyramid scheme by Mr. Polopetsi's friend, but she had a few days, she imagined, to make the necessary arrangements. That would include a frank discussion with Mr. Polopetsi himself, who would have to agree to the risk entailed. She was not looking forward to that conversation, but there was no way round it.

Now was not the time to worry about Mr. Polopetsi; now was the time to announce to Mma Makutsi and to Charlie that the search for Susan's house was over. As she entered the office, they were both there—Mma Makutsi at her desk, and Charlie leaning against the filing cabinet, waiting for the kettle to boil.

Mma Makutsi looked up and greeted Mma Ramotswe with a broad smile. "So you're back, Mma—none the worse for your terrible ordeal."

"I don't think it was quite that bad, Mma Makutsi," said Mma Ramotswe. "But yes, I am now back."

Charlie exchanged a conspiratorial glance with Mma Makutsi. "And there is interesting news," said Charlie.

"Yes," said Mma Ramotswe. "I have some very interesting news."

Charlie looked nonplussed. "No, Mma, I did not mean that you had interesting news. I meant there *is* interesting news."

"Very interesting," said Mma Makutsi. "Something arrived in the post. Charlie collected it this afternoon."

Charlie nodded towards Mma Ramotswe's desk. "It is on your desk, Mma—it's an invitation."

Mma Ramotswe crossed the room. There were several letters on her desk—Mma Makutsi always opened every envelope, irrespective of whether it was addressed to Mma Ramotswe or herself. That, she said, was sound secretarial practice, as advocated by the Botswana Secretarial College. "If one person opens everything," she said, "fewer things go missing. That has been scientifically proved."

Mma Ramotswe picked up the topmost letter. She recognised the letterhead immediately—it was from the Gaborone Chamber of Commerce, on a committee of which she had briefly served the previous year. They still wrote to her from time to time, notifying her of talks or events that might interest her. So the invitation was from them . . . probably to one of their drinks parties, which she always politely declined as they went on for far too long and you always ended up hungry at the end.

"The President and Council of the Gaborone Chamber of Commerce," she read out loud, "have great pleasure in inviting you and one guest to the presentation of the Woman of the Year Award to . . ." She hardly dared read on, but then there was the name, and she breathed a great sigh of relief. ". . . to Ms. Gloria Poeteng."

Mma Ramotswe looked at Mma Makutsi, who was beaming with pleasure. "Well," she said, "that is very good news."

"It was a close-run thing," said Mma Makutsi. "It could easily have gone the other way. I'd heard that Violet Sephotho was everywhere, telling everybody to cast their votes for her."

"Well, it didn't work," said Charlie. "Nobody must have voted for her."

Mma Ramotswe was not so sure. "Oh, I think she has her supporters. Perhaps this other lady, this Gloria Poeteng, asked more people to vote for her than Violet did. It could be as simple as that."

"We must go, Mma. You and I should accept the invitation. We can represent the agency."

Mma Ramotswe shrugged. "Violet will be there," she pointed out. "Remember that she will be the runner-up."

"I know that, Mma," said Mma Makutsi. "That is why I'm particularly keen to go. It will be a great pleasure to see Violet get second prize. She will not like that, you know."

Mma Ramotswe did not like the thought of going off to crow over somebody, even somebody as unpleasant as Violet Sephotho. But Mma Makutsi was adamant. "We must be represented," she said. "It is good for business."

Mma Ramotswe did not argue. She understood why Mma Makutsi should feel as she did. Over the years Violet Sephotho had shown her contempt for Mma Makutsi, right from those early days at the Botswana Secretarial College; she had missed no opportunity to mock or belittle her, and had even tried to lure Phuti away from her. There was no excuse for such behaviour, in Mma Ramotswe's view, and if Mma Makutsi should take some pleasure in witnessing a defeat of Violet, then that was understandable. Of course you should never rejoice in the misfortune of another—the Bishop had said something about that in his last sermon at the Anglican Cathedral and Mma Ramotswe had thoroughly agreed with him, even if now she found it difficult to remember his exact words. Still, she could recall the general gist of his remarks well enough, even if she could not really quote them to Mma Makutsi now, it being difficult to quote words that you've somehow forgotten.

"Very well, Mma," she said. "We shall go. Will you send off a reply . . . or should I do it?"

"Gladly," said Mma Makutsi, reaching for a piece of paper. "I shall write and accept without delay."

"Without delay," echoed Charlie. "Those are very good words, I think. Without delay. *Please will you pay my bill without delay. Please leave without delay. Please improve your attitude without delay . . .*"

Mma Makutsi shot Charlie a warning glance. Their working relationship had improved beyond all measure—she attributed that to his growing up at last—but there were still rough edges to it. In particular, she did not like it when Charlie appeared to mimic her, although he always denied that he was doing it.

It was not this issue that Mma Ramotswe was thinking about, though; she was contemplating the delicacy of asking Mma Makutsi to do anything these days. She had hesitated before asking her to write the reply to the Chamber of Commerce invitation, but in the end that proved easy enough because it was something that Mma Makutsi was especially keen to do. The difficulty lay more in those routine tasks that she did not enjoy so much, or in respect of those instances that unambiguously involved one person giving an order and another complying. Was she still entitled to ask Mma Makutsi to take a letter that she dictated? That had been simple when Mma Makutsi had been the agency's secretary, but as she had been promoted, becoming an assistant detective and then an associate director and then co-principal director (had she remembered that correctly?), could you say to a co-principal director, "Please take a letter, Mma Makutsi"?

Mma Ramotswe thought you could not. And yet if you could not ask Mma Makutsi to take dictation, then whom could you ask? Charlie? The problem with Charlie was his spelling, which was erratic. He was willing enough to transcribe what you said, but it took a great deal of time, as he had no knowledge of shorthand and wrote out every word with intense concentration and a frown on his brow that made one imagine that there was some fundamental problem with what was being said in the letter.

So if Mma Makutsi was too elevated now to perform ordinary secretarial tasks, and if Charlie, although willing, was not much good at them, what was she to do? Should she write her own letters? Many quite high-ranking people did that these days—Mma Makutsi had pointed out an article in a magazine she received, *Secretarial News,* which suggested that now the secretarial role had been transformed into an executive one, people who previously relied on others to type their letters were now typing them themselves. "That's the future," said Mma Makutsi. "That's the way things have been going, and I spotted it a long time ago, Mma. It is not news to me."

Of course none of this applied to filing. That was, as Mma Makutsi had often said, an art, and it was an art that she was both keen and proud to practise. Moreover it was not a skill that could be acquired by anybody—you had to have the right sort of mind to do it properly. "Some people think they can file, Mma," she said, "but they are wrong. Filing is not a mechanical business—you have to under-stand *why* a particular letter should go in a particular file."

But now the reply to the invitation had been typed and Mma Makutsi was reading through it. "I shall sign it for both of us," she said. "That will save you the bother, Mma Ramotswe."

"But it's no real bother, Mma," Mma Ramotswe said.

Her protest went unheard. The reply was folded and put into an envelope.

Mma Ramotswe looked out of the window. The sky was heavier now and that meant there was a prospect of rain—not that day, per-haps, but some day soon; rain—the country's relief, the blessing for which the land called out so desperately.

Charlie addressed her: "You said something about interesting news, Mma."

"Oh yes. Interesting news." She sat back in her chair. "This busi-ness of Mma Susan's house . . ."

Charlie's face lit up. "You've found it, Mma?"

"Yes, Charlie, I've found it."

Charlie clapped his hands together enthusiastically. "Well done, Mma. I thought we would never find it. All those houses . . ."

Mma Ramotswe noticed that Mma Makutsi looked doubtful.

"Are you sure, Mma Ramotswe? Many of these houses look the same, you know."

"I am very sure, Mma. I have been to the Botswana Housing Commission and checked their records. It's all there. The name of the doctor on the lease is there, Mma. Her father's name."

"Well that settles that," said Charlie. "Where is it?"

"It's exactly where Mma Rosie said it was. Right next door to me, as it happens. It's an extraordinary coincidence, I know, but I have checked everything. It is my neighbour's house."

Mma Makutsi fiddled with a piece of paper on her desk. "That doesn't prove anything about that woman," she said quietly.

"What woman?" asked Charlie.

"That woman who claimed to be Rosie. That woman we had in the car. The one whose story was inconsistent."

Mma Ramotswe drew a deep breath. Whenever an argument arose, a tactic that she had long practised was to imagine herself in the skin of the person disagreeing with her. It was a simple device— one she had learned from her father—and it seemed to work. Obed Ramotswe had employed it when negotiating the purchase of cattle. If you thought yourself into the skin of the other side, he said, then you might see the shortcomings of the cattle you were trying to sell. And if you did that, you could address those issues. Yes, that cow was a bit thin, but she had been in an overgrazed area and time was needed to get her back up to her proper weight; and yes, that bull *was* limping, but there was a positive side to it: a bull who limped would not wander, would not waste the energy he needed for his real task on pointless meandering through the bush—such a bull would be on permanent duty, and surely that was a good thing, was it not?

Now, sitting at her desk and facing Mma Makutsi on the other side of the room, she imagined that she was the one behind that other desk, behind those outsized spectacles with their round lenses, with that whole hinterland of Bobonong and the Botswana Secretarial College behind her, not to mention the ninety-seven per cent. What would you see from such a position, and with what eyes would you see it? You would see a desk with Mma Precious Ramotswe behind it, looking back at you; Mma Ramotswe, who started the business and still owned it, who was widely known as *the* private detective, when nobody, or virtually nobody, knew that there was a Mma Makutsi in the business too, who had dealt with many delicate cases rather successfully, but who never really got the credit; who had to contend with Charlie and his young man's impetuousness; who had to answer the telephone and then pass on the caller to Mma Ramotswe because nobody seemed to call and ask for Mma Makutsi in the first instance. That is what you would see.

The insight was instructive.

"Mma Makutsi," said Mma Ramotswe. "I can understand why you are suspicious of that woman."

"Good," said Mma Makutsi. "Because she is suspicious—it's not a case of my making things up."

There was quick reassurance. "You would never do that, Mma. You are very careful with your facts."

"Good," said Mma Makutsi. "Because I am. I'm very careful with the facts."

"But," began Mma Ramotswe. "But how . . ."

Mma Makutsi was staring at her. The spectacles flashed a warning—a shard of light from the window flashed across the room like a signal from a mirror held to the sun.

The issue could not simply be ignored, and Mma Ramotswe persisted. "But how could she have identified the right house if she was an impostor?"

The question hung in the air between them, almost tangible in its awkwardness.

Mma Makutsi sucked in her cheeks, and for a moment, and without thinking about it, Mma Ramotswe did the same. It was a consequence of the exercise in empathy; having imagined herself to be Mma Makutsi, the sucking in of cheeks when faced with a difficult question seemed entirely natural.

"She might have known the real Rosie," said Mma Makutsi. "She might have been a friend of that woman—a sister, even. If that were so, then she would have known quite a bit about the family. She would have known where they lived because the real Rosie would have told her."

Mma Ramotswe thought about this. Mma Makutsi was right—up to a point—but you could be right but still be unreasonable. It was feasible, but then all sorts of alternative—and unlikely—explanations of anything were perfectly feasible, and you could not go through life suspecting that other people were impostors. Holding such a default position would make life impossible. You would think of everybody whom you met: *You might not be who you claim to be.* It would be impossible. You would have to ask everybody for identification the moment you met them.

"I think we're going to have to trust her, Mma Makutsi. She spoke about a dog's grave in the garden, and it's there, you know . . ."

"There are dogs' graves all over the place," said Mma Makutsi. She spoke with determination in her voice that Mma Ramotswe realised was not going to be shifted easily.

"Dogs' graves all over the place? But there aren't, Mma. They are very unusual. We do not give dogs graves—we bury them and then just leave them covered with bare earth. They may be our friends, but we do not mark their passing very much."

"That is because they do not have souls, Mma," said Mma Makutsi. "Dogs do not have a soul inside them. They are just meat."

Mma Ramotswe looked at the window. It needed cleaning, as the dust had built up. But there was the branch of the acacia tree outside—the branch upon which those two doves so often sat. Did they not have souls? Those loyal spouses? Did they not mourn when one of them died, and how could you mourn if you had no soul? And if birds had souls, then how much more likely was it that dogs did too—dogs who, if they could talk, would have so much to say to us about the world and its smells.

"I do not think that a dog is just meat," said Mma Ramotswe.

"Well, I'm sorry to say it, Mma, but you're wrong."

It rarely came to that. They rarely ended up in such an impasse, and Mma Ramotswe did not want to remain there. "Perhaps we are both wrong, Mma," she said mildly. "Perhaps you are a bit right and I am a bit right. But perhaps we are both mostly wrong, and the answer lies elsewhere."

Mma Makutsi appeared to consider this. "Possibly," she said. "But unlikely. I think I am right about that woman, Mma, but I am not going to insist. You can treat her as genuine and then you will get a nasty surprise, I think. But I will not say, 'I told you so,' Mma. I will not say that."

Mma Ramotswe closed her eyes. It helped, she found, to close her eyes. In any situation where you encountered something you did not like, or something you could not deal with, you had only to close your eyes. It always worked.

"You're very kind, Mma Makutsi," she said, opening her eyes again. "But perhaps we should have a cup of tea now, because tea is always very welcome after one has been thinking very hard, as we have been doing."

Mma Makutsi smiled. "You're right about that, Mma," she said.

Even if you think I'm wrong about other things, thought Mma Ramotswe. But she could not say that, and did not—possibly because Mma Makutsi had succeeded in making her think that she might be wrong after all.

MMA MAKUTSI LEFT THE OFFICE that afternoon an hour early, giving Mma Ramotswe the opportunity to phone Susan and arrange to see her the next day. Could they meet, she asked, at the coffee place at Riverwalk? It was a good place to talk, and she had something important to tell her.

Had she found the house? Yes, she had. And Rosie? Had she found Rosie? There was a moment of hesitation, but then she said, "Probably. Yes, probably." They would talk about it the following morning.

"I'm so happy," said Mma Susan.

Mma Ramotswe thought about that. People who said they were happy were often unhappy—not at the moment when they said they were happy—they might be happy right then, but before that. Happiness was like sunlight; we only really noticed it when there were clouds about.

She put down the telephone. There was a noise directly outside the door—a scratching, and then a bump. She stood up and walked across the room. Something told her to be careful; it was broad daylight, even if it was the late afternoon; Mr. J.L.B. Matekoni was still in the garage, as was Fanwell. But there was an unexplained noise . . .

Fanwell's dog, Zebra, looked up at her. He was sitting directly outside the doorway, his tongue protruding from his mouth, a moist pink band. He was panting.

"So it's you," she said.

Zebra looked at her, with complete trust.

"Do you have a soul, Zebra?" she asked.

There was movement. She looked up. Mr. J.L.B. Matekoni had emerged from the garage and was staring at her in a puzzled way.

"Why do you ask that dog if he has a soul?"

Mma Ramotswe sighed. "It's very complicated, Rra. You see . . .

Well, you see: Mma Makutsi said dogs were just meat inside. Those were her actual words."

"She's wrong," he said.

"I think so. I think dogs might have a soul."

He wiped the grease off his hands. "Same thing with cars," he said. "They have souls—or some of them do. Old cars have souls. Modern cars . . . well, I think the Japanese don't put souls into them. They save money, perhaps, by not putting in a soul."

She laughed. And then she thought of something. "Mr. J.L.B. Matekoni," she asked, "do you think that our souls grow as we get older?"

He did not answer immediately, but when he did, she thought his answer quite perfect. "Yes," he said. "Our souls get wider. They grow like the branches of a tree—growing outwards. And more birds come and make their homes in these branches. And sing a bit more." He stopped, and looked a little awkward. "I'm talking nonsense, Mma."

"You're not," she said.

She looked down at Zebra. The protruding tongue was even further out of his mouth now and his eyes, for some reason, seemed to have widened. She could not help but smile, and she thought for a moment that he was grinning back at her; but that was just the way some dogs looked, she reminded herself—they were satisfied with the slightest scraps of human interest, and their grin was no more than a reflection of that.

Zebra had found his way back to the garage, presumably in search of Fanwell. He could be taken back to Zebra Drive, but she wondered whether that was more than a temporary solution to his problems. He was, in a sense, an orphan dog, and there was often no place for such dogs unless . . . The idea struck her suddenly, but with great clarity. Of course there was a place for him—it was so obvious.

CHAPTER TWELVE

REMEMBER TO FORGET

SUSAN WAS ALREADY THERE when Mma Ramotswe arrived at the café in Riverwalk. She saw her sitting at an outside table, under the shade of one of the large standing umbrellas, looking out over the market traders' stalls.

"I wish I needed more scarves," said Susan. "These ladies make such fine scarves, Mma Ramotswe."

"And wooden hippos, Mma? Do you wish you needed more wooden hippos and elephants?"

Susan laughed. "Yes. But people do buy them, don't they? I saw somebody buy one a few moments ago—a big wooden hippo with tusks carved out of bone."

Mma Ramotswe sat down opposite Susan. It was not a comfortable chair; too small, as so many chairs were. The trouble with café furniture was that it was not made for traditionally built people. What were they meant to do? Remain standing while all the modern-shaped people perched on these small stools and chairs?

She surveyed the row of wooden carvings that a hopeful trader had lined up at the foot of one of the stalls: lion after lion, giraffe after giraffe, all caught in the same pose as their neighbour. "There are some people who like such things, Mma Susan," she said. "It reminds them of Africa, I think."

Susan nodded. "Perhaps." She paused. "I prefer the memory of things you can't carve in wood."

Mma Ramotswe waited for her to expand on this.

"The sky," she said, and looked up. "That. And the air . . . That special air you have. The air in the morning, before the heat of the day. The smell of rain—when it eventually comes. That special smell, Mma."

Mma Ramotswe knew what she meant. "It is a very good smell, Mma."

"You can't record any of that in wood, can you?"

Mma Ramotswe shook her head. "No. You can't."

"Or paint it. Or draw it. Or take a photograph of it."

"No," agreed Mma Ramotswe. "You can't do any of those things, Mma."

A waitress began to hover. Mma Ramotswe ordered tea for herself; Susan already had her coffee.

"You said you'd found the house, Mma Ramotswe?"

Mma Ramotswe confirmed that she had—and told Susan where it was.

"It is right next door to me," she announced. "I could not believe it at first. But sometimes the things you're looking for are right under your nose, Mma."

She put a finger directly under her nose and suddenly, uncontrollably, felt the urge to sneeze. It was a forceful, voluble sneeze, a convulsion of the upper part of her body; cathartic in its intensity.

Susan looked concerned. "Are you all right, Mma?" she asked.

Mma Ramotswe wiped her eyes. "Yes, thank you, Mma. I have sneezed."

"Yes, I noticed."

The waitress reappeared. "Do you need water, Mma?"

Mma Ramotswe shook her head. "No, thank you, Mma. I shall wait for my tea."

The waitress did not leave. "Because that was a very big sneeze. Perhaps some water . . ."

"There is no need, Mma. Thank you."

"But water is free, Mma. There is no charge for water."

Mma Ramotswe exchanged a glance with Susan. "In that case . . ."

The waitress was all efficiency. "I'll fetch you a glass of water, Mma."

Susan smiled. "That wouldn't happen elsewhere, you know, Mma Ramotswe. You can sneeze away for hours in some places, and nobody would pay much attention. But here . . ."

Mma Ramotswe dabbed at her eyes again. "It was because I pointed at my nose. I think that's why I sneezed."

The waitress appeared with a glass of water. "This is for your sneeze," she said, as she placed it on the table. "You should drink it, Mma, before you sneeze again."

"I'm not going to sneeze again," said Mma Ramotswe. "That sneeze was just a . . . just a one-time sneeze."

"If you sneeze once," said the waitress, "then you can sneeze again. My aunt, my late aunt, sneezed many times . . . before she died."

Mma Ramotswe took a sip of the water. Turning to the waitress, she said, "That water was exactly what I needed. Thank you, Mma."

The waitress nodded and went back inside.

"What I really want is tea," confessed Mma Ramotswe. "But we shouldn't talk about me and all this sneezing of mine."

"One sneeze," said Susan. "And that waitress should not try to alarm you with stories like that."

Mma Ramotswe smiled. "I'm not too worried, Mma."

"This house," said Susan. "Is it really the place?"

Mma Ramotswe was sure about it, and she conveyed that certainty. "It is definitely the right house. I have checked with the Botswana Housing people and it is in the records. It was let to the hospital authorities and they allocated it to your father. It is on Zebra Drive. So I think that—"

Susan stopped her. "Zebra Drive?"

"Yes. That's where I live. It is not a very big road—not many houses. I've lived there since I came to Gaborone and started my agency." She paused. "Do you remember something, Mma?"

Susan looked uncertain. "It sounds familiar. I think that my parents must have talked about it, but that was years ago. They loved Botswana. They often spoke about it. They said it was a very good country."

"My late father loved this country too," said Mma Ramotswe. He did, she thought; he did.

Susan looked over her shoulder, towards the entrance to the café. "They're taking their time with the tea."

"They must be busy in there."

"They might have forgotten about us."

Mma Ramotswe smiled. "Perhaps I should sneeze again. That will bring the waitress out."

Susan steered the conversation away from sneezes. "Tell me about Rosie," she said. "You've found her?"

Mma Ramotswe explained that the house had been identified by somebody claiming to be Rosie. There were other reasons, too, for her to think that she was genuine. "Did you have a dog when you were a girl?" she asked.

Susan shook her head. "No, I didn't have a dog."

"Are you sure?"

The tea arrived. "I hadn't forgotten about you," said the waitress. "Our kettle is broken, you see, and it takes a long time to boil."

"Like a watched kettle," said Susan. "They never boil."

"The important thing is that the tea is here," said Mma Ramotswe.

"And now you would like something to eat?" asked the waitress.

"No," said Mma Ramotswe. "We are fine, Mma. We have everything we need."

"You're sure?"

"Yes, Mma. I'm quite sure."

The waitress looked disappointed as she walked away.

"That is a very unusual waitress," said Mma Ramotswe. She was puzzled by the dog story. Rosie had brought it up quite naturally, as part of her spontaneous outburst in the car, and she felt that this added to its credibility. And then there had been the rectangle of stones in the yard; that could have been anything, of course, but she had treated it as confirmation.

"Why do you ask if I had a dog, Mma?"

She explained, and Susan listened intently. "But I don't remember any of that," she said after Mma Ramotswe had finished. "May I ask her about it?"

"Yes. I shall try to arrange for you to meet her soon."

Mma Ramotswe took a sip of her tea. It was cold. She looked at her watch. She had told her neighbour about Susan and her quest, and he had agreed to stay in to show them round the house; she did not want to keep him.

"We must go, Mma," she said. "I have my van parked nearby. We can go to see . . . your house."

Susan looked at her in a way that Mma Ramotswe found slightly disconcerting. It seemed to her that it was almost as if she was reluctant to go; and yet this was what she had come all this way for. Of course there were some people who did not want to find what they were looking for; she had observed that before. It was very strange, but it did happen. And why? Was it because what they were looking for was not what they were really looking for . . . so to speak?

MMA RAMOTSWE GOT ON well enough with Mr. Vain Kwele and his wife, Daffodil, even if they did not see a great deal of one another.

Daffodil was listless in her housekeeping, and showed no pride in the place. She spent much of her time sitting on her verandah, paging through old copies of magazines, while Vain, whose lucrative bottle store had a competent and conscientious manager, spent much of his time on his private pursuits, one of which was collecting maps. One room of his house was devoted to his map collection, stored on roughly constructed shelves and in stacked boxes. This room, which Mma Ramotswe had glimpsed only briefly on a couple of occasions, was more than usually dusty. "It's the Kalahari's fault," Vain had said to Mma Ramotswe. "What can anybody do if they live so close to that place. That's where all this dust comes from, you know."

Mma Ramotswe had offered to lend them her powerful vacuum cleaner, but had been politely rebuffed. "That is very kind of you, Mma," he said. "But vacuum cleaners and maps do not mix. What if it attached itself to one of my maps? What if it sucked one up entirely? What then?" He spoke as if he feared that entire regions, entire countries could be lost in this way; whole swathes of territory would be siphoned up, lost to view and to memory.

"I don't want to press you, Rra," she said. "I was just trying to help."

"You are very good, Mma."

Of course she knew it would take more than a vacuum cleaner to bring order to that house; what was required was a change of attitude by Daffodil. But she could not say anything about that, and had resigned herself to the fact that her neighbouring property would be ill-kempt indefinitely.

Now, with the van parked outside the neighbour's gate, she was making her way up the bare and dusty front path towards the Kwele verandah. Vain was waiting for them, and greeted Susan with elaborate courtesy. He explained that his wife was out, but that he would tell her about the visit when she returned. He asked her where she lived now, and expressed the wish one day to see Toronto, of which he had heard so much.

"I have several maps of Canada," he said, as Mma Ramotswe introduced her.

"Then you will know where to go if you come and see us," said Susan.

"They are out of date, I think," said Vain. "You must never rely on old maps to navigate. You might suddenly find there is a dam—or worse still, a hole—directly where you want to go. I would need to get a much better map."

They went inside, where Vain invited them to sit down. "Mma Ramotswe has told me all about your search," he began. "And now you have found the house where you lived. After all these years, that's something to think about, isn't it, Mma?"

Mma Ramotswe watched. Somebody had once told her—it may even have been Mma Makutsi, she thought—that you should watch where eyes went. If you could see what people were looking at, if you were ready to note where their gaze alighted, then you learned a lot about them. Now, as she sat in the Kwele living room, she saw Susan's eyes drift round to the door that led to the back of the house. She did not seem to be interested in the living room, but surely she must remember that better than anywhere else in the house. People lived in their living rooms, after all.

"I can show you round," said Vain. "I imagine that it's very different from those old days, but the walls are in the same place."

"That would be kind," said Susan.

Again the eyes, after politely going to Vain, returned to that door to the back.

Vain rose to his feet. "We could start," he said. "That is, we could start if you're ready, Mma?"

Mma Ramotswe and Susan stood up.

"The kitchen is back here," said Vain. "I think it would have been there in your day. Kitchens stay put, I think—don't you, Mma?"

"You would not want your kitchen to wander," said Mma Ramotswe.

Vain laughed. "You certainly would not. You would have to say: Where is my kitchen today? How am I to cook if it keeps going off somewhere?"

Susan did not laugh; she barely smiled.

"Here," said Vain, "is the kitchen."

Mma Ramotswe could not help but note that the floor was dirty. That was Daffodil, of course; no self-respecting Motswana lady would let her kitchen floor get into such a state. She knew nothing of Daffodil's background, other than that she came from somewhere down near Lobatse. Perhaps that was it; perhaps people in Lobatse were a little bit slacker about these things. Or perhaps it was just because she was the product of a slack home where the mother was not particularly good: good mothers taught their daughters to keep a kitchen clean, and really good mothers tried to teach their sons that too these days, because it was not fair that women should have to do all the domestic work and it was about time the men took on their share. Perhaps that would change; perhaps Africa would begin to see just how unfair it was that half humanity should do most of the work about a house. Perhaps men would stop their posturing and talking and expecting women to cook all their meals and . . . Or perhaps not. Look at Charlie. Only the other day he had said how much he was looking forward to getting married one day and having a woman to do all those things for him. And when Mma Makutsi had exploded and taken him to task for saying that, he had been genuinely surprised. So perhaps talk of change was premature.

Susan stood in the middle of the kitchen. She was staring out of the window at the back of the room, out into the yard.

"The kitchens in these houses are all very much the same," Vain said. "The Commission used the same design up and down the country, but it was a good one, I think. A place for a fridge; a place for the stove; three store cupboards; a place for a table." He paused, and glanced at Mma Ramotswe. He too had seen the direction of Susan's gaze.

"Do you remember the garden at the back, Mma?" he asked. "There was a washing line there, right outside the window, but my wife moved it to the side of the house because there was some grass there and if the washing fell onto the grass it got less dirty."

Susan, who had been largely silent, now spoke. "There was a servant's block there, wasn't there? One of those small houses?"

Vain nodded. It was a standard arrangement, and still was: at the back of a house of that size there would be a small building—two rooms and a bathroom—that made up the servant's quarters. That was where the maid or the man who worked in the garden might live, depending on the domestic arrangements of the particular household. And having a servant was not a sign of wealth or privilege—even a modest establishment would have a maid, as this was an important way of providing employment that would otherwise not exist.

"We knocked that place down," said Vain. "My wife does not like to have a maid in the house. She says that a maid can get in the way and might steal. She is very worried about people stealing from her."

"There are many maids who are one hundred per cent honest," said Mma Ramotswe. "I have one. Mma Makutsi has one. There are many such people."

Vain looked at her reproachfully. "I am not saying that all maids are dishonest, Mma. I did not say that. I am just saying that there are some who are. That is all."

"I'm sorry, Rra," said Mma Ramotswe. "I did not mean to accuse you."

"Why did you knock it down?" asked Susan in a strained voice.

"The roof needed replacing," said Vain. "It would have cost more to replace the roof than to knock it down."

Susan moved towards the door. "Will you show me where it was?"

Vain seemed taken aback by the request, but agreed to do as asked. "The yard at the back is a bit overgrown," he said. "That is deliberate. We do not like people to think that we have a lot of money because our yard is all set out nicely. People come and ask you for money if they think you can spend a lot on your yard."

"But there may be snakes," said Mma Ramotswe. "If you let things grow too much, then snakes move in. They like gardens that are not looked after very well . . . Not that I'm saying that yours is like that, Rra. I am not saying that."

Vain frowned. "There are no snakes in my yard, Mma Ramotswe. That one you trod on the other day did not live here. He was passing through. There are some snakes that pass through."

Now outside, they followed a small path, barely discernible after years of disuse, to an area of flat ground. On this there were signs that once there had been a building—remnants of the concrete foundations, covered here and there by soil, but poking up out of the ground in an unmistakable rectangular pattern. There were a few half-shattered breeze-blocks of the sort used for constructing cheap buildings, now crumbling with the passage of years; there were some fragments of corrugated tin, left over from a roof that must have been taken away to make a coop for hens or something of that sort. There were the remnants of a termite mound, built to take advantage of the bits of wood that the demolition had left lying around, but long ago abandoned by ants that had gone elsewhere to raise a new tiny city.

Mma Ramotswe realised immediately that this was a place of special interest for Susan. She watched her client's expression. She watched her as she looked, and then looked away. That came with pain.

"Are you all right, Mma?" she asked.

Susan seemed to shake herself out of her mood. Turning to Mma Ramotswe, she smiled as she said, "Of course I am, Mma Ramotswe. I'm just thinking." She looked about her, and pointed to a corner of the yard abutting on Mma Ramotswe's yard. "We kept hens, you know. We kept them down there. They were moved there because there was a cockerel who used to wake my mother with his—"

"Boasting," interjected Vain. "Those guys make such a noise, don't they? *Yok, yok, yok* . . ."

Mma Ramotswe looked at him with amusement. That was not the sound a cockerel made—not in her view. "A cockerel that made a sound like that would not be feeling well," she said, with a grin.

Vain took the jibe in good spirit. "Perhaps you're right, Mma. I'm not good with sounds."

"Cockerels go *croo, croo, croo,*" said Mma Ramotswe. "And their wives go *pock, pock, pock.*"

Mma Ramotswe saw that Susan had turned away. She spotted the furtive movement, the reaching for a handkerchief, or a tissue, and the wiping of the eyes. She regretted the levity of her exchange with Vain; this was not the moment to discuss the language of chickens.

She laid a hand gently on Mma Susan's shoulder. She reminded herself of what had been said about her parents: the mother dead and the father in a home, his memory gone, his past deleted. "I understand, Mma," she whispered.

Mma Susan half turned, but did not look at Mma Ramotswe. She reached up and touched the hand upon her shoulder, acknowledging the sympathy. "It was so long ago," she said. "Things look different, I think."

"They will do," said Mma Ramotswe. "We want them to look the same, but . . . well, they change. People move things about."

She thought of Mochudi, and of how she often made that short journey back into her own past. As she saw the village regularly, changes did not surprise her; a new road, a recently constructed building, a wall painted a different colour—these were things that you took in your stride as part of the organic aging of the world about you, but then you looked at an old photograph and saw the place as you had known it in your youth and you were reminded then that the world was slipping away, slowly slipping away.

They walked back towards the house. Vain was talking about

somebody who had lived on the other side of the road for a long time, but Mma Ramotswe did not listen. She was thinking of the futility of Susan's quest. Why would somebody spend such a great amount of money—it must have been expensive for her to travel all the way from Canada—just to stand here in this desolate, ill-kept yard and remember a chicken coop and a servant's room? It was an absurd thing to do—a self-indulgence in a world in which so much better use could be made of that money.

But then she reminded herself that it was not for her to enquire as to why people asked her to uncover information. Once she started to do that, she would rapidly talk herself out of a job and the No. 1 Ladies' Detective Agency might as well close its doors. If she had to assume responsibility for the use every suspicious wife might make of information about the secret life of her husband, she would end up having to decline too many cases. She knew very well that she could not heal such marriages; that she and Mma Makutsi ended up giving clients ammunition to use in rows and showdowns, but she had to live with that. People were entitled to know about the bad behaviour of others; people were entitled to know if they were being betrayed or cheated, or somehow let down. Some wanted vengeance—which Mma Ramotswe would never recommend—while others sought freedom or, at least, to know where they stood, and such people were entitled to this knowledge, just as Mma Susan was entitled to this curious, nostalgic trip to discover something that she had once had, but had no longer. How others spent their money, thought Mma Ramotswe, was not her business. We might want others to spend wisely, but if they did not, then it did not fall to us to stop them.

Vain gave them tea on the verandah.

"It is a very good idea to go back," he said as he passed Susan her cup. "I went back to see the school I attended, you know. And you know what it's like, don't you?"

He looked at Mma Ramotswe, as if expecting confirmation.

She said, "It's very small. Everything is so small."

Vain nodded vigorously. "Exactly! It's much smaller." He took a sip of his tea. "Why do you think that is, Mma Ramotswe?"

"Because we were small ourselves, Rra?" She thought about it further. Yes, we were small and so things around us were bigger. Now that we were bigger, things were smaller. Was that the way it worked?

Vain looked thoughtful. "Probably. Or should I say, possibly." He paused. "Do you think that the world looks bigger to a very small person? I'm not talking about children here; I'm talking about those people who never grow because they are just meant to be small. There is one such person who goes to the dance competitions. He dances with a very tall lady, although she has to bend down to hold him. People love it."

"People can be cruel," said Mma Ramotswe.

"Oh, they are not being cruel," said Vain. "They are just laughing."

"He may not see it that way, Rra."

Vain shrugged. "He may not see it at all, Mma. Down there, he doesn't see very much, I think."

"I don't think he sees the world any differently from any of us," said Mma Ramotswe. "We all see it the same way, I think—after we have stopped being children."

She wondered whether she, a traditionally built person, saw the world differently from the way in which a thin person might see it. She thought not.

She glanced at Susan. "Are you pleased you've been able to see this house?" she asked.

It was a rather direct question, and one she realised that perhaps she should not ask in the presence of a third person, but she wanted to move the conversation on from Vain's wandering reflections.

Susan insisted she was pleased. "It has been very interesting," she said. "It is helping me remember."

Then Vain suddenly said, "But remember to forget. Don't forget to forget."

Mma Ramotswe frowned. "Mma Susan has come to Botswana to remember—not to forget."

"I was just saying," muttered Vain. "Sometimes we need to forget as well as remember."

Mma Ramotswe looked into her teacup. The tea he had served was lukewarm; was Vain one of these men who could not even boil a kettle? They existed; they were fewer and further between, she thought, but they still existed. And then it came to her, as the solution of cases often did, in a moment of sudden insight. Susan had come to Botswana to get over that failed love affair back in Canada. It seemed so clear now: she had come to Botswana because she was unhappy, and unhappy people often go away because it is painful to be where they are. This was not about childhood; this was not about Botswana. This was about love and the unrepaired, sometimes irreparable, wounds that love could inflict. So when Vain—of all people—had said something about the need to forget, he had inadvertently given exactly the advice that was needed. She would have to say this to her—gently, of course, and at the right moment, which was not now.

CHAPTER THIRTEEN

THESE PEOPLE ARE VERY CUNNING

MMA RAMOTSWE liked to make lists, and, like all people who make lists, she was inclined to take an optimistic view of their contents. So lists of things achieved—cases closed, and so on—tended to include matters that were almost, but not quite finished, and lists of things to be done by noon embraced tasks that might well not be performed until four o'clock in the afternoon or possibly even noon the following day. This did not involve self-deception . . . well, perhaps it did, but how can anyone manage to negotiate their way through life's complexities without at least a smidgen of self-deception here and there?

Some of these lists were written down on scraps of paper and on a whiteboard on the kitchen wall in Zebra Drive. That whiteboard, on which Puso used to draw pictures of cars and aeroplanes, now hosted lists for other members of the family, the idea being that everybody should look at it in the morning to see what they had to do later that day. So there might be a note reminding Mr. J.L.B. Matekoni to telephone the Botswana Eagle Insurance Company to renew the household insurance; or a reminder to Motholeli to take ten pula to school for her new mathematics textbook; or one to Puso to put his football socks in the wash. Sometimes there were whiteboard lists for herself—of household supplies running low (washing-up liquid, butter, the hot Mozambique peri-peri sauce that Mr. J.L.B. Matekoni liked to put on his roast chicken); or lists of people she had to telephone (her aunt in Mahalapye, Mr. J.L.B. Matekoni's cousin in Maun—the one who needed the cataract operation—Mma Poto-kwane about meeting for tea when she next came into town). Lists, she thought, are the stories of our lives; they give a picture of who we are and what we do every day.

The list that she made for herself that morning, noted on a piece of paper as she sat on the verandah drinking her morning tea, was of things remaining to be done. This started with the name *Polopetsi*: a single word, but one with a whole hinterland of anxiety behind it. This was followed by *Speak to Mma Rosie about meeting with Mma Susan*. That would be relatively straightforward, even if not plain sailing. And then there was *Mma Potokwane/Zebra*. That was problematic.

She looked at the list and tried shifting the items about. It some-times helped, she thought, to put the most difficult matters first in order to get them out of the way. In which case her list for the day would be: (1) *Polopetsi,* (2) *Mma Potokwane/Zebra,* and (3) *Mma Rosie*. That third item—the contacting of Mma Rosie—would not be without difficulty. Mma Rosie had been offended by Mma Makutsi's attitude, although Mma Ramotswe felt that her own dealings with her had been civil enough. But none of these matters, she felt, was entirely easy.

She had arranged for Mr. Polopetsi to come round to the office first thing that morning, and he was already waiting for her by the time she arrived. He was wearing the same jacket as when she'd seen him in the President Hotel, and he was sporting the eagle-motif tie she had given him. There was that crumpled look about him, though, that revealed his concern. She had told him that what she proposed to do was not going to be easy, and that message had sunk in.

"What are you going to do, Mma?" he asked nervously as she unlocked the office door.

"I am going to put on the kettle, Rra," she said. "The day must start with tea."

"Yes, but after that, Mma? What are you going to do after that?"

Mma Ramotswe opened the door and gestured for him to follow her. "I am going to go to the police, Rra. And you're coming with me. I have arranged an appointment."

Mr. Polopetsi let out a groan. "Oh, Mma, I have not stolen anything . . . I would never steal anything. You know me—I am honest, Mma. You know that."

She tried to calm him down. "I know you're honest, Mr. Polopetsi. That is why I am doing what I am doing. If you were a dishonest man, would I bother to do this for you?" She answered her own question. "I would not. But since you are a good man, I will do everything I can, Rra—everything."

He looked down at his shoes. "I do not deserve such a good friend, Mma. You are like Jesus Christ himself."

She could not conceal her astonishment. "I do not think so, Rra. You are very kind, but I would never . . ."

"No, perhaps not. Maybe you are like his sister, Mma."

She frowned. "There was no sister, Rra. We did not hear about a sister."

"Perhaps they did not want to mention her," said Mr. Polopetsi. "Perhaps she did not want any publicity."

Mma Ramotswe raised an eyebrow. Mr. Polopetsi could say some very strange things, but then so could Mma Makutsi and, come to think of it, Charlie and Fanwell too. In fact, *everybody,* it seemed, could say odd things.

"But let's not get involved in all that," she said briskly. "The police are not going to arrest you . . ." She almost said *yet,* but stopped herself just in time. "We are going to help the police, you see, and in return I shall ask them to help us."

Mr. Polopetsi looked doubtful. "I do not see how I can help the police, Mma. I do not see it."

She explained it to him, and he listened gravely. "But will it work, Mma?"

She tried to sound confident. "I hope so, Rra." She looked at him intently. "How much money have you got, Mr. Polopetsi? How much in total? In savings, cattle—the lot?"

He winced. "I have fifty cattle of my own, Mma. They belonged to my wife, but she has given them to me."

She let out an exclamation. "Fifty, Rra! That's a very good herd. And are they in good condition?"

He nodded, and inclined his head towards the window. "They are over that way—near the Limpopo. There is still water over there."

She took out a calculator that she kept in her top drawer, and keyed in some figures. "In that case you can pay everybody back," she said. "There will be enough to give all the people you recruited into the Fat Cattle Club their money back."

Mr. Polopetsi's mouth opened silently. He seemed to shrink even further, all but disappearing into his jacket. Soon there would just be clothes visible, and no man, and one would only know that he was there when the clothes started miraculously to move by themselves.

"I'm very sorry, Rra," she said. "But there is no other way." She paused. She felt for him—of course she did; the pain of selling cattle was something that any Motswana instinctively understood. It was like selling one's children—not quite as bad as that, but approaching it.

They drank their tea in silence. Then Mma Ramotswe sighed, stood up, and announced that it was time to leave.

"I am ready," came a voice from somewhere within the jacket. It was a thin, distant voice—rather like the voice of Mma Makutsi's shoes. "I am very nervous," it continued, "but I am ready."

"You do not need to be nervous," she said, trying to sound as cheerful as she could. She knew, though, that she sounded far from confident.

MMA RAMOTSWE HAD KNOWN Superintendent Mphapi Bogosi since childhood. He had been a keen tennis player as a boy although there had only been one racquet in the village at that time and he had been obliged to play against a wall. Later on, when he had graduated to a proper tennis court with a real opponent, his talent had come into its own. By the age of eighteen he was in the national team, and had remained there until a knee injury had obliged him to retire from competitions. By that time, he had joined the police on their rapid promotion scheme, and was now the head of the section devoted to drugs and vice. "I am not in charge of rock and roll yet," he was quoted as saying. "But no doubt that will come."

Their lives had touched at numerous points, although never professionally. He had been amused by her decision all those years ago to found the No. 1 Ladies' Detective Agency and had expressed his doubts—not in a condescending way, but out of the belief that there would be nothing for her to do.

"People won't pay good money to have their problems solved," he warned. "They will take them to their friends and ask them to do it for nothing."

He had been prepared to acknowledge his mistake, and often complimented her on the success of the agency.

"If you ever retire, Mma Ramotswe," he said, "come to us. We will make a new post for you: 'Head of Difficult Cases,' or something like that."

"I could not bring myself to arrest people," she said. "I would feel too sorry for them. I would let them off with a warning."

He laughed. "Even the really bad ones?"

She hesitated. "Maybe. I don't know. But of course the really bad ones are often just the unhappiest ones. People are bad for a reason, Rra."

His answer came quickly. "Because they are made that way. They have a bad nature. That is their design, so to speak."

She shook her head. "Were they bad babies?" she asked. "Are there any really bad babies?"

This required further thought, but he answered eventually. "Yes," he said. "There must be bad babies. You see the way they look when they cry. They're angry. They can't do anything bad yet, but when they get round to doing things, then they are bad." He paused, smiling. "Or perhaps not, Mma Ramotswe. Perhaps you have a point. Perhaps the badness comes a bit later."

"Because bad things have been done to them. Bad upbringing. Parents drinking. Parents fighting. The baby watches all this and—"

"And thinks that's the way to behave? Yes, you're right, Mma Ramotswe."

Now, standing before a door marked *Superintendent P. Bogosi,* she thought of the boy she had known in Mochudi and of what had become of him. Could she ever have imagined that the child knocking a tennis ball against that wall would one day have a door like this, with his name on, with uniformed officers at his beck and call and a secretary to say: "The superintendent will see you now, Mma"?

She led Mr. Polopetsi into the office with her. The superintendent stood up and smiled at her, extending his hand to shake hers, before he turned and did the same to Mr. Polopetsi. From within the crumpled jacket a hand came out, half hidden by a sleeve that caused the policeman to fumble as he searched for it.

"This is Mr. Polopetsi," said Mma Ramotswe. "He is the man I spoke to you about. He is the one with the information."

Mr. Polopetsi looked about him nervously. The room was sparsely furnished, but there was a small bookshelf on which there was stacked a pile of copies of *The Botswana Penal Code,* a book entitled *The Reality of Addiction,* and a lever-arch box file labelled *Zambia/Angola.*

The superintendent invited them to sit down on the metal chairs in front of his desk. These were not chairs designed for comfort; these chairs were for those facing even harder and more uncomfortable furniture in the future.

"I would like to have more comfortable chairs in this place," said the superintendent. "Maybe one day they'll get round to improving things here."

"I am quite comfortable," said Mma Ramotswe. "Traditionally built people, you see . . ."

She did not finish, as the superintendent burst out laughing. Mr. Polopetsi, still looking frightened, merely glanced at Mma Ramotswe.

"How's the tennis?" asked Mma Ramotswe.

"I'm still coaching," he replied. "We have some very good younger players coming up. There's a young man from up north with a really powerful backhand. You remember that Swedish man who lived here? Mr. Ogren? He's set up a tennis camp in Maun and he's getting some strong players through."

"That's good work," said Mma Ramotswe. "Tennis is . . ." She searched for what she wanted to say about tennis. What was tennis? What could one say about it?

"Good for you," prompted the superintendent. "If everybody played tennis, I'd be out of a job. No crime. No drugs. No nothing. Tennis players don't go in for things like that."

There was a brief silence. Then the superintendent cleared his throat.

"Now then," he said, turning to Mr. Polopetsi, "I understand from Mma Ramotswe that you have been approached by a certain gentleman. I understand that he proposed a trip to Zambia."

Mr. Polopetsi nodded. "That is correct, sir," he said. "I had no idea—"

The superintendent waved a hand. "Oh, I'm sure you didn't.

Mma Ramotswe has told me that you are not the sort to get mixed up in these things. I trust her judgement." He paused briefly. "But you have obviously been drawn into bad company."

Mr. Polopetsi looked miserable. "I did not know about these things, Rra. I was unaware."

"Yes," said the superintendent. "These people are very cunning. They get hold of people who are not suspicious of others. You are not alone, Mr. Polopetsi. There are many people who are sucked in that way."

Mma Ramotswe leaned forward. "He will do everything to help," she said. "He has agreed."

The superintendent looked pleased. "Good. In that case we can—"

"But," interjected Mma Ramotswe, "there is that other matter I mentioned. That commercial issue. All the people who invested because of Mr. Polopetsi are getting a full refund. They will not be complaining."

"In that case," said the superintendent, "we can disregard that. We are not interested in commercial issues unless there has been fraud." He looked intensely at Mr. Polopetsi, as if to assess him as a possible fraudster.

"There has been no fraud," said Mma Ramotswe quickly. "At least not by Mr. Polopetsi. There has only been a misunderstanding, and all the people he spoke to are, as I say, getting that refund."

"Then we can get back to this other matter," said the superintendent. "You have been asked by this man to bring a consignment of illegal drugs over the border."

"I do not want to go to Zambia," said Mr. Polopetsi.

The superintendent assured him that he would not have to go anywhere. "All we want from you is a statement about what he asked you to do—along with some details of where you were meant to go in Zambia and who you were meant to meet there. We have other evidence against this man, and once we have your statement then we will be able to proceed against him for attempted importation. That will be enough to put him behind bars."

Mr. Polopetsi looked alarmed. "I will have to stand up in court?" he asked.

The superintendent nodded. "I shall be there. Don't worry."

"And I shall be there too," said Mma Ramotswe.

"There you are," said the superintendent. "It'll be simple."

"Mr. Polopetsi will do it," said Mma Ramotswe firmly. "There will be no problem."

The superintendent sat back in his seat. "Mma Ramotswe tells me you are a chemist, Mr. Polopetsi. Is that true?"

"I teach chemistry," said Mr. Polopetsi. "I used to be a dispensing chemist, but I am no longer that."

"Interesting," said the superintendent. "We have a lab—you know, a police lab—but we can't get anybody to run it. There's not all that much work for it to do and the government won't pay for a chemist. So it sits there unused and we have to send our samples off—at great expense, I might add—to a lab over the border. It's a big waste of money, if you ask me. Now, if we could find somebody who could do the job part-time for us, and cheaply enough . . . well, it would be very convenient." He looked at his fingernails. "Just a few hours a week, of course. Not very much. And not much pay, I'm afraid."

Mr. Polopetsi suddenly brightened. "But I'd like to do that, Rra. I enjoy lab work."

"My goodness," exclaimed the superintendent. "These things sometimes arrange themselves in the strangest way. What a coincidence that I should talk about our lab problems and there you are, sitting right in front of me. That is very odd."

"Very odd," agreed Mma Ramotswe.

CHAPTER FOURTEEN

I WOULD LIKE SOME FAT CAKES, MMA

THE CORRUGATIONS on the road out to the Orphan Farm were worse than usual following the prolonged dry season, shaking Mma Ramotswe's tiny white van with the unrelenting determination of a terrier with a rabbit. In the back of the van, holding on to Zebra's collar, Fanwell bounced up and down, as did the dog.

"Slower, Mma!" shouted Fanwell, but his voice was drowned in the rattles and other protests rising from the van's chassis, and Mma Ramotswe, a believer in the theory that a badly corrugated road was best tackled at speed—allowing one to fly across the top of the bumps without descending into the valleys between them—merely drove all the faster.

By the time they reached the gate, Fanwell had abandoned Zebra and was concentrating on supporting himself. The dog was lying on the floor of the van, apparently trying to sleep; now, as they drew to a halt under an acacia tree, Zebra sat up, sniffed at the air, and uttered a low bark.

"He obviously enjoyed the trip," said Mma Ramotswe over her shoulder, as she turned off the engine. "Dogs like cars, don't they?"

"I think he was knocked unconscious," muttered Fanwell. "And so was I."

They left the van and walked over to the small office building from which Mma Potokwane ran her domain. Two children, a boy and a girl both about five or six years old, sat on the cramped verandah outside the office, mutely staring at Zebra. As Mma Ramotswe approached, they looked up and gazed at her with wide, rheumy eyes. Around their eyes flies were crawling.

Mma Ramotswe frowned disapprovingly, and bent down to brush the flies away.

"You must not let those flies sit on your face," she said gently in Setswana. "Why not find something to brush them away with?"

The children looked up at her uncomprehendingly. "They do not speak Setswana," said a voice from inside the office. "They've just been brought in and they haven't said a word."

"Kalanga?" asked Mma Ramotswe.

Mma Potokwane shook her head. "We assumed that, but apparently not. One of the housemothers speaks a bit of Kalanga and she tried to get them to say something, but she said they did not understand her at all."

Mma Ramotswe fished a handkerchief out of the pocket of her blouse and passed it to the girl. The child took it gingerly and dabbed at the boy's eyes, then at her own.

"That's better," said Mma Ramotswe encouragingly. "Keep the flies away."

"I think they both have an eye infection," said Mma Potokwane. "The nurse is coming to take a look. She'll give them some eyedrops. It usually clears it up." She turned to Fanwell. "And here you are, Fanwell. We don't see very much of you, do we? How is your auntie?"

Mma Potokwane and Fanwell's aunt had been childhood friends, and Mma Potokwane always asked after her.

"She is very well, Mma," said Fanwell. "She is getting fatter."

"That's good," said Mma Potokwane. "She always enjoyed her food. I remember that. She was very fat when she was a girl—very fat."

Mma Potokwane looked at Zebra. "And this dog?" she asked. "What does he want?"

"The same thing that all dogs want," said Mma Ramotswe. "Some-where to live. Some people to look after him and give him food." She hesitated briefly before adding, "And children to play with."

Mma Potokwane did not respond for a few moments, but then she turned to Mma Ramotswe and shook a finger in admonition. "Are you trying to tell me something, Mma Ramotswe?"

Mma Ramotswe affected nonchalance. "Are we trying to tell Mma Potokwane something, Fanwell?"

Fanwell was more direct. "Yes, Mma. We're asking her to—"

Mma Ramotswe cut him short. "What Fanwell means is that we were wondering whether one of the housemothers might like a dog to play with the children. He's a very friendly dog."

Mma Potokwane looked down at Zebra, who stared back up at her, his tail wagging to and fro.

"He likes you, Mma," said Fanwell.

One of the children—the boy—now reached forward and patted Zebra on the head. The dog, surprised at first, moved towards him and licked eagerly at the child's face. He licked around his eyes, mak-ing the boy chuckle with joy.

"That's the first sound he's made," said Mma Potokwane. "The first sound since he came here."

"See," said Fanwell. "This dog is good at looking after children. He's cleaning up that boy's eyes."

"*Inja*," said the child.

"That's Zulu," said Mma Ramotswe. "Or Ndebele, or Siswati—one of those Zulu languages."

"Then I can speak to them," said Fanwell. "My grandfather went to the mines over there. He learned Zulu and he taught me. I prac-tised it with him a lot. I am very good at languages, *Bomma*. You may think I'm useless, but I know a lot of words."

"Ask them their names then," said Mma Potokwane. "And we don't think you're useless."

Fanwell handed Zebra's lead to Mma Ramotswe and crouched down beside the children. They watched him solemnly.

He uttered a few words slowly, holding the boy's hand as he spoke. The effect was immediate, the girl reaching over and taking his free hand while the boy gripped tightly. The girl whispered something to him, and Fanwell nodded.

"She is asking for water," he said. "She says that she will tell us their names once they have had water."

Mma Potokwane went into the office and returned with a cup of water. She passed it to the girl, who drank half of it before giving it to the boy. He drained the cup and handed it back to Fanwell. This was followed by more whispering.

"She says that they are brother and sister," said Fanwell. "She says that she is called Buhle. That means beautiful. And her brother is called . . ." He leaned forward and asked the girl. "Sfiso," he said. "I don't know what that means, but it is a name they use."

Mma Potokwane asked him to find out where they were from. "And their parents," she said. "Ask them where their parents are."

Fanwell posed the questions. The boy remained silent, but the girl spoke freely.

"I cannot understand everything she says," said Fanwell. "But she says that their parents are late. She says they have been late for months. She says they were very thin."

Mma Potokwane caught Mma Ramotswe's eye. That was the prevailing euphemism: the slim disease.

Fanwell continued his translation. "She said that they were brought to Botswana from Swaziland by an aunt and left here. She said there is nobody to look after them in Swaziland. The aunt has gone, she says."

Mma Potokwane sighed. "Not an unusual story," she said. "Nobody to look after children somewhere else—dump them in Botswana and then go home to wherever you come from."

"That's not fair on you," said Mma Ramotswe.

"It's even less fair on the children," said Mma Potokwane. She sighed again. "A child is a child. We shall not turn them away."

Mma Ramotswe looked at Zebra. "I shall take the dog back, Mma," she said. "You cannot look after the whole world."

Mma Potokwane turned to her friend. She knew how much she owed Mr. J.L.B. Matekoni. He had nursed their old pump for years, he had fixed the Orphan Farm van, he had tinkered with the hot-water system and kept the boilers going for far longer than their allotted, biblical span. She owed Mma Ramotswe many favours, and she could not recall Mma Ramotswe ever calling them in. A dog would be popular with the children, and they would give it the love it needed. There was only one answer.

"He must stay," she said. "He can be the father of these two children. He will love them."

"You are very kind, Mma," said Mma Ramotswe. "There is nobody kinder than you."

She meant it, and as she spoke, she thought how strange it was that we so very rarely said complimentary things to our friends, and how easy it was to do so, and how it made the world seem a less harsh place.

"The dog is very happy, Mma Potokwane," said Fanwell. "He will be a very good dog out here. He will make the children happy."

Mma Potokwane nodded. "We must drink some tea," she said. "We have dealt with several problems very quickly. Now we should have tea in case any further problems arise."

"I hope they do not," said Mma Ramotswe.

"So do I," said Fanwell. "I am very grateful to you, Mma Potokwane, for taking this poor dog."

Two out of three, thought Mma Ramotswe: Mr. Polopetsi, and now Zebra—both crossed off the list with no complications at all. Now all that remained was the easiest task of all: bringing Rosie and

Susan together—an easy task, it would seem, and one that should have every bit as satisfactory an ending as this one.

But then a feeling of foreboding set in. It was insidious in its onset, but by the time Mma Ramotswe had dropped Fanwell off at his uncle's house in Old Naledi, she was beginning to feel less confident about seeing Rosie. She was not even sure that she would find her— she knew that she worked in a bakery out towards Kgali Hill, but she had no telephone number for her, nor a home address. And she was not even sure about the location of the bakery—new businesses were springing up all the time—and closing too—and bitter experience had taught her that tracing people at their work could be difficult: people changed jobs, went off on holiday without warning, and even occasionally used assumed names at work in order to avoid tax.

Fanwell, though, said that he knew exactly where the bakery was, and had given her precise instructions. "You go up Kudumatse Road, Mma," he said, "and then you are in Extension 23. That is where that man who was having that affair with that lady lived—the man who was married to that lady wrestler—you remember her, Mma? Charlie told me all about that case."

Mma Ramotswe nodded. The No. 1 Ladies' Detective Agency had been approached by the wife of the errant husband and had quickly laid bare what was happening.

"I felt very sorry for that man," said Fanwell. "He didn't know what was coming to him. Is he out of hospital yet, Mma?"

"I think he is," said Mma Ramotswe. "I saw him at the shops at Riverwalk. He was reading a long shopping list in the supermarket."

"He has learned to be obedient then," said Fanwell.

Mma Ramotswe smiled. "Be careful when you choose a wife, Fanwell."

"I shall be very careful, Mma. I will not marry a lady who likes to wrestle."

"I think that's wise, Fanwell—on balance."

He grinned. "Do you think anybody will marry me, Mma Ramotswe?"

She did not hesitate. "There will be young women, Fanwell. They would love a nice young man like you."

"And Charlie?" asked Fanwell. "Will anybody marry Charlie?"

She remembered the man in the housing office and his request that she should help him find a bride. She had rashly offered to help, but how could she? How could she assume responsibility for all the disappointments of the world—for all the yearnings and searches of those who had not found what they wanted to find? Was that her role in life?

Fanwell wanted an answer. "I asked you, Mma: Will anybody marry Charlie?"

She said that the answer was yes, but she saw greater difficulties there. "Charlie is a very big man with the ladies, Fanwell, as you might have observed. Men who are very big with the ladies often have no judgement as to what qualities to look for in a wife. It's the same with the ladies who are very big with the men—they often don't understand what will make a good husband."

Fanwell looked thoughtful. "A good husband? Like Mr. J.L.B. Matekoni? He's a good husband to you, Mma, I think."

Mma Ramotswe smiled. "He is the best husband in Botswana, Rra. That is well known."

"Better than Phuti Radiphuti, Mma? He is a good husband to Mma Makutsi, I think, but maybe not as good a husband as Mr. J.L.B. Matekoni. Perhaps Phuti is a Good Husband, Division Two."

Mma Ramotswe dealt with this quickly. "I don't think we should compare people, Fanwell. I would not say one is better than the other." She gave him a warning look. "I wouldn't like Mma Makutsi to hear that I had been saying that her husband is not as good as mine."

"Oh, I would not tell her that, Mma," protested Fanwell. "I wouldn't go and say that to her face." He paused. "But if you had to choose, Mma—let's say that you were an unmarried lady and these two men were standing in front of you, Mr. J.L.B. Matekoni and Phuti Radiphuti—which one would you choose? Which one would you walk up to and say, 'I would like you to be my husband'?"

She brushed the question aside. "You can't ask people that, Fanwell. It's like those questions where you say there are three people in a big balloon and one has to be thrown out in order to stop the balloon from crashing. You can't answer those questions—not really."

But Fanwell liked the idea of such a quandary. "Oh, I like the sound of that, Mma! That is very good!" He thought for a moment. "Let's say that we have a balloon just like that, and it's flying across the Okavango Delta and there are all these hippos and crocodiles down below. Let's say that the people in the balloon are . . ." He scratched his head. "All right, Mma, there's Mma Potokwane in the basket under the balloon. And then there's Nelson Mandela—before he died, of course. And then there's . . ." He waited for a moment before revealing the identity of the third passenger. "Violet Sephotho. Yes, Violet Sephotho is the third person. And you're the pilot, Mma, who has to throw one of them out. Which one would it be?"

"Do you think you know the answer I'm likely to give?"

Fanwell looked smug. "I think I know the answer, Mma."

"Then why ask the question?" said Mma Ramotswe, and laughed. "Anyway, Fanwell, you were telling me the way to the bakery."

"Well, Mma, once you are in Extension 23 you take a road off to the left. That is called Monganakodu Road and there is a big church on the left up there. They're always singing. The bakery is behind that place, Mma. That is where you'll find that bakery. It is called Fresh Time Bakery."

She nodded her thanks, and then her thoughts returned to the balloon and its passengers. Of course she would have to throw Violet Sephotho out of the basket in order to save the other two, meritorious lives, but it would not be easy. She did not approve of Violet, but she had never forgotten that she was a person too and had the rights that went with being a person. Mma Ramotswe could never inflict pain on another, and Violet Sephotho would require rough handling to be helped over the edge. Mma Ramotswe would do it—if she did it at all—with real regret, apologising to Violet even as she pushed her over the side. "I'm so sorry, Violet. I wish I had an alternative, but I simply don't. You'll have to go. I'm so sorry." But then she thought: no, I could never push Violet Sephotho over the side, even if the balloon was going down. We would have to take our chances for a bumpy landing; I could not do it, I could not push another person overboard.

The instructions were clear enough, and she drove there by herself, without telling Mma Makutsi. The handling of Mma Rosie was now a matter for her and her alone, and she would have to be very careful not to ruffle feathers.

She parked in the broad sunlight, as every available bit of shade was already taken. Then, leaving the van, she walked over the road to the bakery, from which, in the still air of the afternoon, the delicious smell of baking bread drifted—along with something else, and halfway across the road she realised what that was: fat cakes. She stopped for a moment and sniffed at the air: she was on duty and should put all thought of food out of her mind, but fat cakes . . . She tried to remember when she had last eaten one. Two weeks ago? That was a long time ago and there would be no guilt now in buying one—possibly two—of the famous confections and eating it, or possibly eating both of them, in the van. Indeed the purchase of fat cakes might even count as a legitimate expense in the case, just as buying a cup of coffee did when one was waiting for somebody whom one was following.

She opened the door of the bakery. Now the delicious odour was all about her, and there, on a tray on the counter, was a freshly baked batch of fat cakes, their pores exuding tiny succulent drops of nectar, the sweet perspiration of the confection itself.

A woman behind the counter greeted her politely, and Mma Ramotswe returned the greeting.

"I would like some fat cakes, Mma," Mma Ramotswe began.

"Then you have come to the right place," said the woman, gesturing towards the tray. "These are very fresh, Mma. And they are very delicious—probably the most delicious fat cakes in the country."

"That is a big claim, Mma," said Mma Ramotswe.

"We are confident of it, Mma," said the woman, somewhat formally. "We don't make such a claim lightly."

Mma Ramotswe smiled. "I'm sure you're right, Mma. But I would like to ask you something: Is Rosie in? I've been told she works here."

For a moment the woman hesitated, and Mma Ramotswe thought that perhaps she had come to the wrong place altogether. But then the woman nodded towards the back of the bakery. "She's back there. Would you like to speak to her?"

"I would," said Mma Ramotswe. "If you could fetch her, Mma. I will not take up much of her time."

The woman disappeared, leaving Mma Ramotswe contemplating the tray of fat cakes. There were other delights too: on a shelf near the window several richly iced birthday cakes sat ready for purchase— a generic cake for a boy, decorated with icing-sugar footballs and cars, and one for girls, all pink and frilly. Mma Ramotswe smiled: Mma Makutsi would take strong exception to that if she told her about it. And there was a sense, too, in which she herself objected to the forcing of children into such roles; boys should be allowed to be frilly if they wanted, and girls to play football and play with cars; it was just that there were so few boys and girls who wanted to follow such independent instincts. Puso would never agree to wear anything too colourful—khaki was his preferred colour—and Motholeli showed no interest in football, in spite of her brother's attempt to invoke her support for the Botswana Zebras team. "They're silly" was all she had said. "Don't waste my time with silly football things." Of course cars were different; she loved cars and was on course to be a mechanic in the fullness of time, apprenticed, she hoped, to Mr. J.L.B. Matekoni in Tlokweng Road Speedy Motors.

Rosie appeared quite suddenly, wearing a voluminous set of white overalls and dusting the flour off her hands. For a few moments she looked confused, as she evidently tried to place Mma Ramotswe. But then she remembered, and her brow knitted into a frown. It was not a good sign, thought Mma Ramotswe.

"I am sorry to disturb you here," Mma Ramotswe began. "I would have visited you at home, but I do not know where that is."

Mma Rosie pursed her lips. "It is not here," she said. "It's somewhere else."

"Of course, Mma. I know this is where you work. And may I say, those fat cakes smell very, very good."

She had not expected that to work, but it was worth trying. And for a brief moment a smile of satisfaction crossed Rosie's face. Almost everybody, thought Mma Ramotswe, likes to be complimented on their work—there were few exceptions to that.

"Yes, they are very good," said Rosie. "They're very popular."

"I'm not surprised," said Mma Ramotswe. "I am sure there will be fat cakes in heaven—if we ever get there."

Again there was a brief smile, and then the question: "What do you want, Mma?"

The woman who had been behind the counter when Mma Ramotswe entered the bakery was still there. She was listening, although she was busily pretending to be concerned with sweeping some crumbs off the floor.

"I wonder if we could talk outside," said Mma Ramotswe, her voice lowered.

The woman looked up sharply. "It is a private matter, Mma," Mma Ramotswe said to her.

The woman returned wordlessly to her sweeping.

Rosie hesitated, but then she put her cloth down on the counter and walked round to join Mma Ramotswe on the other side. Together they made their way outside, where they stood, partly sheltered by a tattered awning on the side of the bakery, and where Mma Ramotswe began the conversation as tactfully as she could.

"I am very sorry, Mma, that there was a misunderstanding between you and Mma Makutsi—"

She got no further.

"Misunderstanding?" Rosie exploded. "Is that what they are calling big-time rudeness these days? Misunderstanding?"

Mma Ramotswe sighed. "I am so sorry, Mma. I can see that you were upset. All that I am asking is that you understand—"

"Understand a misunderstanding? Is that what I have to do? I go to your place because you asked me to—in the paper, you asked—and then I find that I am the number one suspect of a very strange lady with big glasses."

"You were never suspected of anything," said Mma Ramotswe in as conciliatory a tone as she could manage. "And I have said that I am sorry, Mma. I am truly sorry."

"*You* are sorry, Mma? And what about the lady with the big glasses? Where is she? Has she come to say she's sorry? She has not. She's still sitting somewhere suspecting innocent people."

Mma Ramotswe was silent for a moment. The way to defuse anger, she thought, was to allow it an outlet. Anger was like a volcano; you had to wait until it discharged before you could approach its crater.

After a while, Mma Ramotswe mentioned Susan. "She wants to see you, Mma. This has nothing to do with Mma Makutsi—it's Mma Susan. She is the one you must think of here."

Mma Rosie thought for a moment. "But this Mma Makutsi—what about her?"

Mma Ramotswe said that she did not think Mma Makutsi need be involved. "This will be a meeting between you and the Canadian lady, Mma. That's all it will be."

Rosie fiddled with the strings of her apron, nervously twisting them round a finger. "Then let her come to me."

Mma Ramotswe felt a surge of relief. "Oh, I'm very pleased, Mma. That's very good news. I shall go and speak to Mma Susan—"

Rosie raised a hand to stop her. "No, Mma. I meant that your Mma Makutsi should come to me. She must come to me and apologise. As for this Mma Susan—I have changed my mind, Mma. I do not want to see that lady."

Mma Ramotswe looked up at the sky. Pride, she thought—it was such an important factor in the way in which people led their lives—and such an unnecessary one. Yet one could not wish human failings out of existence—pride, jealousy, anger, resentment: these were all things with which people cluttered their lives. Life would be so much easier if they were not there, but they were, and we had to find a way round them.

Mma Ramotswe struggled to control her irritation. "But why did you contact us, Mma, if you didn't want to see her?"

Rosie shrugged. "I was curious, Mma. That's all. I was curious." She paused. "Now I'm not curious any longer."

Mma Ramotswe was at a loss as to what to say. She was used to cases collapsing, but it always took her unawares.

Rosie looked as if she had just remembered something. "She was a very difficult child, that one."

"Oh?"

"Yes. She was headstrong. She was disobedient. I always said: that one will be a big problem for somebody when she grows up."

Mma Ramotswe waited, but nothing more was said. So she said, "Children are often difficult, Mma. I think we all were ourselves, were we not? And then they grow up."

Rosie shook her head. "Some are like that, Mma. Others are bad."

"Are there really bad children, Mma?"

Mma Rosie seemed surprised that the question was even asked. "Of course there are. There are many."

"I see."

Rosie looked pointedly at her watch. "I am on a shift here," she said. "I can't stand outside talking all day."

"Of course not, Mma. You've been very kind." Mma Ramotswe paused. "I should like to buy some fat cakes, though."

Rosie nodded. "The other lady will look after you."

"And perhaps you'll change your mind," said Mma Ramotswe.

Rosie shook her head. "I never change my mind, Mma."

Back inside the bakery, Mma Ramotswe asked for half a dozen fat cakes. These were taken from the tray and placed in a brown paper bag. Smudges of grease appeared through the paper, promising delight ahead. She paid the woman behind the counter and returned to her van. Just one, she thought; she would eat just one fat cake at this stage, and then perhaps she would have another later on, after she had spoken to Mma Makutsi—a reward for the completion of a task that she suspected would not be easy.

She sat in the van and took a single fat cake out of the packet. It did not last long. She hesitated. It had not been a particularly large fat cake—a bit undersized, in fact—and that, surely, was justification for having another one. This second one, she told herself, is yesterday's fat cake. She had not eaten one yesterday, when she might well have done so. This one, therefore, did not count, and a third would not count either, as there had been no fat cake on the day before yesterday. But the line would have to be drawn there. Firmly.

She finished the third fat cake and licked the last traces of sugar off her fingers. She felt pleasantly full: three *small* fat cakes was not excessive, but was enough to take the edge off your hunger and equip you for whatever lay ahead. Whatever lay ahead . . . She reached forward to place the key in the ignition, but then stopped herself. The concern she had felt in the latter part of her conversation with Rosie returned, and now it was accompanied by an even more disturbing thought. *What if both she and Mma Makutsi were wrong? What if this case were about something else altogether?*

CHAPTER FIFTEEN

DO NOT BE AFRAID
TO PROFESS FORGIVENESS

THESE ARE VERY SMALL CABBAGES," said Mma Makutsi. "But when the rain comes they will grow so quickly, Mma Ramotswe. You'll see."

They were standing in the vegetable patch that Mma Makutsi and Phuti Radiphuti had carved out of the virgin bush that was their yard. Or rather, that had been created by the man who worked in their garden, a taciturn man in a battered hat, who now stood respectfully to one side while his employer showed her visitor his handiwork.

"Mr. Moepi is very good with cabbages," said Mma Makutsi, nodding in the gardener's direction. "What do they say of people who are good at growing things? That they have green fingers? Like leaves. Like grass. Green fingers."

The gardener looked down at his shoes.

"He is very modest," continued Mma Makutsi.

Mma Ramotswe glanced in Mr. Moepi's direction. Mma Makutsi had a tendency to talk about people in their presence as if they were not there. "The garden is looking very good, Rra," she said, smiling at him. "Even in these dry conditions you are getting somewhere with it."

"Yes, he is," said Mma Makutsi. "And he is going to grow a lot of beans this coming season—just like Mr. J.L.B. Matekoni."

The gardener shifted from foot to foot.

"Now we can go inside," said Mma Makutsi. "We can leave Moepi to water the cabbages. We take water from the outlet pipe in the kitchen. It's our washing-up water that we use. Moepi wastes nothing in this garden, do you, Rra?"

The gardener adjusted his hat.

"No, you see he doesn't," said Mma Makutsi.

They began to make their way towards the house. "He is a very good gardener," said Mma Makutsi. "He doesn't speak very much, as you can see, but he is very good at growing things. He comes from Lobatse. He used to have a job in the hospital for mental illnesses. He was a gardener there."

"Oh yes," said Mma Ramotswe. "I think the patients like to work in the gardens. It helps them to get better."

"In some cases," said Mma Makutsi. "In other cases it is not much help. Mr. Moepi told me that one of the patients hit him over the head with a rake."

"I'm sorry to hear that," said Mma Ramotswe.

"Yes. But these things happen, Mma. Nobody is to blame."

Mma Ramotswe assured Mma Makutsi that she had not been thinking in terms of blame.

"You see," continued Mma Makutsi, "if you're confused you may not know what you're doing. It's like being asleep. Then you wake up and you find you've done something you didn't mean to do."

Mma Ramotswe nodded. "That must be true, Mma. It must be very sad for these people."

They reached the house. Itumelang, Mma Makutsi said, was sleeping, but Mma Ramotswe could peek in on him if she wished.

"I'd love that," said Mma Ramotswe. "But first, Mma, we must talk. You and I must talk."

Mma Makutsi stiffened. "About this Mma Susan business?"

Mma Ramotswe nodded.

They were on the verandah; Mma Makutsi indicated a corner where three chairs were ranged around a table. "We can sit there, Mma. It's a good place to talk."

Once seated, Mma Ramotswe took a deep breath and began. "I need to tell you something, Mma Makutsi," she began. "I think I've been wrong."

Mma Makutsi, who had been frowning, now smiled. "About that Mma Rosie? Yes, Mma, I thought you were wrong. I am sometimes wrong myself, you know, and I'd be the first to admit it, but this time I thought, *Mma Ramotswe is wrong.* That's what I thought, Mma."

"But not about Mma Rosie," said Mma Ramotswe hurriedly. "Or maybe wrong about her as much as I was wrong about Mma Susan. She is the one I may be most wrong about."

This confused Mma Makutsi. "Mma Susan? Why are you wrong about her?"

Mma Ramotswe sat back in her chair. "Of course I may be wrong in thinking I'm wrong. That's also possible, Mma."

"No, I think you're right," said Mma Makutsi. "I think you're right about you thinking you're wrong."

They looked at one another for a moment, and then Mma Ramotswe laughed. "You never know, do you, Mma?" she said. "You never know when being wrong is right."

"No, that's never . . . ," replied Mma Makutsi. "It's never right to be wrong." She paused, and looked up at the ceiling for inspiration. "Of course, it may be wrong to be right—"

Mma Ramotswe interrupted her. "Or, rather, to think you're right when you're wrong."

"That's it, Mma. That's what I was trying to say."

They both sat in silence for a moment as they gathered their thoughts. Then Mma Ramotswe said, "You see, Mma Makutsi, it suddenly struck me that Mma Susan might not have liked Mma Rosie."

She watched for Mma Makutsi's reaction: sometimes Mma Makutsi rejected her notions out of hand, but this did not happen now. "Not liked her? Perhaps . . . But why, Mma? Why do you think that?"

Mma Ramotswe recalled the visit to the house on Zebra Drive. "When I took her to see my neighbour's house, she didn't seem all that interested in much of it. She hardly looked at the living room, you know. But when it came to the servant's block—where Mma Rosie would have lived—well, that was different."

"In what way, Mma?"

"Her whole attitude changed, Mma. She became tense. You know how people are when they find themselves in a place that . . ." She struggled to find the right words. ". . . in a place that's . . ." It came to her suddenly. "In a place that's *painful* to them." That was the word; that was exactly right, and now it became clear to her. There had been pain—a long time ago—but the memory of that pain had now come back.

She had not been sure how Mma Makutsi would respond to this; she had very little evidence, after all, to justify the inference. But she need not have worried.

"But that's it!" exclaimed Mma Makutsi. "But that's what happened, Mma. That woman was cruel to her. She's come to . . ."

"Confront her?" suggested Mma Ramotswe.

"Exactly, Mma. That's exactly what she's come to do. She's come to confront her. I felt unhappy about both of them, you know, Mma. I didn't like that Mma Susan because I thought she was not telling the truth about something. And I didn't like that Mma Rosie because I thought she wasn't telling the truth either."

"But you thought she was lying about being Mma Rosie," said Mma Ramotswe. "Isn't that different, Mma?"

Mma Makutsi did not think so. "No, it was the same sort of thing, Mma. That's what counted—it was the same sort of thing."

They were silent for a moment as they considered the implications of what had just been said. At last Mma Makutsi spoke. "Some people who look after children are cruel, Mma. Aren't they? It happens."

"Yes, it does. And it can leave very deep scars, Mma. Very deep."

Mma Makutsi nodded. "I had a teacher once who was like that. I was a little girl then and there was a teacher at the school who was very strict. He had a stick and he used to beat the boys—he did not beat the girls, but we were very frightened, Mma. We thought he might beat us too one day, but he didn't have time to do that. He was too busy beating the boys."

Mma Ramotswe shook her head. "There used to be far too much beating . . . In fact, Mma, any beating is too much. There should be no beating at all."

"But that is not the way the world is," said Mma Makutsi. "There is still beating going on. There are still people who beat others because they think it's the right thing to do."

She was still thinking about the teacher. "You know, Mma Ramotswe," she continued, "when I came down to Gaborone, I still sometimes remembered how frightened we had been. I thought of that teacher with his stick. And then, when I went up to Bobonong one time, I saw him in the street outside the general store and I wanted to go up to him and say, 'Where is your big stick now, you big bully?' That's what I wanted to do. And I also thought: Wouldn't it be good to have a big stick and to beat *him*?"

"Did you go up to him?"

Mma Makutsi nodded. "Yes, I walked up to him and said that I was pleased to see him and I hoped he was well."

"While all the time you wanted to beat him with a big stick?"

"Yes, Mma."

Mma Ramotswe smiled. "I think that was better, you know. I think it's better not to beat people with big sticks, even if they deserve it."

Mma Makutsi looked rueful. "I sometimes still think about getting a stick and going back up there to beat him."

"But you never will, you know, Mma Makutsi."

"Probably not."

Mma Makutsi was still puzzled over Susan's motivation. "I can't quite understand it, Mma. It's one thing for me to go up to Bobonong, but for that lady to come all the way from Canada . . ."

"Oh, that will not be the only reason," said Mma Ramotswe. "I think that Mma Susan has done this because she's unhappy about something else. She's unhappy about that man she loved and who doesn't love her any longer. She is very unhappy about that. And she may be unhappy about her childhood in general—about all sorts of things—and she may not have many people to blame; except for one or two, of course. And so she wants to say something to these people."

"So she thinks she can make everything better by meeting somebody who was cruel to her?"

"Yes, I think so."

"That seems very odd, Mma."

Mma Ramotswe replied that people were odd. "Never be surprised by anything people can do, Mma. They are capable of doing many, many odd things."

"So now we're going to have to tell her that we have found the woman she wanted us to find?" Mma Makutsi asked. "We are going to have to take her to speak to her?"

Mma Ramotswe sighed. "That is a very difficult question, Mma. And I'm not sure of the answer."

"I'm not sure either," said Mma Makutsi. "So what do we do, Mma?"

"Nothing," said Mma Ramotswe. "Nothing yet."

"But we will have to say *something*."

"Yes, but we need to think very carefully about what we say.

And to start with, we may say nothing—and also *do* nothing, Mma Makutsi. Sometimes doing nothing is the same as doing something, if you see what I mean."

"No," said Mma Makutsi. "I do not."

"Well, if you do nothing, then somebody may feel the need to do something, and that means that you're getting something done by doing nothing. It's just that it's done by somebody else, you see."

Mma Makutsi thought about this. Then she said, "I suppose that applies to the making of tea, Mma. That doesn't happen by itself—somebody has to make it."

"You are very right, Mma," said Mma Ramotswe. "And do you know—I have some fat cakes in my van."

"Then I shall put on the kettle while you fetch the fat cakes," said Mma Makutsi. "I haven't had a fat cake for quite a while, you know."

Mma Ramotswe said nothing, but realised, of course, that saying nothing implied something, and that was the inescapable conclusion that she had, very recently, consumed more than one fat cake.

THAT WAS FRIDAY. On Saturday Mma Ramotswe went with Motholeli and Mr. J.L.B. Matekoni to watch Puso playing soccer for his school team against a nearby school. It was a rout for Puso's team, with bruised knees and tears afterwards, and a man-to-man talk from Mr. J.L.B. Matekoni on the need to be a good loser. An ice cream repaired the psychological damage and a sticking plaster the physical; then there was shopping to be done and the evening meal to prepare. None of this activity allowed much time for thought, although occasionally Mma Ramotswe found herself wondering about Susan and whether she should trust the strong instinct she had developed that something was wrong there. On Sunday there was little time for brooding about work either: there was the morning service at the Anglican Cathedral opposite the Princess Marina Hospital, followed by a parish breakfast at which it was Mma Ramotswe's turn to be one of the cooks. She dozed off at one point in the sermon, but felt that she was by no means alone in this, as when she looked about her—as one does after an unscheduled public sleep—she noticed at least three others whose heads were nodding. It was the warmth of the day, of course, rather than what the Bishop was saying. He was talking about forgiveness, which was a subject on which Mma Ramotswe had views. She was in favour of it, and when the Bishop talked about the teaching of forgiveness to children—she was fully awake at that point—she felt as if she might rise to her feet and voice her agreement. That had happened once when a visiting clergyman had been talking about charity; his words had been punctuated at intervals by increasingly loud "hear! hear!"s from a member of the congregation seated in the back row. Seemingly indifferent to the looks of disapproval from neighbouring pews, this person had continued his voluble support for the preacher until, at the end of the sermon, he had announced loudly: "I couldn't have put it better myself!" That had led to laughter, and laughter had defused the tension that had built up until then.

But now, as the Bishop spoke, she restricted herself to just the merest nodding of the head in agreement. "Somebody asked me the other day," he said, "when we should start teaching children about forgiveness. That is the question she asked."

Mma Ramotswe looked up at the ceiling, so high above her in this new cathedral, and at the electric fans suspended from the ceiling, stirring the air so ineffectively with their sluggish blades.

"I was surprised by the question," continued the Bishop, "because I think that forgiveness is one of the first things. Forgiveness is at the heart of the way we live our lives—or should be. So when we teach our children about the things they need to know about the world— about how not to touch fire, about how to wash their hands or put on their shoes; yes, even about the map of our world, about where Africa is, and Botswana, about where the Limpopo runs or the Okavango, about where the great Kalahari lies—all these things, we should also remember to teach them about forgiveness. We must teach them that when another person wrongs us—hurts us, perhaps—we should not strike back, but should be ready to forgive. We must teach them that if we do not forgive then we run the risk of being eaten up with hatred inside, and that hatred is like acid, that it will gnaw and gnaw away. That is why forgiveness must be taught right at the beginning, when we are teaching about these first things."

Yes, thought Mma Ramotswe. *Yes. This is all true. This is all very true.*

"And yet," he went on, "who talks about forgiveness these days, other than the people who come to this place, or to places like this? What politician, what public person, do we hear standing up and saying that we must forgive? The message we are more likely to hear is one of blame, of how this person or that person must be held to account for something bad that has happened. It is a message of retribution—that is all it is—a message of pure retribution, sometimes dressed up in concern about victims and public safety and matters of that sort. But if you do not forgive, and you think all the time about getting even, or punishing somebody who has done you a wrong, what are you achieving? You are not going to make that person better by hating or punishing him; oh no, that will not happen. When we punish somebody, we are often just punishing ourselves, you know. If people lock others away, they are simply increasing the amount of suffering there is in the world; they may think they are diminishing it, but they are not. They are adding to the burden that suffering creates. Of course, sometimes you have no alternative but to do it—people must be protected from harm—but you should always remember that there are other ways of changing a man's ways.

"My brothers and sisters: do not be afraid to profess forgiveness. Do not be afraid to tell people who urge you to seek retribution or revenge that there is no place for any of that in your heart. Do not be embarrassed to say that you believe in love, and that you believe that water can wash away the sins of the world, and that you are prepared to put this message of forgiveness right at the heart of your world. My brothers and sisters, do not be afraid to say any of this, even if people laugh at you, or say that you are old-fashioned, or foolish, or that you believe things that cannot be believed. Do not worry about any of that—because love and forgiveness are more powerful than any of those cynical, mocking words and will always be so. Always."

Mma Ramotswe looked about her. Nobody was asleep now. Seated next to her, a man whom she had never seen before reached into his pocket, took out a fresh white handkerchief, and put it briefly to his eyes. He was by himself, and she thought, *His wife is late.* And she reached out and touched the sleeve of his jacket, very gently and very briefly, and he looked at her with surprise at first, and then with gratitude. There was no need for words, and anyway the Bishop was finishing what he had to say and the choir was rising to its feet.

AND THEN THE WEEKEND was over, seemingly in a flash, and it was Monday morning and time to drive in to the office of the No. 1 Ladies' Detective Agency and to deal with correspondence, with the sending out of invoices, and with all the other matters that usually occupied the beginning of the week. Mma Makutsi was late in, her car having refused to start, and Charlie complained of mild toothache, but otherwise it was a normal morning. Except, of course, for the telephone call that Mma Makutsi took shortly after the second tea break. This was from Susan, and she directed the call immediately to Mma Ramotswe.

Susan's tone was pleasant enough. "You said that you would have information for me," she began. "I'm free at lunchtime. Could we meet?"

Mma Ramotswe hesitated, but she knew that whatever needed

to be done could not be avoided. She suggested that they should meet at the President Hotel. She would book a table on the verandah and be there by twelve-thirty.

"That sounds good," said Susan.

Mma Ramotswe wondered whether it would be all that good. "Mma Makutsi will join us," she said.

"Your assistant?" asked Susan.

They were talking on the speakerphone, and Mma Ramotswe reached forward quickly to cup a hand over the instrument. But it was too late: Mma Makutsi had heard—or thought she had heard.

"Co-director," said Mma Ramotswe quickly.

"The lady with the huge glasses?" asked Susan.

This led to another quick attempt to suppress the broadcast; again too late.

Mma Ramotswe laughed airily. "They're very fashionable, Mma," she said. "I'd like a pair like that myself, but I don't think I could carry them off."

She brought the conversation to an end before further damage could be done. Looking across the office, she saw Mma Makutsi glaring at her.

"I don't think she meant to be rude, Mma Makutsi."

Mma Makutsi looked down at her desk. "I shall forget what I heard, Mma," she said. "It is sometimes better to do that."

"That's very good of you, Mma," said Mma Ramotswe. "That is a good policy."

"Except sometimes," added Mma Makutsi. "Sometimes it's better to remember."

Mma Ramotswe did not pursue the matter. The arrangement had been made, and now, in the two hours before they were due to go to the President Hotel for what she feared would be a difficult meeting, she thought of what she would have to say. It was tricky. If she had been sure that she was right about Susan, then it would have been easier. But any certainty she had felt on Friday had now been replaced by doubts. That, she thought, was the problem with doubts: if you admitted the slightest niggle of uncertainty, even hardly enough to disturb a settled view, it could rapidly become so weighty as to undermine an entire outlook.

On the way to the President Hotel, they did not discuss the case until they were almost at their destination. Then Mma Makutsi faced Mma Ramotswe as she was turning into the road leading to the hotel's parking place and voiced her doubts. "I'm not sure about all this, Mma," she said. "I can't see why somebody would go to all this trouble just to have a row with somebody over something that was long, long ago. It doesn't make sense to me."

Mma Ramotswe sighed. "Nor to me, Mma. And yet . . ."

"And yet we both feel there's something not quite right here."

In Mma Ramotswe's view that was a perfect assessment of the situation. Something was not quite right—but what exactly was it that was not quite right? "We shall have to feel our way through this," she said, as she approached a parking place between two other vehicles—a delivery van and an old green saloon car.

She nosed the van into the space. It was a tight fit and Mma Makutsi, looking out of the window on her side, pointed out that she would be unable to open her door. Mma Ramotswe engaged reverse gear and repositioned the van, this time allowing more room on Mma Makutsi's side.

"That's better," said Mma Makutsi, opening her door before the engine was switched off.

But then Mma Ramotswe saw that she was hemmed in on her own side. "I can't get out," she said.

Mma Makutsi kept her door open. "Then get out this side, Mma. Come over here."

Mma Ramotswe began to slide over to the other side, negotiating her way past the handbrake and gear lever between the driver's and the passenger's side. She stopped. It had looked as if the manoeuvre would be possible, but there was less room than she had imagined and she suddenly realised that she could easily become stuck.

"Breathe in," said Mma Makutsi. "If you breathe in you become smaller, Mma."

Mma Ramotswe inhaled, and then, with a wriggle and a further twist, she was out of the door.

"Perhaps a larger van, Mma . . . ," said Mma Makutsi gently.

Mma Ramotswe shook her head. "There is nothing wrong with my van, Mma. It is the parking places that are getting smaller and smaller. It's not as if the country is shrinking, and yet they are always leaving less and less space for us to park."

"You are quite right," said Mma Makutsi. "Soon there will be no room to park at all and we shall have to drive round and round and then go home."

Mma Ramotswe stood beside the van, adjusting her skirt. As she did so, she became aware that somebody had approached them silently from behind another parked car. It was Susan.

"Is something wrong?"

Mma Makutsi turned round. "No, Mma. We had difficulty parking—that's all."

Susan looked at her watch. "We are both early—will they be ready for us?"

"They always put the lunch out early," said Mma Makutsi. "They'll be ready."

"So," said Susan as they began to walk about the car park. "Have you found her?"

"Yes," said Mma Ramotswe. "I have found her."

Susan seemed pleased. "When can I see her? This afternoon some time?"

Mma Ramotswe drew in her breath. "Why do you want to see her, Mma?"

It took Susan a few moments to answer. "I've told you why, Mma," she said. "You know the reason."

"To make contact with your past?"

"Yes. I told you that right at the beginning."

Mma Ramotswe stopped. They were in the middle of the car park, but there was no traffic.

"But why do you want to make contact with your past, Mma? That's what I'm interested in."

Mma Ramotswe was aware that Susan was irritated. She heard her breathing become more rapid. "With all due respect, Mma," she began, "that's my business."

Mma Ramotswe was now in no doubt. "You want to confront her, Mma—I think you want to confront that woman because she was cruel. Did she mistreat you, Mma? Is that it?"

Mma Ramotswe glanced at the other woman. She saw that the effect of her words was immediate. When she replied, Susan's voice was raised. "Mistreat me? Who told you about that? Did I say anything about it?"

"You did not," said Mma Ramotswe, remaining calm. "But then many of my clients don't tell me the full story." She paused. There had been no further reaction from Susan—just silence, and shallow breathing. But she had said, "Who told you about that?" Those were not the words of one who was denying that anything had happened. *About that . . . That* was something that had happened.

She waited.

"I want to see that person," said Susan eventually.

Mma Ramotswe hesitated.

"I'm serious, Mma Ramotswe. I want to see that person." Susan's voice was uneven now, the emotion breaking through.

Mma Ramotswe took a deep breath. "I'm not sure that it's a good idea, Mma," she said.

"Are you saying you won't tell me where she is?"

Mma Ramotswe closed her eyes. They were fully exposed to the sun, and it was beating down upon them remorselessly. "That is so, Mma," she said. "There is no point in going over very old matters. It's time for you to forget about all that."

Mma Makutsi tried to lead them into the shade, but they did not move.

"She shut me up," said Susan, her voice lowered to a whisper. "My parents were away. She was looking after me and she accused me of taking some cake she had been saving for something or other. She locked me in her room at the back—in the servant's block. She locked me there for a whole afternoon. I was terrified."

"That was very bad," said Mma Ramotswe.

"I've never forgotten it."

"No, so I see."

Mma Ramotswe saw Mma Makutsi frown at the disclosure.

"I was shut up, you know. I was shut in the classroom all by myself. Up in Bobonong. It was for something I didn't do."

Susan ignored this. She was still staring at Mma Ramotswe, and now she said, "So what do you think I should do, Mma? You say there's no point in going over these old things, but what do you think I should do?" Her words were posed as a challenge—and an aggressive one at that.

"Forgive her," said Mma Ramotswe quietly.

This was met with incredulity. "What?"

"Forgive her," repeated Mma Ramotswe. "You see, forgiveness is the only way you can settle these things. Forgiveness is the only way you'll be able to forget this painful episode."

"You're saying I should forgive her . . ."

"That's exactly what I am saying, Mma."

Inside Susan something snapped, and she shouted out: "Her . . . her . . . !" And then, almost blindly, she pushed at Mma Ramotswe. It was somewhere between a blow and a shove, and it had an entirely unexpected effect, almost causing Mma Ramotswe to lose her footing. She toppled briefly and would have fallen had Mma Makutsi not reached out to steady her. There was an involuntary gasp from Susan. "Mma . . . are you all right?" she stuttered.

It took Mma Ramotswe a moment or two to recover. "Yes, Mma, I am all right."

"I'm so sorry," said Susan. "I didn't mean to do that."

"I know," said Mma Ramotswe. "It's over. Think no more about it."

Susan clasped her hands together. "It's all . . ." She trailed off.

"I know, Mma," said Mma Ramotswe. "I know how you feel."

"It's just that . . ."

They were both silent now. The heat was almost unbearable; bright, pressing, unrelenting. Time itself seemed to become languid, its passage marked by the screech of cicadas, but slowly, and almost imperceptibly, the cogs of some great solution, some machine of rescue, seemed to turn upon one another. A dam had burst; somewhere in some guarded corner, a dam had burst.

"I know you're unhappy about something else, Mma," said Mma Ramotswe gently. "We can talk about that later, once we are out of this sun."

"I . . ."

"You don't have to say anything, Mma. You don't have to say anything at all." She looked at Susan, and saw the tears in her eyes. She reached out. "I can take that lady a message," she said. "I can tell you what I think that message should say, but perhaps you can find the words yourself."

Susan nodded. "I'll find them," she said.

They moved towards the shade, arm in arm, following Mma Makutsi, who had already beaten a retreat from the sun and was standing, waiting for them, under the boughs of an acacia tree.

THE PRESENTATION CEREMONY for the Woman of the Year Award took place two days later in the ballroom of the Sun Hotel. Both Mma

Ramotswe and Mma Makutsi were in the mood for a celebration, as several important and long-running cases had recently been put to bed. The Polopetsi business had also been resolved—aided by the painful sale of almost his entire herd of cattle. Mma Makutsi had complained about getting no more than her original investment back, but was persuaded by Mma Ramotswe that this was a much better outcome than might otherwise have materialised. "He has learned his lesson," she said. "He has learned a big lesson, Mma Makutsi."

A satisfactory outcome had also been found for the Susan affair. Susan had abandoned her search for Rosie and had concentrated instead on the couple of friends they had unearthed from her days at Thornhill School. One of these remembered her quite well and had gone out of her way to be hospitable. The last time Mma Ramotswe saw her, Susan was smiling, and that, Mma Ramotswe thought, amounted to a success. The past, she thought, was being remembered, and forgotten, in just the right measure. It had been, though, one of the strangest cases Mma Ramotswe had been obliged to deal with, even if she felt it most clearly illustrated a series of psychological and moral truths. "Forgiveness," she said to Mr. J.L.B. Matekoni. "Forgiveness is often the solution."

He had not been listening to what she had been saying—or had heard only the word *solution*. In his calling as a mechanic the solution to a mechanical problem was often something as simple as a change of oil, and so he made that point now. "A change of oil," he said. "Yes, Mma, that is the solution. I've always said that."

Mma Ramotswe smiled. It was not often that a misheard or ignored question elicited a response that was so perfectly apt. A change of oil . . . yes, that was what we all needed from time to time, whether we were an engine or a person. And there were other similarities to be explored. Engines had to be handled gently, as did people. Forward gears were better than reverse gears—for people as well as engines. There were so many analogies that could be made.

One day, perhaps, she would write them down and add them, as an appendix of sorts, to her cherished copy of Clovis Andersen's *The Principles of Private Detection*—a source of wisdom to which, surely, more wisdom could profitably be added.

At the Sun Hotel a photographer awaited the arriving guests. All Gaborone was there—or at least all of Gaborone that thought it merited the description "All Gaborone." There was the Mayor, and the Minister for Women's Affairs, and the president, vice-president, and secretary of the Gaborone Chamber of Commerce. There was Mr. Spokes "Fast-Time" Pilani, the famous radio personality. There was the manager of the Mercedes-Benz dealership and the chairman of the Water Board. There was barely a figure of note in the city who had not made an effort to attend, and to look at his or her best for the occasion.

And there were the women who had made the longlist, including the runner-up, Violet Sephotho. Of the winner, Gloria Poeteng, there was no sign yet; her entrance would be made on stage and dramatically at the appropriate moment. "She will be looking very good," said one of the waitresses to Mma Ramotswe. "There has been a lot of talk about her outfit."

There was a reception before the main event, and then the guests filed into the ballroom and took their seats. Mma Ramotswe and Mma Makutsi sat as near to the front as they could, hoping to get a good view of proceedings.

"It will be a very great moment when the crown is given to Gloria," whispered Mma Makutsi. "That Violet Sephotho will have difficulty smiling. She'll try, but what is going on inside her will show."

"You never know," said Mma Ramotswe. "And let's not revel too much in her defeat, Mma."

Mma Makutsi was silent, but it was clear that she intended to revel.

The Mayor went up on stage to prolonged applause. His speech, which lasted twenty-five minutes, was all about what he had done to further the cause of women. "That task is never over," he said. "There are always more women."

Following the Mayor's speech there was an address by the Minister for Women's Affairs. This lasted slightly over forty minutes, and was accompanied by a great number of illustrative figures.

"This is a very instructive evening," said Mma Ramotswe. "We are having to learn a lot for our dinner."

They had seen—and smelled—the dinner that had been laid out on long tables at the side of the room. It was worth waiting for, they felt, even if hunger pains made it difficult to concentrate on all the statistics that the minister seemed determined to produce.

At last the minister concluded her speech. "There is only one way for women to stand," she said. "And that is on their own two feet."

Mma Ramotswe glanced at Mma Makutsi, and smiled. "I would have thought that rather obvious, Mma," she whispered.

"As long as they have two feet," responded Mma Makutsi, also in a whisper. "There are some women who may not be so lucky. There was a lady in Bobonong who had only one leg."

Mma Ramotswe hushed her. The president of the Chamber of Commerce was ascending to the podium, ready to make the announcement.

His words, when they came, were simple and direct. "Ladies and gentlemen," he said. "I very much regret that the discovery of certain voting irregularities has obliged the Chamber to change its decision."

"She cheated!" whispered Mma Makutsi. "Violet Sephotho cheated—and they've discovered it. She will no longer be runner-up! Oh, Mma, this is so good . . . I'm so glad we came."

The president consulted a piece of paper. "As a result of this, we have only one name to announce this evening, and that is the name of this year's Woman of the Year—Violet Sephotho."

To ringing applause, Violet walked onto the stage. The president stepped away from the podium and handed her a scroll and an envelope. There were cheers from the back of the hall and applause from all quarters. Lights flashed across the ceiling, glittering lights sending a message of triumph and glory. Mma Makutsi said nothing. She was frozen; turned, perhaps, into a pillar of salt—like Lot's wife.

The presentation over, the crowd made its way to the buffet. In the hubbub of chat that filled the ballroom, Mma Makutsi and Mma Ramotswe were silent, at least for several minutes.

"I have no appetite," said Mma Makutsi at last. "I could not touch food. Not tonight. Not for some days, I fear."

"Come on, now, Mma Makutsi," said Mma Ramotswe. "Worse things have happened."

"I cannot think of anything worse than this, Mma," said Mma Makutsi. "My heart is broken, broken, broken."

Mma Ramotswe fetched her a plate of food from the buffet, but she simply toyed with it. After twenty minutes, during which they sat in morose isolation, Mma Ramotswe suggested that it was time to go.

"We can slip out," she said. "All these people are too busy admiring one another."

They made their way towards the door, and it was there that they met Violet Sephotho, her scroll under one arm and wearing the Woman of the Year ribbon.

Violet seemed surprised to see them. "I had not expected you two," she said. "But it is very kind of you to come and share my evening. Thank you."

Mma Makutsi swallowed hard. Mma Ramotswe, though, bowed her head politely. "It is a very great evening for you, Violet. Congratulations. I am very happy for you."

She nudged Mma Makutsi, who looked up slowly. "Yes," she said. "I am happy too, Violet."

If there was any irony in Mma Makutsi's words, Violet did not notice it. "Thank you so much," she said. "I hope you have had a good meal too."

Mma Ramotswe extended a hand to Violet, and Violet shook it.

Then, after only a few seconds of hesitation, Mma Makutsi did the same.

They left, and outside in the car park, under the high sky of stars, they stood for a moment to breathe in the cool night air.

"You did the right thing back there," said Mma Ramotswe quietly. "There is nobody—nobody—whose hand you should refuse to shake."

"Even the Devil's?" said Mma Makutsi.

Mma Ramotswe thought for a moment. Then she gave her answer. "I used to believe in the Devil, you know, Mma. Now I don't. So there can be no question of shaking a hand that doesn't exist."

Mma Makutsi awaited an explanation.

"You see," said Mma Ramotswe. "He's not a separate person. He's inside us. He's there inside people—as part of what they are."

"I'm not sure," said Mma Makutsi.

"Well, I am," said Mma Ramotswe.

Mma Makutsi shook her head in disbelief—not about what Mma Ramotswe had just said, but about what had happened. How could it be that Botswana of all countries—the country that paid more attention to doing what was right than so many other countries—how could Botswana, of all places, choose as its Woman of the Year a person as self-seeking as Violet Sephotho? Did people not realise? Were people such poor judges of character as to be unable to see Violet for what she was?

She expressed these thoughts to Mma Ramotswe, who listened carefully.

"Mma Makutsi," she said, her voice quiet and even, "there are many things in this world that are not right. You only have to look about you and you see them."

"But, Mma, everybody should know about Violet Sephotho."

"I'm afraid they don't," said Mma Ramotswe. "Or if they do, they don't care, or they even admire qualities like that."

"Selfishness? Wickedness? Is that what you're saying, Mma?"

Mma Ramotswe thought for a few moments. "They might not see them as that. They might think that people who are flashy—"

"She's definitely that," interrupted Mma Makutsi.

". . . or shallow—"

"And that too," said Mma Makutsi forcefully. "She's as shallow as the far end of Gaborone Dam after a long drought. That's how shallow she is, Mma."

"And so people might vote for somebody like that because they think that's what a woman of the year should be—ruthless, Mma. They think that a woman of the year should be a real go-getter, determined to succeed."

Mma Makutsi shook her head again. "How can this be, Mma? How can people be so wrong?"

Mma Ramotswe smiled. "Fortunately nobody will pay much attention. I don't think that Violet will be remembered for long."

"I wouldn't be so sure about that," muttered Mma Makutsi. "I wouldn't be surprised if she gets *Woman of the Year* painted on the side of her car."

Mma Ramotswe laughed. "I hope she does that, Mma. Imagine how we'll all laugh when we see that car go by."

Mma Makutsi looked outraged, but only for a short time. Then she started to grin. "It is quite funny, isn't it, Mma? Violet Sephotho elected Woman of the Year because she probably paid people to vote for her. And all those officials being fooled into thinking she deserves it. There is a funny side to it, isn't there?"

"Just," said Mma Ramotswe. "But even when there's a very small funny side to something—very small in this case—it makes it easier to bear, don't you think, Mma?"

Mma Makutsi did think that, and her mood lifted.

They walked towards the van, so small and shabby alongside all the official cars parked in front of the hotel that night. But there was not one of those cars—not one—that Mma Ramotswe would have accepted in exchange for her van. Not one.

THE NEXT DAY she drove out to the Orphan Farm to visit Mma Potokwane. She had a great deal to tell her friend, who liked to be kept up with developments. There was news of Mr. Polopetsi—Mma Potokwane had not heard about the sorting out of that problem, and would be pleased with the outcome. That had been a troubling situation that could have ended very differently. Then there was the remarkable outcome of the Woman of the Year Award. Mma Potokwane would not be at all pleased to hear that Violet had won that, but she was robust and would get over the shock. And finally there was the Susan story. Mma Ramotswe would enjoy telling her friend all about that and about the outcome, which was clearly a good one. Anger, and its close cousin revenge, had come off second best to forgiveness and to the realisation that current unhappiness is not always helped by delving into the past, but can be dealt with by other, more productive means. "People often make that discovery themselves," observed Mma Potokwane. "All they need is a bit of a push."

They went to visit one of the housemothers. She received them warmly and took them into one of the small bedrooms that made up each house. It was afternoon rest time for the younger children, and there, on the lower bunk, lying head to toe, were the brother and sister whom Mma Ramotswe had seen on her last visit. And on the bed with them, curled up and comfortable—against all the regulations—was Fanwell's dog. When they entered the room he awoke and gave a low, protective growl.

"He is looking after them," said the housemother. "He is very fond of them."

Mma Ramotswe turned away. She did not want others to see her tears.

"It is good to have somebody to watch over you," said Mma Potokwane. "It is very good." And then she looked at her watch. "And somebody to make you tea too."

"That is very good," said Mma Ramotswe, just managing to keep her voice even.

They walked back to Mma Potokwane's office in silence. Above them the sky of Botswana was empty, except for a small corner in the distance, behind the wind, beyond the hills—a small patch of purple that was a great cloud of life-giving rain, the rain the parched land so yearned for; small now, but heading their way like an angel of mercy on great wings.

afrika
afrika afrika
afrika afrika afrika
afrika afrika
afrika